Praise for Beverly Rae's *I Married a Dragon*

"I really love Beverly's take on dragons and damsels in distress. I laughed out loud in places. I recommend I MARRIED A DRAGON."

~ *Romance Reviews Today*

"Deliciously decadent and delightfully witty, I MARRIED A DRAGON, the second book in the PARA-MATES series, is a fun and sexy paranormal romance."

~ *Romance Junkies*

"If you like a paranormal romance with a little bit of everything-from dragons to demons, then give this entertaining and well written contemporary a try; you won't be sorry you did."

~ *Literary Nymphs*

Look for these titles by
Beverly Rae

Now Available:

Magical Mayhem
To Fat and Back
Touch Me
Wailing for Love

A Cannon Pack Romance
Dance on the Wilde Side
Howling for My Baby
Running with the Pack

Para-mates
I Married a Demon
I Married a Dragon

Wild Things
Cougar
Wild Cat

I Married a Dragon

Beverly Rae

Samhain Publishing, Ltd.
577 Mulberry Street, Suite 1520
Macon, GA 31201
www.samhainpublishing.com

I Married a Dragon

Print ISBN: 978-1-60928-075-8
Digital ISBN: 978-1-60504-957-1

Editing by Deborah Nemeth
Cover by Natalie Winters

First Samhain Publishing, Ltd. electronic publication: May 2010
First Samhain Publishing, Ltd. print publication: April 2011

Dedication

Dedicated to all the red-hot lovers and the women who love them.

Knights in Shining Armor and Other Mythical Characters

I married a dragon.

There. I said it. I finally got the words out.

Let's face it. It's not exactly the kind of statement anyone thinks they'll ever make. In fact, "I married a dragon" would fly high on the list of the World's Most Incredible Statements, along with such implausible declarations as "I bit the nose off a grizzly bear" or "I use the Hope diamond for a doorstop".

If you can't believe that an intelligent thirty-five-year-old woman can find herself married to a fire-breathing dragon without knowing who, or rather what, she married, then you aren't alone. I still find it difficult to believe and *I'm* the woman. It's even more unbelievable when you consider how I make my living.

You see, I expose the paranormal hocus-pocus of our world.

Yep, you got it. I'm a real-life paranormal investigator and debunker of all things scary that go bump in the night. Do you hear strange noises in your house? Call me. I'll find bats—the non-vampire type—in your attic. Are Grammy's favorite knickknacks moving from the curio cabinet and to the kitchen counter when nobody's at home? I'll nab the neighbor's teen while he's doing a little B&E, playing his not-so-funny poltergeist joke again. Got a psychic charging you big bucks to contact Uncle Marty and get him to spill his ghostly guts on where he hid his lottery winnings? Better keep your job. You'll need it once I show you Madame Sheneeka's arrest record for running a not-so-supernatural scam.

Yeah, I know. Some people do believe in werewolves, demons and other creatures of folklore and mythology. Shoot, even my best friend from college is a believer. We used to get embroiled in heated discussions about the possible existence of supernatural beings Jenn called Otherworlders. At the time, I thought she was eccentric and, yes, maybe skirting the fringes of wacko.

Now I guess I owe her an apology.

Ah, yes. I can almost see your bemused smile. Dragons don't exist. Therefore, I must be telling one whopper of a story. But don't break out the laugh track too fast. Sure, I understand your reluctance to accept what I'm saying. But trust me, when my hubby morphs to full fire-breathing size, it's hard to miss the guy.

I bet you're wondering how I couldn't see my future husband for what he was. Well, let's just say when in his human form, the man could give a movie star a run for the ladies. Women *and* men stop and give him a double take. So how does someone find a dragon, much less marry one? The truth of the matter is that I didn't find him. In fact, he'd been searching for me. That's right. My handsome draggy-poo found me.

Before I knew it, I became Christina Taylor-Delcaluca. Delcaluca is an ancient name running through several generations of—wait for it—dragons. But who knew? I'd assumed (and you know what happens when you assume)

Delcaluca was an old Italian name. Not a name associated with the Dragon Dynasty. (I'll get into the dynasty part later on in my story.)

I grew up in Atlanta, with two loving parents who believed that every mystery had a logical explanation and they passed their practical attitudes on to me. After spending a whole lot of time in endless low-paying jobs, I decided to put my drilled-in skepticism to good use by disproving the stories of poltergeists, malevolent spirits, boogie monsters and whatever other creatures poor delusional people believed in. I started a struggling business called Debunkers, Inc. Hey, the money still sucks, but at least I'm doing what I enjoy: dragging the frights of the night out into the light of the day. So you can understand why I didn't realize what my lover was when we first met, can't you? My mind simply wouldn't accept the fact that dragons and other supernatural beings existed.

I met my smokin'-hot (pun intended) hubby at my friend Thad Pittman's over-the-top birthday bash on Lake Lanier. Thad—pronounced Tad for reasons known only to him—Pittman is one of my best friends. Too bad he's gay or I'd have considered hauling his handsome bod into bed. Anyway, I was at his party when I decided I needed a breather from the wild antics of his less inhibited friends.

I stood on a boat dock a few yards away from another dock where a group of partiers were toasting Thad with Dom Perignon champagne. Although he didn't make much money as an actor or a playwright, he always had cash in hand. In fact, he often joked about the pot of gold hidden away in his basement.

In typical Thad style, he'd decided the best way to break the drought in Atlanta was to offer a sacrifice to the Rain Gods. The sacrifice, of course, wasn't the champagne. I mean, the man's not stupid, just sometimes certifiable. No, the sacrifice consisted of Thad and the others pouring bottled water onto the dry edges of the lake. They did this while imploring the Water Witch and other imagined deities to bring in the clouds, which, of course, was sung to the tune of "Bring In the Clowns". Fortunately for me and anyone else within hearing distance, the singing transitioned from off-key harmonics to overly dramatic prayers aimed at the cloudless sky.

"Rain, baby, rain!" Thad raised his arm in the air, then turned the water bottle over, letting the liquid pour into the parched ground surrounding the dock. Several years of drought conditions had left many of the boat docks high and dry. Thad's friends did the same, echoing him by adding their own pleas.

"Let it rain, Cloud King!"

"Shake, rumble and roll, Oh, Great Thunder Lord!"

"Powerful Lightning Wizard, we call on you to make it rain!"

"Flood me, Downpour Diva!"

"Oh, brother." I forced myself to stay on my dock and not rush over to stop them. All I saw was a group of intoxicated people wasting perfectly good bottled water. (Yeah, I know. Sometimes I can be a real killjoy.) But after finishing my latest assignment—debunking yet another supposedly haunted house—Thad had ordered me, with a firm and not-so-subtle command, to not mix my business with his pleasure. Since it was his birthday, I did my best to honor his wishes, although a big part of me wanted nothing more than to go home to my tiny overpriced studio apartment, curl up with a good autobiography and scarf down a pint of Ben and Jerry's newest flavor.

Thad waved to me, calling me over to join the fun, but I shook my head. I took another sip of my champagne and moved farther out on the dock, going almost all the way to the edge before I could see any water through the gaps between the boards. I took off my shoes, settled down on the edge and let my feet dangle in the water. With a heavy sigh, I took another drink and looked up at the moon. In a rare fanciful mood, I let my mind wander and tried to imagine a real man staring back at me. I sighed again. My love life was as dry as the Georgia ground. *Sheesh, when I start fantasizing about the man up there, it's time to get laid. Waay past time.*

I gulped down the last drops of my drink and closed my eyes, listening to Thad and his buddies stumbling up the sloped hillside to his rented lake house. *I should rejoin the party.* Instead of hopping up and rushing off to do my BFF duty, I rested my back against the wood and searched the clear skies for any sign that Thad's sacrifices had worked. *Yeah, like that'll happen.*

A splashing sound interrupted my contemplation and I turned my head to gaze over the smooth surface of the lake. Another splash, sounding closer, brought me to a sitting position to scan the glassy water closer. My mind was already working on the most logical explanation.

Probably just a fish. I frowned at the water. Then why didn't I see any ripples? Unless it had been a very small fish. But then the sound wouldn't have been so loud. Giving the lake another look, I decided to let it pass. I was supposed to be off duty, anyway. Telling myself to follow Thad's order to relax, I leaned back down on the dock and tried to chill.

A dark form, shrieking loud enough to pop my eardrums, flew over the corner piling and aimed straight for me. One red eye glared at me from the middle of a grotesquely-formed head, and razor-sharp fangs flashed in the moonlight. All of this happened so quickly, I didn't have time to react. Fortunately for me, I didn't have to.

A figure dressed in black jumped between the thing and me. I gasped, frozen to the spot as my hero reached out a large hand covered in some kind of golden leathery material and grabbed the watery beast. Stunned, I squeezed my eyes shut and shook my head, hoping that when I opened them again, I'd realize my eyes had been playing tricks on me. *Did I drink that much?*

Another shriek filled the air, only this time terror mixed with ferociousness in the sound. A *crack* had me opening my eyes to see my hero, his back turned toward me, flinging a limp and obviously dead *thing* away from us.

The man must've played major league baseball or shot the put—*put the shot?*—in the Olympics, because the attacking fish-thingy soared through the air, going the impossible distance to the middle of the lake. My mouth dropped open and I was powerless to close it. No one could throw anything that far. Not even an Olympian. Several seconds later, the thing hit the water and disappeared into the black depths.

"Omigod!"

The man whirled to face me and I knew at that exact moment one of two things had happened. Either (1) I'd swilled a shitload of champagne or (2) I needed more relaxation than even Thad knew. Why? Because for a second, I would've sworn the face of my champion had changed from a man to something else. Something not quite human.

Fear and surprise had me closing my eyes again. Releasing pent-up anxiety, I repeated an impromptu mantra three times. *I am not drunk. I am not drunk. I am not drunk.* Maybe I should've said *I am not crazy. I am not crazy. I am not crazy.* Either way, I didn't look forward to opening my eyes and finding out which condition I was in.

The rational me, however, knew I had to. Holding my breath, I peeked and found myself staring into the most gorgeous green eyes I'd ever seen. He'd moved closer and was kneeling beside me. His face—a chiseled movie-star face even Thad would envy—was so close I could've nibbled on his lips. And oh, how I wanted to do just that! Among other parts of him, of course. You know. Just a nibble or two.

Thankfully, my eyes were functioning quite well. With a quick glimpse at the rest of his body, I registered the black pants and black silk shirt he wore. The *V* formed by the open collar of his shirt highlighted a hard chest and a small sideways figure eight tattoo at the base of his throat. I wondered briefly why he'd chosen to tat his throat, but that was the least of his allure. His air of sophistication mixed with a natural casualness reminded me of a James Bond type. He definitely did not look like the average renter at the lake. Although he didn't wear a tie or a belt, an expensive gold watch adorned his wrist and two rings, one on each hand, sparkled under the moonlight. A lot of men can't get away with wearing diamonds, but this guy sure could. Hell, he could've gotten away with anything. And I do mean anything (wink, wink).

An after-five stubble formed a *U* from one ear, around his chin, and up to the other. Still, I knew he would look rugged even clean-shaven. Dark hair, curling a bit at the ends, framed his tanned face. I could never get enough of staring at him even if I stayed with him for a thousand years. *Wow, where did that thought come from?*

Swallowing, I forced my brain train to hop onto the rationality track again. But the brain train would only creep at minimum speed. I waited, letting the train chug along until, at last, it gained enough momentum. I gulped again and attempted to open my mouth to speak—at exactly the same moment he ran his tongue over his upper lip. The train ground to a screeching halt with the conductor hopping out of the engine to inspect the roadblock derailing my thoughts. Unfortunately for me, one of the cars broke free, jumped the track and careened toward the depot called my mouth.

"Ahwkern."

One perfectly groomed eyebrow arched upward.

"Ehhhh...bwa...errr. Ugh."

Humor twinkled in those brilliant green eyes. He tilted his head at me. "Are you trying to speak?" He narrowed his eyes at me. "Are you *able* to speak?"

Holy crap. Barry White move over. His voice was the voice to end all voices. If every woman in the world could hear the deep, rich timbre coming out of his mouth, they'd slap duct tape over other men's pie holes. I doubted I'd ever want another man to speak to me after hearing this guy. And all I wanted at that moment was to hear him speak again. I didn't care what he said just as long as he said it to me. Too bad I still had my runaway brain train to contend with.

Come on, Chrissy! Don't let this chance pass. I'd never found myself face to face with a real, live god-like male before and I couldn't blow this opportunity. I cleared my throat, shook my head to remove that mental roadblock and tried again, hoping I could convince him that I wasn't the Speechless Wonder. "Wow. That was quite a throw."

Yeah, I know. It wasn't the cleverest remark anyone had ever made, but, hey, at least he could understand me.

"Thank you."

"You're welcome." I cringed inside and promised I'd enroll in an impromptu public speaking class the very next day.

The tips of his mouth curved upward and I reached out to touch them. (Seriously! I actually reached out to touch them.) Obviously, the village idiot had jumped on the caboose and been promoted to conductor.

But here's the really good part. Instead of jerking away or

scowling at me, he took my hand and pressed his lips to the center of my palm. The action from any other man would have seemed corny, but not this guy. He was definitely the coolest of the cool.

Of course, I reacted in my own cool and collected fashion—not. Instead of playing Cinderella to his Prince Charming and acting all classy and charming, I stopped breathing. I swear I did. I physically held my breath. Then, as if I couldn't act like more of a dumbass, I giggled.

Omigod. Please let me die right now. I just giggled at the man. And not a tickling, sweet-sounding ingénue-type laugh, mind you. Oh, no. I had to let loose with an all-out-there, teeny-bopper crush titter. Had I no shame left? Amazingly, however, he didn't appear to notice.

"Are you all right?"

Thank goodness I'd dressed for the party in nice slacks and a flattering blouse instead of wearing my usual lake wear of tattered jean shorts and faded halter top. I nodded and hoped playing the silent and semi-cute damsel-in-distress would be my best option. At least until my mind started performing at its usually high-functioning level.

Still holding my hand, he helped me to my feet, glossing over my total awestruck stupidity. Feeling something wet at the corner of my lips, I clamped my mouth shut. *Did I almost drool?*

"I'm sorry, but did you hear me? Are you all right?"

His concerned gaze stuck with mine, holding both my attention and my heart. "Uh, yeah." *Damn it, Chrissy, you can do better than that.* "I mean, yes. I'm fine. Thanks to you." At last, the entire brain train was back on course and moving down the track toward Cognitive Ability Land. I glanced down at my hand in his, wanting to take full pleasure of the remaining time he would hold it. He was bound to let go soon. I mean, that's the saying, right? All good things must come to a finish? *Damn those stupid sayings.*

Instead, he took my other hand. Pleased by this unexpected development, I looked into his handsome face and found him studying me. Yet instead of matching his gaze again, I lost my nerve and turned toward the lake. "What was that thing, anyway?"

He released my hands—*No! I promise to never say another word if you only take my hands again*—and looked out to where the thing had disappeared into the murky depths. "I'm not sure. I've never seen anything like it before. Have you?"

"Never. To tell the truth, I'm not even sure I saw what I think I saw." Growing more comfortable with him, I smiled and ventured into Talking To a Gorgeous Guy Land. "The whole thing happened so fast. I mean, one minute this fanged sea monster was flying toward me, ready to chow down on my neck. Then in the next minute..." I let my smile grow wider. "In the next minute, you're standing above me, saving me from a brutal attack." *Wow. Do I sound dramatic or what?* Thad would've loved to hear me talking like one of those people who actually believe in monsters and shining knights.

His smile carved dimples into his cheeks. *Holy crap. Can the man get any sexier?* Although his dimples fascinated me, I let my gaze drop to his nether regions—his mountainous nether regions. *Is that Pike's Peak under his slacks? Do I dare hope the attraction isn't one-sided?*

He cleared his throat—omigod, had he seen where I'd been looking?—whipping my attention back to those dimples.

"A bit dramatic, don't you think?"

Does he mean my description of my rescue? Or his tented pants? Both are quite dramatic. But I didn't mind that he thought I was over-the-top. Not as long as he kept looking at me that way. “Maybe.” Resorting to a cliché girlie gesture, I tossed my hair over my shoulder and smiled. “Maybe some of Thad’s theatrical personality has rubbed off on me.”

His smile grew into a good-natured grin. “Oh. So you’re one of the happy group that was pouring water into the lakebed?” He glanced up at Thad’s rented home, then back to me. “Did you pray to the rain gods too?”

Oh, crap. I’d assumed he was another actor-friend of Thad’s. He was simply too hunky not to be on the stage or in the movies. Although I was okay with letting him think I had a flair for the dramatic, linking me to the drunks up on the hill was a different matter. I considered my options and decided I’d best not answer. I didn’t want him to think I was that loony. “Oh, so I take it you’re not here for Thad’s birthday party?” *Duh.*

The dimples deepened, making me wish I could tickle each one with the tip of my tongue. This man made me hungry. And I’m not talking about my favorite late-night snack from the drive-through.

“No. No, I’m not.”

My curiosity won out over my nervousness. “Then you’re staying in one of the other rentals? Or is this your permanent home?” *Please, God, don’t let him be a tourist. Please let him live in the area. If not, I’ll have to move.* My sudden contemplation of moving to wherever this handsome stranger called home surprised me. But the shocked feeling soon morphed into an incredulous one when I realized I’d meant it. He was the type of man a woman would move heaven and earth—much less the meager contents of a studio apartment—to be with. After all, I could do my work anywhere mysterious things happened, and believers in the supernatural would fork over their money to have me prove them sane.

I already had half my apartment packed and ready to go

when he not only didn't break me out of my fantasy, but gave it another sprinkle of fairy dust. *Sheesh! Fairy dust? When did I start thinking like one of my clients?*

"Actually, yes, I do live here."

Omigod, dreams do come true. What next? Will he invite back to his castle? "You're kidding. Really?" I couldn't help it. I grinned like he'd combined my two favorite holidays, Christmas and Valentine's Day. I nearly spread my arms wide to receive my presents.

It's true. I was stone-cold, head-over-heels in lust—*dare I say* love*?*—with the man and I didn't even know his name. What was happening to me? I didn't believe in love at first sight any more than I believed in the Loch Ness Monster. Yet here I stood, ready and hoping he'd whisk me away to his kingdom. Yep, my prince had arrived, not on a white stallion, but in expensive Italian loafers.

"Actually, not here at the lake. I live in Buckhead. Do you know the area?" He wrapped an arm around my waist and escorted me down the dock.

Yeah, right. Like anyone living in or around Atlanta wouldn't know Buckhead. I inhaled, catching the scent of an intoxicating aftershave, and wanted nothing more than to lean into him. Not simply *on*to him, but actually *in*to him, melding my body with his. My normal sensible nature, however, had to pick that moment to regain its rightful place in the hierarchy of my personality. Instead of leaning, I maintained a few dignified but torturous inches between our bodies. Although my libido shouted at me to hug him, lick him, devour him, years of practical thinking kept the urges at bay. "Of course, I do. In fact, I don't live very far from there."

What I'd said was partially true. Although my apartment wasn't geographically far from the affluent area, it was light-years away in terms of accommodations. The wealthy of Atlanta lived in the prestigious Buckhead area with its million-dollar mansions, elegant shopping and world-class restaurants. I wasn't a gold-digger by any means, but I have to admit I was thrilled that my newfound love was not only dashing but loaded.

"I'm glad."

I almost stumbled at those two sweet words. Fortunately, he caught me, bringing me against his hard body and effectively killing my practical oh-so-not-wanted-right-now side of me. With my hands pressed to his chest, I looked up at him and whispered, "You are?"

"I most definitely am."

Wow. Omigod. Wow. My little brain train chugged to an abrupt stop again. "Wow." Had I said that last *wow* out loud? From the sparkle in his eyes, I realized I must have.

"Most definitely wow." He bent over and touched his lips to mine.

A burn—faster, hotter than any burn I'd ever experienced—flashed through me, torching urges and desires I'd thought had dried up and blown away. My legs melted under the intensity of the heat, and my fingers turned clawlike to grasp the sleek material of his shirt. I moaned at the taste of him, warm, musky, mysterious. Taking my moan as a welcoming response—*hell, yes!*—he deepened the kiss and slid his tongue between my parted lips. Slowly, in what could only be described as an imitation of what his shaft could do inside another part of me, he stroked his tongue alongside my cheeks and over my tongue, then drove deeper still.

I couldn't help it. I moaned again, hoping he'd interpret it correctly, scoop me into his arms and ravish me. *Ravish? Since when did I talk like the heroine of a romance novel?* He nibbled at the corners of my mouth and I answered my question.

Instead, he broke off the kiss—*no, don't stop!*—and took a moment to look into my eyes. I held my breath, partly because I didn't want anything to break our connection and partly because I'd eaten onions rings earlier.

He cupped my head, bringing my mouth to his again, and skimmed his teeth over my lips. I exhaled and then inhaled sharply. He skimmed across once more, this time nipping my lower lip, coaxing—*yeah, like I need coaxing*—my mouth to open wider. He wrapped one strong arm around my waist and I let him support me. Closing my eyes, I whimpered into his mouth and his hold tightened on me.

Please, never let go.

I couldn't think of anything else. Only that I'd waited for this moment all my life and couldn't stand it if he stopped now. I slid my arms over the silky smooth material, exulting in the feel of his muscular body beneath.

I'm not certain how long the kiss lasted, for a minute or for a decade, but however long it was, it wasn't long enough. Most definitely not long enough. I could have stayed in his arms, his mouth on mine, his tongue tasting mine forever. Unfortunately, I knew all too well that life is not a fantasy and this moment had to end. *Damn, double damn.*

Still, once the kiss ended, I made no effort to move away from him. In fact, if he ever wanted me off his bod, he'd have to be the one to make it happen. I swore right then and there that I would never go very far from him. Ever. As in *for*ever. Amazingly, I sensed that he didn't want me off him, either.

We kept our arms locked around each other and leaned back only as far as was necessary to see into each other's faces. A small smile echoed the knowing look in his eyes.

Wow.

I've never been really good with change. Especially big changes. Especially big *and* fast changes. But no one would have known it from what happened next.

For the next few hours, we sat on a bench by the lake, talking and cuddling. His name was Kaine Delcaluca—has any name ever sounded so perfect?—and he was an entrepreneur dealing in rare artifacts. Cynical me figured that meant he was a dreamer and probably couldn't hold down a job for long. He was probably living off family money and would lose his trust fund once they got a load of me. (Yeah, I'm definitely a glass-half-empty kind of gal.) But I didn't care if he was rich or a beggar. Just listening to his voice was enough for me.

Whenever I spoke, telling him about my business, he listened intently, eating up every word, every syllable. It's corny, I know, but I drank him up as much as he drank me up. If someone had asked me, I would've told them we were lost lovers, separated by time and finally reunited. I felt like I'd known him for hundreds of years and couldn't imagine living the rest of this life without him.

This was why, of course, I ended up hopping on his private jet and flying to Las Vegas that same night. Later, I would realize who, or rather what, my husband was.

I'd married a dragon.

Viva Las Vegas, Baby!

"Omigod, omigod, omigod!"

I grabbed for dear life, clutched at the sheets and screamed my pleasure. "Omigod, Kaine, suck on me. Suck harder. Omigod, yes!"

He grabbed my legs, dragging my body toward the end of the bed. I lifted my head just in time to see his face disappear between my legs. I couldn't watch for long, however. The sensation of his mouth on my sensitive area jolted me and I jerked my head backward. I screamed again and was thankful Kaine had booked a luxury—and soundproof—villa at the Bellagio Hotel in Las Vegas. Otherwise, who knew how many hotel guests would call the manager to report a woman screaming in dire danger? Danger of exploding from too many climaxes, that is.

He clutched my thighs—*please don't notice the cottage cheese cellulite*—and flung them over his shoulders. I giggled and moaned in rapid succession, delight and lust mixing in a torrential downpour flowing from my pussy. He nipped me and my yelp dissolved into another moaning giggle.

Mewing sounds of delight, I concentrated on the sounds coming from between my legs. Hell, the sounds were almost as good as the tongue stroking my tender nub up and down, and all around. The man was a machine, lapping, sucking, stabbing. My body tightened and I tried to relax, wanting to enjoy every second of the ecstasy shaking my body. "Omigod, Kaine. I've never had anyone go down on me like—Omigod!"

"You say *omigod* a lot, don't you?" His chuckle wafted over my tender skin.

"Not really." He added his thumbs to the action, spreading my folds even wider. I gasped and clutched the bedspread. "It's just—omigod—you're the first one who's ever—omigod—rated so many omigods before."

"The first one?"

I reared up to find him silently questioning me. "Seriously. But why are you stopping?"

He arched an eyebrow at me. "The first one out of...a lot?"

What the hell? "Please tell me you're asking because you're jealous and not out of a perverse pleasure of knowing the exact number." I scowled at him and fought to hang on to the bliss I'd enjoyed moments before. "Because I don't think this is the best time to be exchanging numbers."

He blinked as though my response was totally not what he'd expected. Then, with a curt bob of his head, he grinned and tucked his head down again. He blew air onto my aching clit and then reversed it by drawing my nub into his mouth.

The tension grew stronger until I feared I might pass out. Talk about embarrassing. *Don't pass out. Don't pass out.* Hell, I didn't even want that swirling black-behind-the eyes feeling that I sometimes got when a really big *O* hits me. No way. I wanted to experience every little sensation, sound and touch of this one. But I was defenseless against the whirlwind of sexual hunger ripping from my abdomen through my chest to tingle its way up and down my spine. The Climax of All Climaxes took hold and I felt my entire body give into the brilliant release. I inhaled, held on and rode the tidal wave to the top of the crest.

Shudders cascaded inside me, bursting from my core to spread quickly outward along my skin.

The effect was so intense I couldn't gather enough breath to say anything. I settled for letting my mantra echo in my head. *Omigod. Omigod. Omigod.*

Abruptly, startling me out of my orgasmically induced trance, Kaine moved swiftly from between my legs to stretch his body over me. He took my breasts in both hands, fondling them while his thumbs crossed back and forth over my nipples. I gasped, raking in a huge gulp of air, my eyes widening at him. The impression of his gaze boring into me was splendid and, amazingly, revved my sex-engine again.

He pressed my breasts against his cheeks and rubbed his face against my nipples. I clutched his hair, keeping him in position, and wondered how anything so simple could feel so incredible. I jiggled my breasts, hoping to bring him the same amount of agonizing pleasure he was giving me. "How do you like them babies, big guy?"

He chuckled, a deep, rich sound that rumbled against my chest. Keeping his head entrapped, I moved my tits in opposite directions, causing a friction of the carnal kind along his cheeks. He ran his hand down my body to cup my bottom with one hand, then grabbed and squeezed. I returned the favor by pressing my boobs harder against his face. A delighted "Yes!" vibrated against my skin.

At last he broke free of my mammary prison and, taking my tit in his mouth, he tugged on breast and buttock, pulling me on top of him. (In case you haven't noticed, we're very athletic in our lovemaking.) I rubbed one breast against his face, exciting me, and if the throbbing dick between my legs was any indication, exciting him as well. He moaned and I couldn't keep the smug grin off my face.

I felt his shaft straighten, threatening to burst before either of us wanted it to. With any other man I would've worried about a premature ending to our lovemaking, but Kaine had proven time and time again during our week together that his endurance had no limits. The man, simply put, had the Energizer Bunny of Cocks. An image of the famous bunny sporting an enormous penis flashed through my mind. *Hump away, bunny-boy. Hump away.*

"Ah, my Chrissy-doll. Switch around and let me taste you again."

I've never liked pet names, but I absolutely loved it when he called me Chrissy-doll. Being called a doll was more than this girl had ever counted on. I'd been called broad, babe, and bitch (a lot), but never doll and I liked the new pet name. This hunk of a man calling me doll made me feel petite and, miraculously, zapped away the extra hump in my butt that no miracle diet had ever managed to eradicate.

"So soon? But don't you want me to blow you now?"

I waited to see which answer he'd give me. He could give me (1) the PC correct answer of "Oh, no, honey, I'd rather please you" or (2) the probable truthful answer of "Yeah, you're right—it is your turn after all." And if I were the one being truthful, I'd have to say I was rooting for option number one. Yep, I admit it. I'm a glutton for...well, for getting eaten. I'll spread my legs and offer my pussy for consumption anytime, anywhere. But only to Kaine, of course.

"Oh? Maybe. But let me go down on you again first."

Ya gotta love the guy, right?

With a happy giggle, I twisted in the opposite direction. His ramrod cock hovered above my face and I reached up to wrap my fingers around its thick trunk.

"No, not yet." He straightened his legs, keeping his prize

out of easy reach and dipping his upper body lower. He had, in effect, told me to "Look, but don't touch." I grumbled and settled for watching the lengthy shaft bob around like a piñata I wasn't allowed to break. Oh, but how I wanted the candy within.

His very talented tongue found the right spot with deadly aim. He toughened his tongue to lash at me, wanting to take every drop, refusing to allow even one drip of moisture to escape.

I whimpered with need and tried to pull him down. What every other lover in my life had lacked, Kaine had in spades. "Taste me. Lap me up the way I like you to."

Although our vows—hurriedly spoken in front of a Madonna-clad male minister at one of more luxurious chapels on the Strip—hadn't said anything about obeying, my sweet hubby minded his new wifey-poo, grasped onto my clit and started sucking. Forgetting my earlier thoughts about being overheard, I cried out, relinquishing my tenuous hold on yet another release. Still he hung on, torturing me more, even when I tried to break away.

Darting his tongue inside my cave, he worked his fingers over my aching clit, pressing and tweaking my nub to match the rhythm of his tongue. I grabbed his granite-hard legs and clung to him. Cry after cry racked out of me until one last scream ripped free along with another even longer climax.

Do I have anything left in me? "Kaine. Kaine. Wow, oh, wow, Kaine."

He freed my tortured pussy and swiped his tongue along the inside of my leg. "Mr. Delcaluca to you, baby."

I somehow managed to laugh in between gasping for air. "Baby? It's Mrs. Delcaluca now, dude, and don't you forget it." *Holy crap, I'm married!* If I had a penny for every time I'd had that same thought this week, I'd be rich enough to pay the rent on my studio apartment.

Kaine finally freed me and I pushed him over, intent on giving as good as I'd gotten. Hey, I may want what I want when I want it, but that didn't mean I wouldn't want to give him what he wanted too.

Going to my knees, I positioned my upper body so my breasts would hang over his tight abdomen and clasped his dick in my hand. With a lick of my lips, I lowered my mouth, covering as much of him as I could. My only wish at that moment was for a bigger mouth.

The exquisite feel of my lips wrapped around his manhood shook me to the core. I'd never liked giving head before, but with Kaine, it was different. His scent, his taste were more than sweet. In rapid strokes, I licked his lollipop for all its yumminess. With each of my pulls, I drew him in, holding him longer than the pull before. My breasts rubbed against him, sending bursts of pleasure through me and, hopefully, through him.

He ran his hands down my back, then squeezed my butt cheeks, spreading them, kneading them, making me wish he'd take me doggy-style. Yet I couldn't, wouldn't let go. Not yet.

I tracked my fingers through the dark patch of curly hair and dipped lower into the crevice between his crotch and leg. I found the soft balls below and fondled them, earning a low moan from Kaine. He shuddered and bumped his hips higher, thrusting his cock deeper into my mouth.

But Kaine wasn't one to sit, er, lie by and do nothing. Sliding his hand from my ass and over my leg, he opened my folds and pressured my swollen clit with his thumb. "You drive me crazy, Chrissy-doll. I love the smell of you. The taste of you. The feel of you."

I mewed a soft sweet sound of gratitude and rubbed my tits against his abdomen as much for my benefit as his. Wanting to tease him, I took my mouth off him, then ran my tongue over and around his dick.

He continued his finger-work on my clit and fondled my breast with his other hand. "Chrissy-doll."

Hearing my name said with such emotion, such lust, sent a fresh burst of juice out of me. I wanted to take him into my mouth again, but I had to admit, I wanted something else more. "I need you inside me."

"That would most definitely be my pleasure." Releasing a low rumbling sound, he pushed me off him and positioned me on my side. Flinging his body on top of me, he paused and sought my eyes.

"Ready?"

I made a face at him. "Are you freakin' kidding me?"

He laughed and bent his head to my breast. He bit and tugged on each nipple and I wrapped my legs around him. He swirled his tongue around my tit, unleashing a ring of fire in my womb. Moving to the other bud, he lazily swirled his tongue around this one, until at last he sealed his mouth over it, clamped his teeth gently at its base, and sucked.

I gritted my teeth against screaming his name. Whether from the delight at the sensations rippling through my tit or from the vexation of his not plunging into me, I didn't know. Finally, he slid his cock over my pussy.

Too bad it wasn't what I was hoping for.

"Kaine, I swear to God if you don't fuck me, I'm gonna rip off your dick and feed it to the white tigers at the Mirage."

He cocked his head at me, a bemused expression on his face. "You never told me you were so..."

"Be careful what you say, Kaine." I reached down to take his hand. Although I didn't make him stop his methodical rake over my clit, I still craved more.

"...ferocious." He hiked an eyebrow at me. "I *like* it."

With an animal-like growl, he plunged into me. I gasped, then cried out.

Kaine pushed my legs over his arms—thank goodness for my Pilates classes—giving him better room to do his job. He stroked me from the inside, rubbing his cock along the sensitive nerves within my sex. I squeezed my muscles, determined to keep him within me for as long as possible.

Panting, I met every one of his thrusts with one of my own. Hot juicy warmth rushed from me, covering him. Closing his mouth over mine in a frenzied heated kiss, he roared his climax, mixing his breath with mine. I held him to me, drinking in both of his releases and let loose with yet another one of my own.

Kaine collapsed on top of me, his weight pressing down, but I didn't mind. With a satisfied smile, I ran my hands over his back, massaging him as he lay unable to move, awakening not only the nerves in his skin, but the fantasy of what lay ahead. "Umm. You feel good on top of me."

His low chuckle warmed my neck. "Umm. You feel good under me."

"Then it's official. We feel good together."

He rewarded my humor with another chuckle to tickle my neck.

"You know, we might want to leave this room at some point. Maybe gamble, see some shows." He slid off me and came to rest at my side. Unable to bear not having his skin touching mine, I took his arm and slung it over my body. "Then again, maybe not."

Kaine smiled at me, then nibbled my shoulder. "Your wish is my desire. Tell me if you want to see a show, go out to dine, go shopping, go for a swim...whatever you want. You only need to ask. I don't want you to think I'm holding you prisoner."

"Ooh. Does that mean you'll put me in handcuffs?"

"If that's your fondest desire."

The man did have an old-fashioned way with words at times, but I liked it. I cuddled into him, deciding to give my "fondest desire" some thought. Instead, my mind wandered to the day we'd first met. It may have been Thad's birthday, but I'm the one who had received the best present.

I'd had him pegged as having old family money. You know the type of man I'm talking about—the kind who has enough moolah in the bank so that he never has to worry about working to pay his mortgage, but not enough dough to retire early.

But, boy, was I wrong. This dude had a lot of money. I'm talking about Bill Gates or Oprah kind of money. When he'd proposed, however, I hadn't known the full extent of his wealth because it hadn't mattered to me. Seriously. I would've said yes if he'd been a janitor or even unemployed. I mean, love is the most important thing, right? (Yeah, I know. I would've scoffed at such a statement a few days ago, but now it seemed undeniably true.)

But I have to admit something else. As the old saying goes, it's just as easy to fall in love with a rich man as it is a man with no pennies. Or however the saying goes. Yep, at the risk of sounding like a money-hungry gold-digger, I was damn glad I'd fallen for a rich one.

I grew up with lower-middle-class parents who had, due to a tragic car accident, left me orphaned and living with an unmarried, barely-making-ends-meet aunt. I had, inadvertently, dropped myself into the *lower*-lower-middle-class by way of my rather unique and non-lucrative occupation. Not that I'd cared before, but now that I'd seen what money could buy, I wasn't about to play the poor snob enough to snub my nose—or my wallet—at my fortunate turn of circumstances. Besides, Kaine loved spending money on me, er, us.

Kaine rented a beautiful wedding chapel in the marriage-happy desert town, booting all the other couples ahead of us in line out of the pristine white house. They didn't mind, however, once he handed them a thousand-dollar poker chip for their inconvenience. Then he arranged to stay at the best accommodation, including private butler and maid service, in a fancy hotel. In blissful wedded happiness, we hopped into the waiting stretch limousine and glided down the Strip.

You got it. I was living the champagne-and-roses life, lying next to the man I loved. And even though I know it's kind of rude to say so, I can't help but go there.

Eat your heart out, ladies.

"Chrissy-doll..."

I batted my eyelids at him. I couldn't believe it. Batting eyelids was so *not* the type of thing I'd do. Or at least it wasn't until I met Kaine. "What's up, big guy?" I grinned, knowing he'd understand what I really meant by *big* guy.

"We didn't discuss this, but—"

I laughed. "We didn't have time to discuss a lot of things." I wiggled my eyebrows in a so-so imitation of Grouch Marx. "Especially since *coming* in Vegas." I winked at him, hoping he'd catch my innuendo. Again, not something I would normally do, but a girl in love does silly things.

He quirked an eyebrow, mimicking my eyebrow play. "Very, very true."

I reached down to grab his Big Guy and was shocked when

Kaine took my hand away. Wow, talk about a short honeymoon. Headache already? However, I decided to keep my thoughts to myself—for once. Instead I cocked my eyebrow at him (ahem!) with a pointed (like he should be) look. This eyebrow-versus-eyebrow thing might have to go to the mat. Preferably the mattress. (I'm on a roll.)

"I'd like to talk about children."

I froze as though someone had dumped a bucket of ice on me. First, Big Guy was off limits and now he'd brought up the ultimate libido-buster: children. Was he trying to kill the attraction between us?

"Chrissy-doll, are you all right?"

Somewhere deep inside me, a molecular army of child-bearing DNA lit an emergency flame, thawed me out, and went into hiding. Was the man insane? Did he expect me to give up my pursuit of the magical miraculous butt-buster already? Talk about humps! I immediately envisioned my body with not only my little hump on the rump, but a bigger bump in the front.

"Children? Tell me you're about to say you've had a vasectomy. Because if you have, it's totally cool with me." I waited—hell, prayed—to see him confirm a little snip-snip to his dick-dick. But it seemed my luck had run out. "Holy crap, are you seriously talking about rug rats? Seriously? What happened to the honeymoon? What happened to just you and me having fun for a while? And I'm talking a *long* while."

As in a lifetime.

He pulled away—*oh, no he did-n't!*—and I gaped at him. My hope that he was joking vanished along with the sparkle in his eye.

"Yes, I'm serious. I'd like to have a child as soon as possible."

As soon as possible? Now I was the one pulling away. Away

and straight out of the bed. "Are you frickin' kidding me?" I wrapped the sheet around me, scanned the room and searched for a hidden camera. "Tell me you're punking me." I laughed—or at least I tried to—but the noise sounded more like a croak. "This is a joke, right?"

But his expression left no doubt. The man wanted a baby-mamma and he wanted her now. My legs suddenly lost their strength, and I barely managed to sink into one of the cushy armchairs near the bed.

Kaine was up and moving toward me. "Chrissy-doll, I had no idea you'd react this way. Don't you like kids?"

I tilted my head and peered at him, hoping a different angle would make me see the upward turn of his lips signaling his mirth. I held on to the dying dream that this was a bad joke, but knew that particular funeral had my beloved dream lying four feet under and sinking straight to Hell. "Uh, sure I do." As long as they were someone else's. A tickle of apprehension latched onto the back of my neck. *No. Don't go there. Don't think about it.*

He visibly sighed in relief. *Uh-oh.* Time to nix his dream in the butt. Or however the saying goes.

"Hold on, sport. Let me clarify. I like kids in television commercials, on billboards hawking cereal, and in someone else's arms, far, far away in a whole different universe than mine. But real kids screaming, pooping and getting dirty within a hundred yards of me? Not a chance."

The pained expression on his face threw me for a loop and, so help me, I relented a little bit. "Are you like dead-set on having one? And definitely only one?" An inner voice screamed at me, warning me not to go down this path. I suddenly wished I could take back my questions.

I prayed he'd say no—to the first question, that is. Failing help from above, I hoped he would want just one. The thought of two or more children clinging to my shirttail was simply too unbelievable to imagine.

"I must have a child. And soon." His gaze bore into me and I knew, without a doubt, we had hit a deal breaker. If this man didn't get a baby from me, he'd go elsewhere.

And, frankly, that just pissed me off.

"You *must*? What does that mean? And isn't this something you should've mentioned before we got hitched?" Never mind that I'd never brought up the subject either. He started to open his mouth, but I didn't want to hear anything like *baby* or *pregnant* or any other word not in my vocabulary. "You'd better start taking hormone treatments because if anyone in this marriage is getting knocked up, it ain't gonna be me!" I didn't give him time to retort. Instead, with a dramatic whirl of my sheet, I stomped toward the combination bathroom and dressing room.

"Chrissy, come back here!"

Not Chrissy-doll. Just Chrissy. *Figures.* I glanced back at him and scowled as hard as I could, then renewed my trek to safety. *Yeah, right. Not a chance, dude. I'll be damned before I let you command me like some antiquated housewife from the 1950s Me-Man-You-Wifey era.* "Not on your life."

"We need to talk about this."

I hurried through the bathroom door and whirled to face him again. Putting all my anger behind my glare, I stuck out my chin and took the enraged woman stance; one hand on a hip and a look that could wither flowers right off their stems. A momentary silence rested uneasily between us until I slowly raised my hand, palm out. "See this? Learn how to use yours. Because until this baby talk ends, that's all the sex you're getting."

With a *harrumph*, I stepped back, never taking my eyes off him, and slammed the door.

Two hours later I knew I'd gone overboard. Yeah, I can be a bit of a drama queen. Couple that with a big mouth and trouble usually isn't far behind. How was my sweet new hubby supposed to know that kids scared the crap out of me? That's right. I'm afraid of kids. Bring on the haunted houses and spooky graveyards, but keep those precious little tykes on the playground and out of my sight. Why? Hey, I have good reasons. The first reason being named Desmond Donaldson.

When I was a teenager babysitting for mall-cruising cash, I landed a job sitting with the Donaldson family. No one, including my aunt, however, bothered to tell me Desmond's nickname. Having gone through twenty-two sitters, angelic-looking Desmond had been dubbed Dessy the Demon. Oh, he wasn't an actual demon—at least, I didn't think so at the time—but I'd have bet he could make a real demon run screaming home to Papa Satan. My one and only night with that little baby-faced horror made me swear off kids forever.

Picture this. I'm sitting on the sofa watching a movie after getting the cute, lovable Dessy to bed. At that point, I couldn't believe my luck. What other parents were willing to chuck out fifty dollars for three hours of babysitting? Being an intelligent girl, I wasn't about to question their generosity—at least not until I heard a loud *boom*.

I raced down the hallway toward little Dessy's bedroom, but when I shoved at it, the door wouldn't open. What could've exploded in his room? I shouted for Dessy, terror twisting my heart. His calls for help cut through me. Imagining him trapped inside, body brutally torn apart by the mysterious blast, I did the only thing I could to do. I rushed to the living room and called nine-one-one. Smart move, right?

Not so much.

To say the demon child had set me up to embarrass the hell out of me is an understatement. With neighbors watching, a television crew filming and his parents wringing their hands next to the ambulance, I made my way out of the house, intent on nothing more than going home and never having anything to do with another child. An unhurt Desmond followed behind me, grinning from ear to ear, his hand firmly clasped in a firefighter's. Another firefighter walked behind them, holding what was left of the box of fireworks Dessy had set off in his room.

Need I say more?

Actually, I guess I should. To be honest, the Dessy the Demon story was what I told people who were either brave enough or rude enough to ask about my possible fertility. The real reason, the one that tore at my gut every time I thought about having a baby, wasn't something I was ready to think about, let alone share with anyone else.

How was poor Kaine to know about my tormented past? He'd tried to cajole me out of the bathroom but, after an hour of waiting for me to reappear, he'd apparently decided to let me cool my jets in privacy. I heard the door slam signaling his departure. At first, this made me even madder. *How dare he leave me to stew all by myself?*

Eventually, however, I realized I was acting like an overgrown child. So the man had wanted to have the Baby Talk. Big deal, right? True, I hadn't expected the talk to come during our honeymoon, but I should've known the subject was bound to come up at some point. I mean, he's a virile young man. Why wouldn't he want kiddos? I had to ask myself, had his request warranted my reaction? I cringed inwardly and knew the answer. *Nope. But what should I do now?*

I sat on the toilet with the sheet wrapped around me and stared at my reflection in the full-length mirror on the opposite wall. Damn how I hated it when I screwed up. Especially when I screwed up big time like this *and* looked like a crazy bitch in the process. I eyed the telephone next to the toilet and reached out for the receiver. Should I call him, blare the all-clear signal, and tell him Hurricane Chrissy had blown herself out? Should I tell him I'd like to discuss getting pregnant?

Uh, definitely not. Just because I'd gone ballistic when he'd mentioned having a child didn't mean I wanted to push out a baby. I was ready to call a truce, but not ready to wave the white flag. Sighing, I hung up the telephone.

I needed help with this problem. Unfortunately, Aunt Flo (yes, I've heard all the jokes) had passed away two years earlier and most of my friends weren't very good at doling out advice. Most that is, except Thad, my own personal gay Dear Abby. Again I reached for the phone, then stopped. Getting Thad on the line never worked. Between writing, acting and directing his own theatre productions, he was harder to reach than Oprah's Stedman. Tracking him down was easier done in person, but I was in no position to do so sitting on a toilet thousands of miles away. Instead, I did the next best thing.

I admit it. It's a bit wacky to have conversations with someone who isn't really there, but let's face it, sometimes wacky works. Closing my eyes, I imagined how the conversation would go. Within seconds, I heard the sing-song tones of my friend ringing through me.

"Hel-looo! This is Thad. How may I help you make my day?"

"Thad, it's Chrissy. I need some advice, Oh Wise One."

"No problem, sweet-cheeks. Let Thaddy come to your rescue. Do exactly what I tell you to do. Open your mouth and make an *O* shape with your lips. Now pull his dick out of his boxers, bend over and—"

Typical Thad. "Oh, come on, ya big fairy. You know I don't need help with that." Thad allowed me to call him names because he knew I never meant them in a negative way. Every foul name I called him was filled with unconditional love. Besides, he could sling mud better than I could.

"How would I know that, Miss Bitch-Witch? I've never had the displeasure of having you blow me."

See?

I laughed, my fantasy already making me feel better. "Seriously. I need your help."

"Oh, honey, you've been married less than a week and already needing my fab self's help?" He tsked at me. "No matter. You know I'm always here for you. What's up? Or should I say down? Uh-oh. Is that the area of discontent?"

"I did something stupid." I cringed, reliving the scene in the bedroom.

"So what else is new?"

I shook my head at my imaginary friend. "Kaine brought up the subject of babies and I freaked out. He's gone. I think he's in the casino, but he left me alone in the villa."

The silence in my head lasted too long.

"Thad? Are you there?"

"Not to fear, I'm still here."

Another pause ensued, giving me time to renew the connection to my inner Thad. Who knew I could channel the gay bard so easily? Maybe I was on the wrong end of the paranormal pranks. "Yoo-hoo, did you get distracted by your newest boy toy?"

"I wish. Seriously, here's what you do. You get all dressed

up and go find him. Once he gets a load of you, he'll forgive and forget. You know those heterosexual breeders. They're all balls and no brains."

Could it be that easy? Or did I just subconsciously want it to be? I bit my lower lip. "And then what? He'll bring up the subject again. I know he will."

"Maybe. Maybe not. But in the meantime, you can work on him. And I do mean *work* on him."

I heard Thad's trademark snort and let his words soothe my nerves.

"Get him to see your side of the situation. Oh, and don't you dare play without a condom."

"Don't worry, I won't. As far as I'm concerned, no glove means no love." I frowned and wondered. Did I get an expression correct for once? I'm the worst when it comes to getting those things right. "Besides, I'm still on the pill." Being fearful of pregnancy meant always using at least two forms of birth control.

My interpretation of Thad's laughter filled my ears, lifting my spirits even more. "Good girl. Now get off the toilet and go find your man before some two-bit cocktail waitress snares him away from you."

"Will do, boss." I mentally disconnected, happy and determined to fulfill my mission.

I took his—okay, my—suggestion to heart and hopped into the shower. Making better time than I've ever done getting ready, I tugged on the tight red dress Kaine had bought me, shoved the room key in my cleavage and gave myself one last look in the mirror. I looked awesome, even if I did say so myself. Once I found Kaine, I was bound and determined to take his mind off babies and back on to hot steamy sex where it belonged.

When he got a load of the snug bodice accentuating my girls—and hopefully, garnering admiring glances from other men—he'd forget how badly I'd behaved. Then, after making him suffer over dinner first, I'd bring him back and screw the baby thoughts right out of him.

Although I had my new plan firmly in place, I decided I needed a little more bolstering to my ego. And as all girls know, there's no better way to lift your spirits than to tell one of your girlfriends about your blissful (soon to be blissful again) nuptials. Problem was, I didn't really have many close girlfriends. At least not like the one I'd had in college. Just thinking about Jennifer Randall made me smile. This time, however, an imaginary convo wouldn't work. I scooped up my cell phone and punched in her number. She answered on the second ring.

"Chrissy, is it really you? Shit, girl, I haven't heard from you in such a long time. What've you been up to?"

Suddenly, I was back in the dorm scarfing down greasy pizza and dishing dirt with my BFF. Jenn and I may not talk to each other every month—heck, not even every six months—but we've always had an indefinable connection. You know. Like a personal bungee cord that keeps pulling us back to each other.

"You won't believe it, Jenn. I'm getting married." I don't know why I suddenly couldn't tell her I was already married. Instead, I looked at my face in the mirror and scowled. Hadn't I called her to spread the good news?

I received the obligatory expressions of good wishes. Shoving the question of my marriage denial to the back of my mind, I gushed on. "He's wonderful, Jenn. I met him at a friend's birthday party. The party was at the lake, and this *thing* jumps out of the water, flinging its gruesome body straight for me. Suddenly, this man leaps in between me and this killer fish-thing, and saves my not-so-insubstantial butt."

I bit my lower lip at the silence that followed. *Shoot. Should've kept quiet about the creature from the lake, Chrissy. Knowing Jenn, she's bound to get on the yes-there-really-are-monsters kick and you don't need that shit right now.*

"Are you okay? Were you injured?"

"No. I mean, I'm fine. But this man, my hero, caught this ugly animal seconds before it chomped into me. I didn't see it because I turned my head, but when I turned back around, the animal was dead. He tossed it in the lake."

Another silence. What was Jenn thinking? At this point, I was wondering what I'd been thinking to call her.

"C, is there something else you're not telling me?"

Damn. People have told me that sometimes I need a nudge to spit out my problems. But I didn't have any real problem, right?

"No. Well, okay, something else did happen. When I looked at him, I thought I saw my hero change." I winced. *Why can't I keep my trap shut? Why did I bring that up?*

"Change? Change how?"

"Oh, I'm just being silly. I must've hallucinated out of shock or something." *Way to backpedal, girl.* I forced a laugh. "Something like too much booze."

"C, tell me what you saw. Don't leave out any details. You never know what might be important."

Important? Surely she wasn't thinking this is one of her supernatural things. "Well, I thought—and only for a second, mind you—the man looked like a...a..."

"A what?"

I could hear her struggle to keep her tone level. How I wished I'd never picked up the phone. Make-believe discussions were so much easier to handle. Yet instead of blowing off the whole conversation and hanging up, my mouth took over and left my exit plan in tatters. "A dragon." I quickly executed damage control. "Now isn't that the dumbest thing you've ever heard?"

"A dragon? Are you sure?"

"Of course I'm not. I mean it was just the way his head *seemed* to change shape for a second. Like I said, I'd obviously mixed too much celebrating with an overly active imagination. I shouldn't have any said anything about this. I don't even know why I did. Let's talk about fun things, okay? Did I tell you he's wealthy? Not that that's why I love him or anything."

Another damn silence took over. *Damn, damn, damn.* "Jenn, are you there? Listen, I didn't realize the time when I called you, but I've got to run. I'll send you a photo and you can see for yourself what a major catch I've landed."

"Yes, do. Hey, C, do me a favor. Send me a pic on my phone."

Somehow I didn't think she wanted to gush over my hottie-honey. Worry crept into my heart. "Will do. Bye-bye." At first, I considered not emailing her one of the photos I had stored in my phone. But I reconsidered once I remembered how tenacious Jenn could be. I could either send her one now or have her call me back a few hundred times and coerce me to send one. Checking through my files, I quickly chose the best photo that I had of Kaine and emailed it.

Breathing a sigh of relief, I ran my hands over my dress, repositioned the heavy artillery and straightened to my full height. I was finished making calls. Now was the time to get my man back.

I left the villa and headed for the casino. Once inside the noisy room, I stopped, glanced around at the throng of people and sought out the nearest bar. I might not have known my new hubby for very long, but I knew him well enough to search the nearest watering hole.

Entering the club off the main gambling area, I found Kaine sitting at a table next to a wall. But my man was not alone.

Her long silky hair ran down her neck and wafted over her shoulders to flow in a cascade of beautiful white rain over the rich upholstery of the chair. The length ended an inch below the seat and rippled with every movement of her head. I stared, tried to find signs of peroxide or split ends, and had to fight back a curse when I didn't see even one imperfection. I mean, who has hair like that? Although the oversized, luxurious chair hid her body from me, I pictured an oval face with piercing blue eyes and kissable lips on a come-and-get-sex bod.

The woman must've said something funny because Kaine leaned back in his chair and laughed. Not chuckled. Oh, no. This was one of his rare full-throated laughs. The lean mean envy machine zapped into high gear in less time than it took to growl at her.

What the hell is Kaine doing with some bar floozy? One little argument and he's off and running into some skank's open arms? I didn't care how good-looking this bitch was, he had no right to sit there laughing with her. Had they been together the whole time I sulked in the bathroom?

I threw back my shoulders and strode over to the table. No one was going to take my man, much less some Vegas vixen. Trying to play it cool, I came to a stop behind the White-Haired Witch, tipped my head and regarded Kaine from beneath lowered eyelashes.

He froze, raised drink in one hand, and let his gaze slide over me in an agonizingly slow trek. If he'd looked at me like that at any other time, I would've dropped my thong, slipped onto the table and opened wide.

"Oh, there you are, honey-buns. I thought I'd lost my new *husband*." When he didn't respond, I pushed the issue. "Aren't you going to introduce me to your friend?"

The chair turned toward me and I prepared to launch into my first-ever public cat fight. Yet when I saw who sat before me, all the jealousy and anger rushed out of me like a gigantic balloon with a Texas-size hole.

"You must be Mrs. Delcaluca." The man rose, tossed his TV-commercial glossy hair over his shoulders and offered his hand. I glanced from the stranger to my very amused lover and lifted my limp mitt. He took it and placed his other hand on top of mine.

Eeww. "I, uh..." My tongue stalled.

His eyes sparkled at my distress. Thankfully, he didn't mention my inability to form a complete sentence. "Mrs. Delcaluca, I am so happy to meet you." With a quick glance at Kaine, he added, "She should do very nicely."

Huh? Why did I feel like a heifer in the auction ring? "Thank you." *I think.* Since my tongue had finally found its power again, I used it to give me time to study the person in front of me. "I'm sorry. I didn't mean to disturb you. It's just that I assumed Kaine would be..."

I continued to ramble on, not caring what I said as long as I had time to take in this interesting creature in front of me. His long face, so not the oval one I'd imagined, appeared slightly out of shape, as though his skin barely fit over his skull. A long chin jutted out, making a stubby nose seem even shorter. His dark eyes glittered, reminding me of the cold, uncaring eyes of a reptile. When he smiled—at least I think it was a smile—then closed his mouth, long, pointed teeth barely fit behind thin lips. I shivered, unable to brush off the feelings of disgust and trepidation I felt. Hoping he wouldn't take offense, I pulled my hand out from between his and forced myself not to wipe my palm on my clothes.

"Chrissy-d—" Kaine stopped, obviously not wanting to use his term of endearment in front of the man. "May I introduce, Mr. Tuo Chow? He's a former business associate of mine."

I noticed the brief scowl that flitted across Mr. Chow's features at my hubby's use of the word *former*.

"Former associate, Kaine? I certainly hope not." Mr. Chow tossed his question over his shoulder, but kept his eyes on me.

Had I caught Kaine doing business on his honeymoon? Because I ran my own business, I could understand mixing work with play, but on a honeymoon? Talk about Type-A personalities. Or perhaps it was simply a chance encounter?

"It's nice to meet you, Mr. Chow. Do you do business with my husband often?" Leaning toward appeasing the man, I couched the question in the present tense.

Mr. Chow ran his gaze from my face to my feet and back again in a blatant appraisal of my body. A shiver—and not the good kind—zipped down my spine. "Kaine and I go way back. But, unfortunately, he seems to think we've drifted apart."

The irritated expression on Kaine's face said it all. Chow may be a former associate, but he was no friend. Inwardly, I breathed a sigh of relief. The farther away we kept from this slimy creature, the better.

"We're as close as we ever were, Tuo."

Oooh, s-nap. Kaine had effectively dissed the dude. I instinctively took a step back.

"Then take the bargain I've offered you. I want what you have." Tuo Chow's eyes danced with danger and locked onto Kaine.

Kaine shook his head. "As I've said several times before, the item is not for sale. The Dy—" His gaze flitted to me, then back to Mr. Chow. "My company would never approve of such a transaction."

A hiss from Tuo sent me shuffling over to my husband, who stood and glided his arm around my waist. Tuo hissed again, his eyes glittering.

"Hey, I'm no doctor, but getting too worked up can be harmful to your health. Don't you think you might want to calm down?" Like I really cared about this strange man.

Tuo's fierce gaze drifted from Kaine to me. "Not when your husband is upsetting me." His hard glare settled on my hubby again. "Give me what I want."

"Again, Tuo. You ask for the impossible." Although his body was rigid, Kaine's voice stayed remarkably calm. I bit back a smile of pride.

"I will have what I want, Delcaluca."

I gasped and turned to Kaine. In the instant before he replied, I would've sworn I saw my husband's gorgeous green eyes flash and change to a bright gold. Narrowing my sight, I tried to find the gold again, but it was gone.

"Chow, you tread on dangerous ground." Raw rage masked his calm face. He leaned slightly forward and lowered his tone. "Pursue this and you will regret it."

Holy crap! Did my sweet hubby just threaten a man? I knew I was staring at Kaine, but I couldn't help it. Had he meant what he'd said? Or was this how they negotiated in his line of business?

Sending my husband one last longer, louder hiss, Tuo pivoted on his heel and stalked away.

"Wow." I cocked my head at Kaine and studied him again.

The anger left his features in small waves until, at last, my loving husband had returned. "A little harsh, don't you think? Not to mention how threatening a person can put a damper on any future negotiations."

He sighed and led me toward the door. "That animal isn't worthy of your concern."

I coughed out a short, harsh laugh. "You'd better hope nothing happens to him or someone might think your threat was a serious one. Good thing wives can't be forced to testify against their husbands, huh?" He remained quiet, leaving my joke hanging in the air. "But what was he so upset about? I mean, it's only business, right?"

"Of course. He overreacts, is all."

Although Kaine had briefly explained his line of work, I still had more questions than answers. "Exactly what item were you two talking about?"

He took my arms to pull me around to face him. "Chrissy-doll, we have to have an understanding. You don't need to know the details of my work and, frankly, I'd rather not discuss it with you."

Oh, no way! Did he just tell me to mind my own business? I started to fume, but quickly stamped down the brewing volcano. I'd already had one blow-up with him and I didn't want another one. Besides, I'd give him the benefit of the doubt. I'm sure he hadn't meant it the way it had sounded.

Unfortunately, however, sometimes my mouth doesn't listen to my head. "Are you seriously telling me to butt out? What's next? Patting me on the head and telling me I shouldn't worry my pretty little head about men's business?" *Oops. Watch out for lava!*

Kaine didn't take my bait. Instead of firing back, he pulled me against him and nuzzled my ear. "Please, Chrissy-doll, let's not talk about such things. I only want to spend time with you before we have to fly back to Atlanta. From this moment on, let's not even use the word *business*, much less talk about it. Okay?"

I am such a softie. Part of me wanted to stay the course, but another part of me wanted that worry-free, work-free honeymoon I'd always dreamed of. So, even though my questions were left unanswered, I couldn't resist him any more than I could've resisted a pint of double-chocolate fudge ice cream. And as is obvious from the expanse of my rear end, I rarely put up any resistance to ice cream. "Okay."

Still, when I turned to search the direction of Mr. Chow's exit, I couldn't shake the uneasy feeling that we'd be seeing the odd stranger again.

Purple People Eaters and Other Weirdoes

The plane ride home was almost as romantic as the honeymoon. Kaine thought of everything from the chauffeured limousine to the long-stemmed red roses waiting for me on the plane. He also arranged to have soft music, dim lighting and my favorite meal—a footlong chili-cheese dog with a pile of onions on top with real hand-cut greasy French fries—waiting for me. I knew my arteries were probably well on their way to becoming clogged like the drain in a sorority house, but a girl's got to have some vices, right? Still, the best part was the total absence of any discussion regarding babies. I snuggled into the comfy chair and breathed a sigh of relief.

Kaine, settled into a captain's chair a short distance from me, flashed me a disarming smile. He continued his perusal of the business papers on his lap and swiveled his chair around, placing his back to me. *So the man's a workaholic. Everyone has a few faults and I can think of a lot worse activities for my new hubby to obsess on.*

Outside the runway of Hartsfield-Jackson Airport was growing closer. When the wheels hit the pavement, I popped the last fry into my mouth and thought about the past few days in Vegas. Unfortunately, instead of thinking about the amazing makeup sex we'd had after my tizzy fit, my mind wondered back to the meeting in the bar. What the hell was Tuo Chow? I frowned, perplexed at my use of the word *what*. Of course I'd meant *who*. But something about the man bothered me. Was it just his strange appearance? The way his skin seemed shiny, almost as though it was covered in scales? Or did my feelings of unease come from the guy's creepy personality?

Tuo Chow was definitely odd, but something else kept coming back to bug me. Had I really seen Kaine's eyes flash from green to gold? I'd checked his eyes numerous times since then and found no gold in them. Not even one tiny gold fleck. So had I seen what I thought I'd seen? My gaze darted toward my husband, but he still sat with his back to me.

In my line of work, you get good at asking questions. After all, what better way to find out what's really going on than to just put it out there? Resolving that my marriage would be an open book, I stood and took a step toward Kaine. My man had some explaining to do and now was the time for him to pipe up.

Strains of Thad's voice singing my business's theme song jolted me from my thoughts. With a quick glance at the still-working Kaine, I flipped open my cell. "Christina Taylor. You've reached Debunkers, Inc. Let me take the fright out of your night." I shook my head. I'd tried several slogans and still hadn't hit on the perfect one.

"Chrissy? It's Jenn."

"Hey, Jenn. Wow, two calls in a week. We're on a roll."

Jenn didn't laugh like I'd expected her to. Instead, she replied with a noncommittal grunt and got straight to the point. Yep, typical Jenn.

"C, I don't know how to put this, so I'm just going to spit it out. I'm worried."

"What about?" Had something happened to her husband? She'd gotten married only a short while earlier. Surely their marriage wasn't on the skids yet.

"About Kaine. And you."

Her words took all the air out of me. "Kaine? Why?" She hadn't even met the man and she was worried? I glanced at him to make sure he hadn't heard me, but his back was still toward me. I doubted an atomic bomb could've roused him from his paperwork.

"I got the picture you sent me."

"Yeah?" The hairs on the back of my neck stood up. Not a good sign. Not a good sign at all. "So? Didn't I tell you he's gorgeous? But not to fret. He's definitely a one-woman man."

"That's not the problem."

"Then what?" I tried to keep my tone level, but her remarks were ticking me off. Why couldn't she simply be happy for me like any good friend should be?

"Well, I noticed something in the pic you sent me."

If I could've reached through the phone and pulled her into the plane, I would have. "Jenn, quit beating around the tree. What are you getting at?"

"I noticed the, uh, tattoo on Kaine's neck. You know the one I'm talking about, right?"

Of course I did. Yet for some inexplicable reason, I didn't want to admit it. "Uh, maybe." *Oh, please, girl. Like she's gonna believe that I'm stupid now.* How could I have possibly missed it since I'd licked the area at least a few dozen times in Vegas?

"Are you serious?"

Like I said. She's not buying the dumb routine. I opened my mouth to deny seeing the mark again, but couldn't force the words out. She let the pause between us go on far too long to leave any doubt. She knew I knew she knew I was lying.

At last, however, she spoke up. "Come on, C, the one at the

base of his throat? Are you really trying to say you haven't seen it?"

I still wanted to dodge telling the truth. Or at least the whole truth. "Oh, that. It's nothing."

"Nothing? I don't think so."

"I know so, Jenn. In fact, it's not there any longer." Before I could give it a second thought, my vivid imagination took the reins away from my conscience and played Little Red Riding Hood. *Damn, what a big liar you are. The better to get away with shit, my dear.*

"Huh? It's gone?"

I ignored the disbelief in her tone and trudged on through the mire of deceit. "Yeah. The tat was a joke, a temporary. He washed it off." My stomach did a flip-flop with the last whopper. Why was I lying? Because her questioning bordered on an interrogation?

"Good." I heard the rush of relief behind her sigh. "I'm glad."

"Yeah, no biggie. So you were worried about a silly tattoo?" *Let it drop, Chrissy. Let. It. Drop.* But again I ignored reason and opened my trap. Like a scab you can't help picking at, I kept picking at this sore. "Pretty silly, don't you think?"

"Yeah, I guess so."

Oh, crap. I knew I'd kept this discussion going too long. She still thought something was off. Curse Jenn and her super-sleuth instincts. Sometimes I wondered if she'd missed her calling. Instead of working as a realtor, she should've been a private investigator. Or maybe a secret agent.

"So you haven't noticed anything else strange or weird?"

Now that you mention it... I ignored what the "else" implied because, for once, my mouth listened to my mind. "No. Nada." I bit my tongue to keep from asking *what kind of weird things?*

"Good. That's good."

I could sense the mood lifting on her end and experienced a fresh flood of guilt. "Yeah, it is good. Real good."

"So when's the wedding?"

I should've copped to my deception—*is this the second or the third lie?*—at that point, but I didn't. What the heck was going on with me? Why didn't I want her to know I was married? I dug the hole deeper and this lie was easier than the last. What happened to tell-it-like-it-is Chrissy? "Oh, we haven't set a date yet."

Kaine, who had suddenly turned his chair toward me, furrowed his brows at me in question. I made a funny face and giggled. He smiled in return, pointed toward the cockpit, and headed that way.

"Oh, I see. Well—and I don't mean to carry on about this—but keep your eyes open, okay? I mean, if you ever need me for anything, all you have to do is call."

Oh, hell. Could she be any nicer? *Just ratchet up the guilt, why don't you?* "Thanks, Jenn. I will. And I'll be sure to send you an invitation. Then we can meet each other's hubbies." *Liar, liar, pants on flame.* Or however the saying goes.

At last, however, the rationalizing part of me kicked in. I was actually being nice, too. I mean, why should I bother Jenn with any strange stuff when I knew I'd find a logical explanation? After all, explaining away weird shit is what I do.

During our honeymoon, Kaine and I had agreed on where we'd be living. The discussion, of course, didn't take more than a couple of minutes. I mean, on the one hand, we had my tiny studio apartment. It was cozy, semi-clean, cheap and my *twin* bed took up at least half of the square footage. On the other hand, however, we had his huge home. Hmm, which one to choose. Hey, my mamma didn't raise no pauper—or however the saying goes. I happily agreed to Kaine's place and today was the day I'd finally see my—um, our—new home.

I gazed out the side window of Kaine's limousine and watched the city of Atlanta flash by. Just a few days earlier, I'd been wondering how to pay my rent and now I was on my way to a grand house in Buckhead. Who'da thunk it? Not me, that's who.

Taking another sip of champagne I'd found chilling in the limo's mini-bar, I couldn't help but let out a small sigh of contentment—until I realized we'd veered off course and were heading toward the outlying areas of Atlanta.

"Uh, Kaine, where are we going?"

The corners of his mouth tipped upward, signaling he'd planned this detour.

"What did you do?"

He reached over to place a sweet kiss on my cheek and clinked our glasses together. "I should've known you'd pick up on the change in destination."

"Change? So we're not going to your home?" I'm not a big one on surprises, but let's face it, so far his surprises had been nothing short of spectacular. So instead of letting my nerves get the best of me, I returned his smile. "Okay, dude, spit it out. Where are we headed?"

"To our new home."

Our new home? Had the man forgotten our decision to live in his luxurious Buckhead home? "But I thought we'd agreed I'd move into your place."

"We did."

I tried not to let my irritation show, but the Quiet Man routine was getting old. "Then we're not headed in the right direction. Or did you fib about where you lived?" An uneasy feeling tickled my stomach. Had I been scammed? Was Kaine really who he said he was? Or was he some kind of con man who only pretended he was wealthy? Although if that was true, he'd sure picked the wrong mark. Was I destined to be a guest on Dr. Phil?

"Relax, silly girl." Kaine chuckled and leaned away from me.

"Okay, first of all, never call me silly." In my line of work, I meet truly silly, fearful people. Since I prided myself on my practicality, calling me *silly* was an outright insult. Of course, my new hubby had no way of knowing this so I cut him some slack. This time. "Secondly, I am a woman. Not a girl." I batted my eyelashes at him, lessening the sting of my words. "I would've thought you'd have noticed that by now."

His lustful gaze slipped from my face, ran a quick race over the rest of my body and came back to the finish line of my lips. "Chrissy, trust me. I am very aware and incredibly pleased that you're a woman." He let his perusal make another lap around my body track. "You are the most beautiful, sexiest woman I've ever seen."

Had this guy memorized a book of great lines? Or maybe written it? Yet instead of obeying my heart and falling into his arms, I took a deep breath, secured my raging libido with mental chains and forged ahead. "And last but not least, you'd better tell me what's going on. I realize I haven't told you this before and, in fact, have probably led you to believe otherwise, but I'm not big on surprises. So 'fess up. Where are we going?"

"I told you. We're going home." He glanced away as though

he'd settled the issue.

Could my man have developed a memory problem and lost his way home? But why would the driver have the same problem? I steeled myself against the remote possibility of early Alzheimer's disease and kept the ball rolling.

"Honey, your, uh, our home is in Buckhead." Hopefully, I hadn't sounded too patronizing. But I knew better. Before getting a diagnosis, I'd already started speaking to Kaine like he lacked the mental capacity of a bunny. "We're headed toward Cumming. You know, one of those towns *way* outside the Perimeter."

Like many large cities, a beltway circled around Atlanta. Atlantans, therefore, use the highway to designate areas as being either inside the Perimeter (ITP) or outside the Perimeter (OTP). Kaine's home in Buckhead was definitely ITP and we were headed OTP. Living ITP had always provided everything I'd ever wanted or needed, so I had rarely ventured OTP. Except, of course, for other basic necessities such as work (money) and lakeside birthday parties (booze).

"I know." He twisted back to me and smiled. "But I promise you. We are headed home." His grin grew wider and I suddenly got the image of Jack Nicholson sticking his head through a hole in the door.

"I'm sorry." I figured those words would cover a bunch of different scenarios. Like *I'm sorry, but I don't understand.* Or *I'm sorry I didn't see this breakdown coming.* Or *I'm sorry you've suddenly become a complete moron and can't find your way home.* Or the very popular *I'm sorry, please don't go bonkers and kill me.*

Kaine laughed and pulled me to him. I didn't resist which, to me, proved how much I loved the man. "Chrissy-doll, I know you're confused, but all you have to do is trust me. This surprise is a good thing. I bought you a wedding present."

"Oh." *I'm sorry* suddenly meant *I'm sorry I'm such an idiot.* "Another present?" At least I wouldn't sound like an ungrateful idiot.

Kaine pointed to the ornate gates already sliding open as our car pulled off the road and cruised toward them. The gates opened automatically, sending me into a bit of a panic. I definitely needed an explanation. "Are we visiting someone?"

"No, we're not visiting anyone." He inclined his head, directing my attention to the massive building looming ahead. "We're home."

Although I knew Kaine was loaded—I'm talking both financially and in the lower extremities (ahem!)—I was still unprepared for my first view of our new house. Perhaps the wrought-iron gate and fence surrounding the estate should've given me a clue. Not to mention the beautiful drive passing along the manicured lawn and magnificent topiary. Or maybe the numerous chimneys on the roof. But I just wasn't getting it.

"Home? I don't understand. You live in Buckhead in what I'm positive is a great place. But this—" I gestured at the cream-colored walls. "This is amazing. Hell, this is a freakin' castle right in the middle of Georgia."

"Well, strictly speaking we're not in the middle of Georgia, but—"

"Kaine, shut the hell up and tell me what this is about."

He chuckled again. "I can hardly shut up and tell you anything at the same time."

Our car pulled up to the steps leading to the front door and I fought to keep from fainting. I leaned my body over Kaine's to peer through his window. "Why are we here?"

"Chrissy-doll, I don't know how to say this any clearer. *This* is our new home. I bought it the day after we were married."

I swear I did almost faint then. "Our new home?" Again, I looked up the steps leading to the front, and this time, noticed a man, obviously a butler, standing beside the ornate front doors. "Are you frickin' kidding me?"

Kaine wrapped his arms around me and pulled me close. "No, I'm not frickin' kidding you."

I stared at the only sight more amazing than my new home—my husband. "But why?"

He placed his palm against my cheek and I melted, unable to resist the heat coming from his skin. "Because when you married me, you turned this poor excuse of a man into a king. Isn't it only right that my queen live in a palace?" He smiled and tilted his head. "Or at least the closest thing to a palace that I could find in this state."

I fell into the kiss, forgetting the mansion, the whirlwind marriage—everything except how much I loved him. No Lifetime Network movie had ever been this good.

Kaine kissed me back. Breaking through my lips, his tongue swept through my mouth, running along my cheeks to soak up my taste. He groaned in pleasure, bracing his hand behind my head to tilt it back. His kiss grew deeper, fuller, needier.

I slid down in the seat, ready and willing to do the Backseat Bump. Kaine slid his hand over my chest to cup my breast and I wanted nothing more than to get naked and dirty. Raking his thumb back and forth over my already-taut bud, he pressed his body over mine. I broke off the kiss, but only because I desperately needed air. I glanced toward the driver and the darkened partition separating the front of the limo from us. "He can't see us, can he?"

Kaine's mumbled words warmed the curve of my neck.

I pushed him to a sitting position and kept moving, coming to sit on his lap. "I'll take that as a yes." *Oh, naughty me.*

He pulled open my blouse, breaking the top button, and tugged my skirt up to my hips. I grinned at the sound of my thong being ripped off me. Unhooking my front-clasped bra, he pushed the material out of the way and latched onto my tit. I shuddered at the fierce tug on my nipple and rocked against him, delighting at the feel of the sudden growth underneath me.

"Oooh, I always wanted to screw in a limo."

Swiping his tongue over the top of one breast, then the other, he grasped my shoulders and lifted me more squarely on his protruding cock.

When did he unzip his slacks? But that was a question not needing an answer. He shoved his thick arrow into my target and aimed for my bull's-eye. I inhaled and ground my hips against him.

He lifted me, moving me up and down along his shaft. He entered me again, cramming upward until I was sure I'd see his shaft poking out from my mouth. Not that I was complaining. Hell, no. In fact, I rotated faster on top of him, hoping to drive him even farther into me. Up and up until he touched the top of my head.

Moving his hands to my hips, he held me securely. I rode him hard and wet, holding my breasts to feather against his face in a tease-you gesture. Gripping his shoulders, I bit my lower lip and bumped to his hump. I met his every thrust with an equally strong push.

Push, circle, push. The words became a mantra echoing in my mind. I arched my back, finally giving my breasts to him and he played with them, catching first one, then the other as they bobbed up and down with our movements.

His cock filled me completely, rubbing against the walls of

my cave, making me spill my essence over his shaft. Reaching down, I found my aching clit and massaged it, my fingers matching the circular motion of my hips.

"Oh, Kaine, I love the way you fuck me." I licked my lips and clenched my inner muscles. He ground his teeth, a sure sign that his release was near. "Promise me you'll always fuck me like this."

His golden—*golden?*—eyes met mine and I swear I saw flickers of light in them. "I promise you that and more."

I moaned, readying for the *O* that I knew was near. We'd made love fast and hard, and I loved it. I loved him.

Unfortunately, all good things must come to a finish. "Omigod, Kaine." *Pant.* "We'd better—oh—" *pant, pant,* "—get out before—" *pant, gasp,* "—everyone figuresoutwhatwe'redoing." I hurried the words as the build-up tensed my body, readying for the eruption.

"Chrissy-doll."

Using my pet name was the final straw. My climax ripped through me a second before Kaine's did. I bit the shoulder of his jacket, hoping to stifle the scream of ecstasy tearing loose inside me. Kaine gritted his teeth and placed his forehead on my shoulder, his tortured breaths the only clue to his release.

Finished welcoming each other home, I hurriedly pulled my clothes together and finger-combed my hair. *Figures.* The one time I put my purse with the rest of the luggage would be the one time I really needed my comb.

I helped Kaine clean up, straighten his jacket and zip his slacks. "Are we good?"

The sparkle in his eyes made me wet all over again. "Chrissy-doll, you're not good. You're incredible."

I placed a peck of a kiss on the tip of his nose. "Aw, I bet you say that to all the girls you fuck in your limo."

He grabbed me then, roughly, a stern expression on his face. "Maybe."

Maybe? Shoot, I'd been joking about the other women.

"But I've never said this to any of them." He cupped my face. "I didn't expect to love you. I only thought that you'd give me—"

Give him what? I waited, my heart pounding against my chest, eager hope mixing with a rush of anxiety.

He shook his head, effectively shaking off the rest of his sentence. "I never thought you'd give me so much more. I love you more than anyone and anything in the world."

I swallowed. Oh, sure, the idea of his having had women in the limo before me wasn't particularly my idea of after-sex talk, but he'd sure ended the conversation with a bang.

We looked at each other for a solid thirty seconds before Kaine broke the spell. "Let's go check out our new home." He pushed the speaker button. "We're ready now, Roger." The driver hurried around to the passenger's side and swung the door open. Kaine slid out of the limo, turned and offered me his hand just like the dashing hero did in all the romantic movies I'd seen.

I took it, feeling every bit the queen of the manor, and scooted not-so-gracefully out the door. Straightening up with Kaine's arm wrapped around me, I studied the house. "We are talking mansion for sure. I bet this place has at least ten bedrooms."

"Sixteen."

"And six bathrooms."

"Eleven. Not counting the seven half baths."

I eyed my man speculatively. "And a home theatre?" *Please, oh, please, let there be a home theatre.*

"What mansion would be complete without one?" He touched my chin, then pivoted to face the crowd gathered at the top of the steps. "Want to go inside now?"

"Do bears shit in the trees?"

"I believe the expression is...do bears shit in the woods?"

I rolled my eyes. "Whatever." Grinning, I put my attention on the mansion before me. "Take me inside our new home, lover-boy."

To say I slipped into the lavish lifestyle without a hitch is an understatement. This girl had found her Prince Charming and she wasn't about to lose that stupid glass slipper.

After I met the staff—all twenty-four of them—Kaine escorted me to the enormous master bedroom where I spent nearly ten minutes *oohing* and *aahing* over just the silk bedspread. When he left me alone to get unpacked, I spent another thirty minutes gazing out the six luxuriously draped windows like a queen surveying her kingdom. Although it was still summer, I couldn't help but wish I could start a fire in at least one of the two fireplaces. And the bathroom was twice as big as my studio apartment, with two long counters, the best lighting any girl could ever hope for, and a spa tub that could have easily accommodated six people. To put it bluntly, I was in Spoil-Me-Baby Heaven.

After enjoying an hour soaking in the tub, I wrapped the softest robe I'd ever touched around myself and stepped through a different door and into yet another room, the sitting area between the two enormous walk-in his-and-her closets. As usual, my Kaine had thought of everything. My closet was filled with not only my pitiful poor girl clothes from my apartment, but with designer duds from gowns to jeans. The shoe collection alone took up an entire wall. I've never been a girly-girl and into fashion much, but I have to confess, tears came to my eyes when I looked at my new beautiful wardrobe.

Taking care with my makeup and hair, then dressing in a pair of linen slacks and a silk shirt, I slipped on a bejeweled pair of flats and forced myself to leave my oasis. I was halfway down one hallway when I realized I had no clue where I was. Much less where I should be heading.

"Sheesh, I should've asked for a map." I looked around, trying to determine which way might lead me to Kaine. Maybe I should've stayed in my bedroom. But, money or not, I was not the type of gal to lie around in her boudoir waiting for her man to spare her some of his time. When I'd finally decided to take a stab at a left turn down the other hallway, I heard the unmistakable sound of someone talking. Feeling like a modern-day Gretel, I headed in the direction of the voice.

The door to the room closest to me was open, allowing me to step inside without announcing my presence. (Yeah, yeah, I know I still should've knocked, but, hey, it's my home after all.) The bedroom wasn't as opulent as ours, but it was still plush by anyone's standards. A thin woman stood at an ornate desk on which rested a small cage. Little white mice, all painted with different colored stripes, scurried around the cage, each clamoring to be in the far corner away from the woman. One mouse, painted with a brilliant streak of hot pink, dared to rear up on its little legs, almost as though offering itself in place of the others. I started to speak, then abruptly closed my yap. Something about the intent way she stared at the rodents gave me the creeps.

What the hell was she doing with all those— My brain froze before it could finish the thought. Instead, I gaped, unable to believe what I was seeing. The woman reached into the cage, snatched up one of the frightened creatures and popped it into her mouth. *Omigod! Did she really eat that mouse?* Even though my eyes told me she had, I still couldn't believe it. I stumbled backward, out the door and into the hallway.

"Who's there?"

Damn!

The scratchy-sounding voice sent me running down the hallway. No way did I want to talk to Ms. Mouse Muncher. I kept moving, trying to sort out exactly what I would tell Kaine about my discovery. *Hey, sweet man, guess what I saw. Did you know there's this really creepy lady in the house who likes to eat mice? Please tell me she's not your sister. Or maybe she's in training for the next* Survivor*?* I ran on, figuring if I did, then I'd have less of a chance of meeting up with Ms. Munch-a-Bunch-of-Mickey. After all, who knew what else she might like to pop into her mouth? A bit of ear? A tongue or nose? Or maybe my pinkie finger for a little dessert? My stomach roiled every time I pictured that poor mouse squealing all the way down her throat.

I have no idea how long it took, but at last, I found myself in the grand foyer and at the front door. Part of me wanted nothing more than to escape back to my safe apartment. The other half, the good wifey half, knew I could never leave Kaine in a house with the strange woman. So, with a burst of renewed courage, I dashed toward the study he'd shown me earlier.

Pushing the door open, I strode in, intent on telling my husband exactly what I'd seen. After all, he'd have an explanation, right? Because there's always a logical explanation. "Kaine, you are not going to believe what I saw." My feet thudded to a stop at the exact moment my heart did. My husband, sitting at his desk, looked up from his papers to shoot me a quick smile. Standing over my husband was none other than the Mouse Muncher.

"Hi, Chrissy." He stood and opened his arms wide. When I didn't move toward him, he gave me a funny look and walked over to pull my stiff body against his. "I was about to come and find you." Releasing me, he kissed me quickly, then turned to face MM. "Honey, I'd like you to meet my right-hand lady, my assistant extraordinaire, Miss Hermatilda Fitzwilder."

Holy crap! Usually I'm fairly fast on my feet and able to readily adapt to unusual circumstances. I mean, it's sort of a requirement in my line of work. Yet all I could do was stand and gawk at the woman. My husband, oblivious to the turmoil raging inside me went on with the introductions.

"Fitz was needed elsewhere during the staff introductions, but she's an invaluable asset and has been with me for years. Her family has worked for my family for generations, doing whatever needs to be done. I trust her with my life."

The Thin Woman inclined her head at Kaine. "It is my honor to serve the Delcaluca family. My purpose in life is to attend to *Mister* Delcaluca's needs in every way possible." She shot my hubby a look filled with...love? Yet worse, Kaine gazed at the woman as though she were made of gold.

I studied my hubby's face. Had he noticed the way she'd accented the word *Mister*? As though the *Missus* part—yours truly—of the newly married duo was chopped mouse meat?

"She knows all you could ever want to know about everything and everyone. I don't know what I'd do without her."

Hmm, I don't know, hubby dear. Maybe get a cat instead? I gawked at him. Was he aware that his Gal Friday was a rodent chomper? He wrapped his arm around me and squeezed. "I was asking Fitz if she would help you get settled into our new home. After all, she's the whiz who helped me purchase the place. She's also the one who got everything ready for our return."

So far, Fitz hadn't moved a muscle. She stood stock-still, her rat-snatching hands folded in front of her, her face an emotionless mask, listening to Kaine ramble on about how terrific she was. He kept extolling her virtues, but his voice soon became a distant drone. I locked eyes with Fitz and knew she disliked me, even distrusted me.

"You are correct."

The heavily accented words entered my head before I knew what had happened. Although I hadn't been listening to Kaine, I glanced his way, thinking he'd probably be waiting for me to respond to what he'd said. Instead, I heard the voice again. The very scratchy female voice.

"You are an intruder."

I couldn't believe it. Staring straight at Fitz, I dared her to confirm the unbelievable. *What did you say?*

A tiny smirk lifted the corners of her mouth. *"I am telling you that you are correct. You don't deserve him or this life. Kaine is mine to protect."*

She'd spoken to me without speaking out loud. But how? I knew there had to be a reasonable explanation. Yet I was damned if I could find one at that moment. Why was I having such a hard time explaining things? Had I hit my head without knowing it? Had I gotten drunk and this was all a way-out-there nightmare? I shook my head, denying her words and the idea of telepathic communication.

"I do not care if you believe what is real. Simply know that I will always be by his side. You, however, will not last long." Her smirk grew bigger, but Kaine didn't seem to notice.

Had this psycho rat-gulping bitch just threatened to steal my man? I glared at her, preparing to blast her big time. *Okay, Minnie-mauler, let's settle this right here, right now.* I moved out of my husband's hold to take two steps closer to her. Yet instead of the confrontation I expected, Fitz bobbed her head in deference.

"I am so happy to meet you, Mrs. Delcaluca."

Kaine gave her one of the beatific smiles I treasured. "Good. I'm sure you two will become fast friends."

His gaze fell on me and I almost shouted, "See? He loves me. Take that bitch!" Instead, I kept my mouth shut.

"Now, if you ladies will excuse me, I have a few business matters to attend to."

When Kaine turned to leave, I quickly lost my bravado and wanted to reach out and stop him. But my pride wouldn't let me. *Don't let her see you sweat, Chrissy.*

Kaine had barely exited when Fitz reached into a pocket of her drab gray off-the-rack suit and whipped out a photo. "If she couldn't hold him, you won't be able to do so, either."

Could this bitch get any ruder? I'm not one prone to violence, but I had to clench my fists to keep from snatching her bald. Not that being bald would make her any less attractive. Her emaciated body coupled with a hound-dog face and scraggly dishwater-blonde hair would've scared the varmints she liked to devour. Still, I took the photo.

The woman in the picture standing next to Kaine, arms wrapped possessively around him, was nothing less than movie-star gorgeous. You know the type: sick body like Megan Fox's, hair like Jennifer Aniston and super-kissable lips like Angelina Jolie. I immediately hated her. But so what? Obviously, she hadn't had what Kaine wanted.

Fitz snatched the photo away from me and repeated her previous prediction. "You won't last long." Her two beady eyes narrowed as she looked snidely down her nose at me. "How can you? You don't even know what he is."

What *he is? What the hell does that mean?* I opened my mouth to ask, but Fitz was already striding out of the room. For a skinny skank she sure could move fast. “I hope the rats bite your finger off,” I mumbled.

Mi Familia, Su Familia

I hated to admit it, but the Thin Woman had effectively delivered a punch to my solar plexus without lifting a hand. Instead of knocking her on her butt the way I itched to do, I had no choice except to regroup and live to confront her another time. After all, how would my belting his favorite assistant stack up with Kaine? Not good, I imagined. So, unable to do anything else, I took another accidental scenic route back to our bedroom, all the while thinking about the two other women in my hubby's life. If I'd known, however, that I wouldn't see Kaine until the next morning, I'd have tracked him down and dragged him back to christen our new bed.

Determined to begin our life together in our new home with a night of blistering sex, I stayed up, waiting for Kaine to return. I waited. Then waited some more. Yet, instead of my handsome hunk coming to make his new bride oh-so happy and sexually satisfied, I spent the night listening to strange sounds. Not only did our home have the usual creaks of a house settling, I was positive I heard someone crying. Creepy much?

I opened the French doors leading to the balcony off our bedroom and yes, for a moment, pretended to be a wealthy, sophisticated heiress surveying Paris. I peered into the yard below. A full moon lit the area, helping me see past the

Olympic-size swimming pool and on toward the extensive gardens. A nervous tickle traveled up my spine. *Come on, girl. You check out spooky things for a living. Why are you letting a few weird sounds unnerve you?* Gathering my courage, I remained on the balcony, telling myself to enjoy the serenity of the night. I may not be able to lie well to others, but I can do a bang-up job fibbing to myself. My unwanted friend, Dee Nial, has often been my sidekick. At last, however, I gave up trying to see into the places where only night-vision glasses could penetrate and turned to go back inside.

A howl, deep and rich, echoed through the air, making me swivel toward the yard below. I dashed to the railing and, my hands gripping the white stone, leaned over to stare into the night again.

I gasped, blinked several times and even pinched my arm. Directly below me, standing next to the pool, was a dark form. The creature, too massive in height and width to be called a dog, cocked its head at me. Blazing red eyes hit me, holding me to the spot even though my legs wanted to turn tail and run. Saliva dripped from the side of its mouth as it curled back its lips, exposing fangs that had to be at least six inches long. I swallowed, finally letting my legs take the lead, and took a step back. The creature growled, flashing more fangs. Letting out a sound I will never forget, it howled its displeasure and darted into the shadows of the house.

Holy shit! What is that thing? I came up with an answer, but it was one I didn't want. *A werewolf.* No other canine would stand on two legs the way this one had. No other wolf or dog, not even a Great Dane or St. Bernard, would be as large. But it was the look in its eyes that confirmed it as a werewolf. No wolf or dog—not even Lassie—could claim such intelligence. The kind of intelligence that was all human.

My pulse beat against my chest. I stood, unable to move,

unable to react. Should I find Kaine and tell him what I'd seen? I wanted to. Oh, how I wanted to. But my ego wouldn't let me. No. I wasn't ready to tell him that he'd married a hallucinating looney. Maybe after we'd been married a few years, but now was not the time to go down that particular road. Besides, how would it look for the myth-and-monster debunker to literally start crying wolf? *Were*wolf, that is.

Suddenly I wished for a camera, something to prove what I'd seen. Or maybe disprove my eyes and confirm what I knew. Werewolves didn't exist any more than all the ghosts and ghoulies I'd exposed over the years. Often studying a photo and dissecting the image with technology would prove a person's sight wasn't always trustworthy. I couldn't count the number of times a ghost had turned out to be nothing more than a trick of the eye. This was a hoax. A prank. Maybe one of the staff was having fun with the new lady of the house. Yet, although I wanted to believe my idea, I couldn't rid my gut of the uneasy feeling that what I'd seen was real.

I glanced around the area surrounding the home and worked up the nerve to peer over the edge of the railing. Why hadn't the wolf bolted for the gardens and run into the wooded area beyond like any self-respecting wild animal would do? Why had it gone into the shadows below me, directly under my balcony?

Uh-oh. It went below me. Right below me. My imagination took over, forming a huge woman-eating animal standing underneath me, ready to break through the stone of the balcony. Its claws would dig into my legs, snagging them like hooks into sides of beef, and pull me down into the darkness. *Get a grip, girl. You know monsters don't exist.* Yet, try as I might, I couldn't buy into my own assertions.

Feeling as though I was about to literally risk my neck and the blood pumping through it, I leaned farther over the railing, both hands holding onto the stone with a death grip. *Urgh.* Lousy choice of words. *Death* grip. Why not *life* grip? After all, I was hanging on to stay alive.

It's a sad fact, but true. My mind tends to wander, taking up the most ridiculous thoughts when stunned with fear. But I can't help it. That's just the way I am.

"My kingdom for a flashlight," I whispered, then cringed. The thing probably had super-sensitive hearing and I'd just done the equivalent of whistling for him. I squinted below, willing the dark to change into light. But even the full moon wasn't helping to illuminate the area. Was that lump over there the wolf crouching, preparing to attack? With that unnerving thought, I pushed away from the edge and walked as softly as I could backward toward my room. Sweat lined my forehead and I reached behind me, grasping air when I'd hoped to grasp doorframe. Finally, however, my hands found their mark and I whirled to escape, my heart threatening to burst from my chest. I slammed the doors, rattling the etched glass, and breathed a ragged sigh of relief.

A relief that lasted only seconds. Another howl filled the air. With a girly cry, I twisted the deadbolt and clung to the doorknob. I knew I should've yanked the curtains closed but, much like how we always slow down to see a car wreck, I just couldn't. I had to see what might happen next.

Fortunately, nothing happened last night after I'd garnered my courage and looked beyond the curtains. Nothing except cranking up my vexation with one sexy and absent hubby. I'd managed to build up a full head of steam despite my lack of sleep—or maybe because of it—and was ready to rage at Kaine. I'd spent the night alone, terrorized by demons of unknown origins and I wanted answers. How dare he stay away! What kind of man left his wife alone on the first night in their new home? I stormed out of my room and barreled down the hallway to my right.

"Kaine, you've got some explaining to do." Then a horrible thought struck me. Maybe Kaine had run into the monster I'd seen outside. I stopped, barely missing one of the many maids as she exited one of the bedrooms.

"Ma'am?"

I shook the image of my husband lying bleeding and torn apart out of my head. "What?"

The mousy little woman couldn't meet my eyes. She tucked her chin, letting her fuzzy white hair, brightened by one hot pink stripe, cover her face. When I reached out to comfort her, she gave a little squeal, reminding me of the frightened mice in Fitz's room. "I'm sorry, ma'am. I thought you said something to me." She glanced up with a timid look. "Did you need something?"

"What I need is my husband. Where the hell is he?"

The maid seemed to fold into herself even more and took a quick step away from me.

I immediately regretted my gruff tone. "Damn, I'm sorry." I reached out to take her hand, but she quickly put it behind her back. Why was this poor girl so afraid? "I didn't mean to sound harsh. Seriously." I bent my head, trying to make eye contact with her. "I'm really a pussy cat."

If the girl hadn't appeared frightened before, she sure did now. With another squeak, she backed up again. "Please, ma'am. I'm still learning my new job. I'm doing the best I can."

What or who was she terrified of? After all, almost all the staff was new, hired by Fitz while we were on honeymoon. Was it Fitz? Was she afraid of the Mouse Muncher? Could the human equivalent of a mouse feel the same way towards Fitz that the actual rodents did? "I'm sure you're doing a terrific job. What's your name?"

She paused, looking like she'd forgotten her own name. "Missy." The girl visibly relaxed. "And thank you, ma'am."

I smiled at her, hoping to put her more at ease. "Nice to meet you. But you know what? I don't like being called ma'am. Do you think you could call me Chrissy?"

Horror spread over the young woman's face. "Oh, no, ma'am. I wouldn't dare. Ms. Fitzwilder wouldn't like it."

"Screw Fitz." The retort flew out of my mouth before I could stop it. A brief smile flitted across the girl's face and her eyes lit up. "I mean...considering Fitz works for my husband and now me, I don't think I need to consult her."

Did Missy think Fitz would fire her? Not if I had any say in the matter. Or did the fearful thing think something worse would happen? I pictured Fitz holding the girl up by the ties of her maid's apron, opening her mouth, and preparing to drop the squealing mouse-girl, pink stripe and all, inside. "Still, just so we don't antagonize the b—" This time, I stopped. "How about we compromise and say you can call me Mrs. Delcaluca? But definitely not ma'am."

The sparkle in the girl's big brown eyes was priceless. "Yes, ma'am. I mean, Mrs. Delcaluca. Thank you."

I gave her a little hug, then released her. "Would you please tell the rest of the staff to call me Mrs. Delcaluca too?" Even that formality sounded stuffy to me, but I knew I'd have no hope in getting the staff to call me Christina, much less Chrissy.

"Yes, Mrs. Delcaluca." Her smile was soft yet radiant.

"Great. Now, can you tell me where I can find Kaine, uh, Mr. Delcaluca?"

"I believe he's in the conference room. Ms. Fitzwilder and he went in there about an hour ago."

We had a conference room? Wow. "Fitz, huh?" Had she already shanghaied my hubby? Determined to get to the bottom of his absence during the first night in our new home, I asked Missy to lead me to the conference room. I resolved that if I did nothing else today, I'd make a map of the house.

When I walked through the swinging doors, however, I found Kaine seated at the head of the huge mahogany table with Fitz, computer at hand, holding court at the other end. Again, however, I was waylaid by unexpected people. Seated around the table were ten very distinctive-looking men and women. (Please note that I'm being very diplomatic with my description.)

I halted in my march toward Kaine and momentarily lost the power of speech. Could I ever get my hubby alone in this place?

"Chrissy, I'm so glad you're awake." Just like last time, he stood and opened his arms for me. "Come. I want you to meet my brothers and sisters."

I must've looked like a rabbit caught in a snare, eyes wide and bulging, and my mouth hanging open in a silent scream. You know, kind of like the painting *The Scream* by Edvard Munch.

"He never said anything about brothers and sisters? Are you frickin' kidding me?" The old saying of *you don't just marry the man, you marry the relatives* popped into my brain. Time to meet the family? *How about a little warning, honey-man?*

Kaine wasn't racking up any gold stars, that's for sure. Still, I slammed my mouth shut, paced over to stand next to him, put on my best smile and faced my new homies.

Something was very wrong. Was my shirt open? I dropped

my gaze to make sure I wasn't exposing my rack to my new kinfolk. Okay, boobies covered. So why was everyone giving me such odd looks?

The others continued to stare at me with a mixture of disgust, bewilderment and a whole lot of other emotions I couldn't name. At last, realization of what I'd done hit me. In a flash, my anger was gone, replaced by utter humiliation. I leaned closer to Kaine and whispered, although I was certain they could guess what I was saying. "Did I say that out loud? You know. About the *frickin' kidding me* part?"

"You sure did." Kaine's bemused yet sympathetic expression greeted me, giving me the support I desperately needed.

I cringed, praying with all my heart that I would melt into a sticky pool of nothingness. Anything was better than facing all these people after opening my big yap. "Oh, damn. Sorry, folks." I raised my head, ready to take whatever they threw at me. "Sometimes I have a difficult time with impulsivity." *Great. Now I sound like a mental health worker.* "Uh, or in other words, I talk too much."

"Don't worry about it."

Kaine might have thought I shouldn't worry about what I'd said, but I could see by some of the others' expressions, they sure as hell thought I should. Having no alternative except to shove down the lump in my throat and forge ahead, I slapped on a silly, not-so-brave grin. Kaine started the introductions.

"Chrissy, these are friends of mine. Friends I consider my extended family."

Thank goodness. He isn't actually related to them. I inhaled. *Did I say that out loud too?* I held my breath, checked their faces and saw I hadn't. Relief threatened to buckle my knees. But I still leaned against Kaine for support.

“To my right is Miko. She handles the financial records of my business transactions.”

Miko, a name I might have associated with a diminutive woman of Asian descent, was a large burly Irish-looking woman with arms the size of tree trunks. If the Incredible Hulk had had a sister, she’d have looked like this broad. Curly red hair framed features that could’ve been carved from stone, accented below by rock-hard Schwarzenegger-type bosoms. Her man-hands gripped a black binder and she sat ramrod straight in her chair. Her eyes, the same color as my husband’s, scanned me, giving me a chill. I don’t intimidate easily, but this broad made me want to curl up into a fetal position and whimper for my mamma. I nodded at her, unable to force a smile with her sternness hacking away at my self-confidence.

“And next to her is my Acquisitions Advisor, Thomas Petrosky.”

I tilted to the side to see past Mighty Miko. When I did, I let out a tiny squeak as the round bald head popped out from behind the hulkette. Almost toppling over, I bent even farther to see the rest of him and clamped my hand over my mouth to keep from laughing. I quickly faked a yawn.

Petrosky reminded me of a garden gnome. His round little body—a perfect match to his round little head—was nearly hidden behind the giant woman. His head was only a couple of inches higher than the table, giving him the appearance of peeking over the edge. He’d make one of the Little People seem statuesque. I offered him a smile. He returned the smile, albeit with his gaze fixed on a part of me much lower than my face. *Little People, my ass. This tiny turd is a Little Lech.*

“Next to him is a longtime business associate of mine, Grayson Carnacian.”

My gaze slid from the puny pervert to the man on

Petrosky's left and my smile vanished. The man bent his head to study the papers in front of him, and his dark brown hair, thick and raggedly cut, hung around his shoulders like the crowning glory of a lion. The jeans and wrinkled denim shirt he wore couldn't hide his strong body. Although he was totally relaxed, he also seemed ready to leap from his seat at a moment's notice. Then he looked up at me.

Searing red eyes fastened onto me. *I've seen those eyes.* I swallowed and felt the flush of blood flow from my hairline down to my neck. My legs suddenly wobbled and not in the way Kaine made them weak at the knees. Struggling with the fear crushing through me, I clutched my man's arm with both hands and held on.

Those eyes belong to the animal from last night. But how could that be? Werewolves do not, I repeat, do not exist. Yet didn't I see one under my balcony? A war raged between Logical Chrissy sitting on my right shoulder and Scared-Enough-To-Wet-My-Panties Chrissy on my left shoulder. Frankly, if I'd taken bets on which Chrissy would win out, I'd have chosen the panty-wetter.

I stared, unable to break free of his hold on me. Meanwhile Kaine, apparently unaware of my discomfort—now there's an understatement—kept the introductions flowing from the next person to the next. Yet the wolf man's hold on me was relentless.

What do you want?

His eyebrows rose as though he'd actually heard my unspoken question. Then, with a bemused expression, he gave a slight shake of his head.

I swear I nearly fainted. *Did he actually answer me? Or did I imagine it? Good grief, first I think I hear Fitz and now the wolf man can read my mind. Am I losing my grip on reality?* I could almost hear the *crack* as my belief in logic and practicality bowed under the continuing weight of supernatural events. What the hell was going on?

"Chrissy, are you all right?"

Kaine's voice broke through the spell the man had on me. Although I fought to retain eye contact with Carnacian, Kaine dragged my attention away. Placing his palm on my cheek, he forced my face toward him. "I asked if you're all right."

"Uh, I, uh..."

Kaine's friends tittered at my stutter until he scowled at them. "I see Carnacian's had the same effect on you that he has on everyone."

"He does?" *Does he hear their thoughts too?* I started to look his way again, but decided keeping my face toward my hubby was much safer.

"Yes, he does." Kaine pressed his lips to mine in a short, reassuring kiss. "Don't pay any attention to him. I promise you, he won't bother you again."

Again? Again as in how he's bothering me right this moment? Or as in how he scared the bejesus out of me last night? Do you know about the werewolf?

Kaine released me to confront Carnacian. "Stop. I don't care what time of the month it is, cease what you're doing."

Time of the month? Was he talking about the full moon or a menstrual cycle? But Carnacian was male, wasn't he? I gave his rugged appearance another quick look. After all, ya just never knew any more. But my glance confirmed it. This guy was all testosterone. The only question I had was if he was all man—or part animal.

"I think we've finished for the day. Remember what I've asked of you. Talk to your people and give me your findings by tomorrow night." Kaine slipped his arm around me and murmured parting words to his departing guests. Carnacian shot me one last steely glance, mumbled something I couldn't hear, and left.

At last! I resisted the urge to blow out a breath of relief. I could finally have some time alone with my man. I waited for the last person to leave before doing what I'd come here to do. "Kaine, damn it, where the hell were you last night?"

He put me at arms' length to study me. "Are you all right, Chrissy-doll?" To his credit, he appeared genuinely concerned.

Now it was my turn to examine him. "Am I all right? Are you seriously asking me that?"

This time he dropped his hold on me—along with the concerned expression—and took a step away. "Yes, I am seriously asking you that. However, I'm already rethinking my question." Deep furrows broke into his tanned forehead. "I realize we didn't have a very romantic start to our life in our new home, but it couldn't be helped."

I snorted. Yep, I executed the totally unattractive, never-make-such-an-awful-sound-in-front-of-your-lover derisive snort. And what was worse? I didn't care. "You can say that again. Which necessitates my asking the question again. Where the hell were you last night?" The Mouse Muncher and Wolfie were forgotten. I had my priorities straight.

Kaine shook his head and tidied up the papers on the table. "I can't help it if you don't believe me, but I'm sorry about last night. However, a very troublesome situation demanded my attention and I had to deal with it. I...lost...a valuable acquisition. I was up all night and now I'm exceedingly tired." He left the stack on the table and confronted me. "You have to understand that when a man runs a large enterprise such as mine, there will be times when I have to put business before pleasure."

"So you spent the night, down here, all by yourself, because of some business problem?"

"A very important business problem. And yes, I spent much of the night, down here, mostly all by myself as you put it. However, Fitz and a few of my other associates were in and out."

Did you share a late-night snack with whiskers? But I couldn't get the words out. My practical side simply wouldn't let me go down that path.

"But did you have to work all night?" I knew I'd gone from demanding harpy to whiny wussy, but I couldn't help it. "Couldn't you have at least let me know?" I stepped forward to close the distance between us. "Then I wouldn't have stayed up all night waiting." I'd managed a few hours sleep toward dawn, but I wasn't going to let him know that. Doing so would take away from my pitiful plight.

He tilted his head in that cute way that reminded me of a puppy. "I don't understand. I did send word to you."

"You did? How?" Kaine abhorred using cell phones inside a house, claiming they were supposed to be used for communication only while out and about. Being a cell phone lover, I decided I'd challenge his little pet peeve later. Right now wasn't the time.

"I asked Fitz to tell you."

I couldn't stop the immediate and visceral reaction to the name. Not only did the woman want my hubby all to herself—for whatever reason—she wasn't beneath using subterfuge to make that happen. "She never gave me the message. And by the way, did you know your assistant has a disgusting diet?" Okay, I'd found the path and was skipping down it now.

"What do you mean?"

Why did I get the impression he knew what I meant but didn't want to let on? Still, I gave him the benefit of the doubt. "Kaine, I saw her eat a mouse." He didn't even flinch. I swear. I could've told him she collected Hummel figurines and gotten a bigger reaction. How could the man not even flinch at such an outlandish declaration? "Did you hear me? A mouse. She ate a real, still-alive, twitchin' and wigglin' rodent."

"I'm sure you must be mistaken. Who eats mice except cats and the like?"

Is he saying he doesn't believe me? Or that I'm imagining things? I cringed since I'd had the same thought. "That's kind of my point. No one eats mice except cats and the like." I narrowed my eyes at him. "Don't you believe me?"

He came to me again, his eyes twinkling in mirth. "Are you sure you weren't daydreaming?"

Hey, once you go down the Path of the Ridiculous, you kind of want someone to believe you. No matter how silly you sound. I tried to pull away from him, irritation not letting me snuggle into his embrace, yet he held on. "I know what I saw. And besides that, I saw a werewolf last night. In the garden, right outside our bedroom window."

I know he didn't mean to hurt me with his laugh, but he did. Especially when he let me go, still laughing at me. "Wow, you really did have an off night. Not only does Fitz supposedly—"

Supposedly?

"—not give you my message, then you see weird and supernatural things. All this from the owner of Debunkers, Inc."

I was stunned into silence almost as though he'd landed a one-two punch to my ability to speak. *He doesn't believe a word I've said.*

"Think about it, honey. Isn't it more probable that you were asleep when Fitz arrived at your door? And you simply didn't hear her knock?"

At last, I found my K-O'd vocabulary. "No. I don't—"

"And isn't it more reasonable to assume you dreamed about Fitz eating a mouse and then dreamed you saw a werewolf?"

"No." I crossed my arms. "Okay, maybe I did catch a few winks, but that was early this morning, not earlier when these things happened. And I did not dream about a werewolf. A werewolf I think I met again this morning."

I would've sworn Kaine narrowed his eyes for a second before resuming his I-have-to-patronize-my-nutty-wife serene expression. Had he believed me even for a second?

"You saw the wolf again this morning?"

"Not wolf. Werewolf." I could sense I was losing this argument big time, but I was already too deep in it to wade out. "Carnacian. I'm sure he's the werewolf. He has red eyes, for Pete's sake."

At least this time he chuckled instead of letting out a full-throated laugh. "Well, I can see how someone might think he's a bit of an animal. Knowing Carnacian, however, the bloodshot eyes are probably from a hangover." He gave me a patronizing smile. "Honey, if you saw predator in his eyes, it was all because of how beautiful you are. He may want to eat you, but not in the way you're implying."

"What I saw had nothing to do with sex." Predictably, I wasn't getting anywhere with the werewolf story. "What about Fitz eating a mouse?"

"Look, Chrissy-doll, I realize you and Fitz may have gotten off on the wrong foot, but you can't possibly think she'd eat a mouse, can you?"

When he put it that way, even I began doubting what I'd

seen. "I know it sounds wacko." I fumbled the other thing I wanted to say and passed the ball to him.

"Fitz does keep mice as pets, but I'll ask her to get rid of them. Will that help soothe your nerves?"

I finally recognized this conversation. It reminded me of the discussions I'd had with clients who firmly believed in the ghost haunting them. The ghost that always turned out to have perfectly normal un-supernatural origins. *Oh, hell. Have I become one of those people?* Could Kaine be right? Had I dreamt the whole thing? After all, I had been exhausted from our trip. "Okay. Maybe you're right."

"Of course I'm right." He shot me one of his wonderfully warming smiles and held up his right hand. "I promise we'll have a romantic night tonight. Right after I finish dealing with this mess. Agreed?"

I knew a dismissal when I heard one. Although I wanted to complain and force him to spend the entire day with me, I'd already promised to check out a reported demon invasion in an elderly woman's home. Business was business and needed my attention. Besides, I had no intensions of becoming a rich, pampered wife with nothing to do except play bridge and tennis all day. Plus, I sure wasn't going to spend another night waiting on my dear hubby—no matter how sinfully sexy he was in bed. *Especially* after getting dismissed. Do I sound P.O.'d? Uh, duh.

But my whiny wuss was still in attendance and had to get in the last word. "You promise? Cross your heart and hope to die?" I crossed my heart.

Kaine repeated my gesture, then took me in his arms. "Agreed. And maybe we can even start on a little project of our own."

What did he just say? I pushed away from him, but he held on. "Are you shitting me? We haven't even broken in our new bed and you're bringing up that subject again?" A vise gripped my heart and squeezed, threatening to take my breath away. "Kaine, I thought we got past this in Vegas." Not really, but maybe I could make him believe it anyway. His skeptical frown blew that scheme to Hell and back. "Look, Kaine, I think it's time we sat down and had that talk."

"Well, at least talking is going in the right direction." He tried to nuzzle my neck, but I wasn't having any of it.

"No, I mean... You see, my parents... That is to say..." Okay, so maybe I was having some of it. And it was adversely affecting my thinking. "Kaine, stop!" I wrenched out of his arms, madder at myself than at him. I'd told him about my parents' accident, but had never spoken about how their deaths had affected me. I'd spent years burying those emotions and didn't want to undo all that now. But how could I make Kaine understand my position without spilling my guts? This totally sucked.

"Okay, okay. I get it."

"You do?" Could he read my mind? After all, if Fitz and Carnacian could hear my thoughts—*Wow. Do I really believe that?*—why not a little mind-reading by my husband?

"You want to do this the right way. Talking as in pillow talk. And you're right. The conference room is hardly the place for this discussion."

"Uh, no, not what I meant." Shoot. Why can't supernatural powers exist when you really need them?

He twisted me around and pointed me toward the door. "Chrissy-doll, you are distracting me from solving my problem. Now get out of here so I can get this matter resolved and devote my evening to my sexy wife."

I had to admit it. Another delay in the baby talk was peachy-keen with me. "Just make sure you keep your promise, big guy." I gave him a quick grin for the compliment and scooted out the door. Hey, I might've been mad, but I wasn't about to burn any beds. I turned the corner in the hallway and ran straight into the Mouse Muncher. If only I could burn her bed. With her in it. Inwardly I scowled at the thought. Since when had I become so mean? "Fitz." I could've sworn her nose rose two inches higher on the Snoot-ometer.

"Miz-z-z-z. Taylor."

Is she hissing at me? I sneered and felt the palm of my hand itching. If ever anyone needed a bitch-slap it was this bitch. Okay, just call me the Mean Girl. "The name is Mrs. Delcaluca."

"Ah, yes. So it is." Her steely gaze ran the length of my body.

"You betcha it is. And you'd do well to remember that." I hiked my nose higher, determined to match her snooty to snooty.

Yet, instead of sassing me again, she gave an imperious sniff and pivoted away

"Fitz, why didn't you give me the message K—Mr. Delcaluca sent me last night?" When she turned toward me again, I had to make a fist to keep my hand from smacking the smirk off her face.

Again she perused me as though I was covered in cow dung. "He deserves better than you."

"What?" Had she really said what I thought she'd said? "Who do you think you are?" I tried to keep the next question from popping out, but I couldn't stop it no matter how hard I gritted my teeth. "And why the hell not me?"

"*I* am the one who protects him. And *you*—" the sneer dripped from her tone, "—are the one who won't—" her gaze ran down my body again, "—or can't give him what he needs." Once she'd finished, she wheeled away and kept on walking, head held high and scrawny butt swaying.

I gaped after her, dumbstruck. Had Kaine told her of my reaction to having a baby?

Preggers, Schmeggers, Keep Your Scepter Away From Me!

I was still grumbling at Fitz's remarks two hours later while standing outside the home of Mrs. Twillierson in the town of Norcross. After finally locating my old car—I couldn't see myself using the limo without Kaine, much less one of his fleet of imported cars—I finally found my way to my appointment. If nothing else, at least my studio apartment had been semi-centrally located. I glanced back at my Honda (200,000 miles and counting) and sighed. With fuel prices going up, I could plan on spending a lot more on gas. Oh, sure, I could've used the gas card Kaine had given me or one of his expensive cars, but this girl had to retain a tad of independence. Married to a rich man wasn't going to change my determination to make Debunkers, Inc. a success, and that included paying for business expenses like gas.

Poor old lady Twillierson greeted me with a heroine's welcome. She tugged me inside her home, swept me into her tiny living room and pointed at a spiky-haired teenage boy plopped in front of an older television. Clutching the game control in hand, he terminated six gargoyles in the World of Warcraft and never gave me a glance.

"Get rid of it," she hissed.

I scanned the area around him, and except for the fact that

the place needed a good cleaning, I couldn't see anything out of whack. "Get rid of what, ma'am?"

She harrumphed and edged closer to the boy. Although we weren't being quiet by any means, he still didn't appear to notice us. Instead, he remained motionless, aside from the lightning speed of his thumbs on the controller's buttons. Dressed all in black with studded wristbands and several piercings, his persona screamed Emo.

"Get rid of *that*." She flicked her hand toward Emo Boy, then shuffled backward when he yelled his dismay at the loss of one of his warriors.

I still wasn't sure I understood what she meant. "Are you telling me to get rid of him? Your, uh, son?" No way was the old biddy this young kid's mom, but I'd learned early on in my career to not make assumptions, especially when talking about a woman's age.

Mrs. T. shook her head vehemently, making her blue curls bounce. "That thing is not my grandson." She waved for me to come closer so she could whisper. "It's a demon. What kind of a supernatural expert are you, anyway?"

A demon. Goodie. The old girl's gone goofy. I'd run into other clients who'd thought their pet or loved one had suddenly gone over to the dark side and communicated with beings from down under—*way* down under—but I didn't think wearing depressing clothing meant you'd gone evil. I choked back a laugh and retained a professional demeanor. "Ma'am, how do you know he's a demon?"

"Just look at him." Her mind may have slipped its hold on reality—something I could now relate to—but she was still a sweet old lady. "My grandson is a good boy. A well-dressed boy. He'd never wear all those devil-worshiping clothes if something hadn't taken him over. He's possessed. I know it." Tears sprang into her eyes, ratcheting up the sympathy factor in me.

Aw, hell, a crier. I hated criers. Those were the clients who made me want to close my business and work at a fast food joint. “Maybe he’s trying out a new style. You know. Like all teens do.” *Come on, Mrs. T., get a grip.*

She stared at me with suspicion. If I didn’t play this right, she’d believe I was in league with Satan. Then things would get really interesting and not in a good way. “That’s not it. Why else would my grandson do *that*?”

I followed her outstretched arm and noticed the jar of steel bolts on the floor next to him. As if on cue, he reached over, pinched a bolt from the jar and popped it into his mouth.

Wow. Talk about getting your daily dose of iron. Before I could say anything, he’d popped and swallowed another one.

“Okay, I’ll admit that’s strange. But it doesn’t make him demon-possessed.” Besides didn’t teenagers often act like demon-possessed people? “Have you asked him why he’s eating those?”

When in doubt, ask. And always go for the simplest and most logical explanation. An image of Fitz swallowing a mouse flashed through my brain and I quickly kept it moving right on out of there.

“Why the hell would I ask him anything? He might eat my face. Or tear my heart out. Don’t demons eat hearts?” Mrs. T. shivered at the thought.

“Uh, so I’ve heard.” Last time I’d checked, soap operas didn’t delve into the antics of demons. Yet no matter where this lady had gotten her ideas I wasn’t about to argue with her. “Do you mind if I ask him?”

She scrutinized me, obviously trying to judge whether I knew what I was doing. At last, she nodded. “Fine. But don’t go blaming me if he tears out your heart and sends your soul to the devil hisself."

At least I now knew imagination didn't atrophy when you got older. "I promise I won't blame you." I decided to fight fire with flame—or however the saying goes—and squatted down beside the kid. I watched him play the game a few minutes, then jumped in with the universal teenage word of greeting. "Hey."

His eyes darted my way, finally acknowledging my presence, then darted back to the obviously more important game. "Hey."

"My name's Chrissy." Having been a teenage girl at one time, I knew teen boys rarely plunged into a conversation quickly. "Warcraft, huh? Cool game."

"Yeah."

The old lady gave me another harrumph. *Better get moving, Chrissy, before Grandma decides to take us both out.* "So, I'm kind of curious. Why are you eating the bolts?" A rather nasty-looking dwarf bit the dust and I let out a shout of triumph. If nothing else, the kid was a whiz at Warcraft.

"I dunno."

Great. Slammed into a non-verbal wall already. "Uh-huh. Like maybe you saw them lying around and decided they looked tasty?"

He snorted, the teen's version of a laugh. "Naw. My friend Josh and I have a bet."

Figured. But at least his responses were getting longer. "What's the bet? Who eats the most?"

"Naw. Too easy."

I mentally took out my pliers, determined to get more information from him. "Okay. Then what's the bet?"

"Whoever gets taken to the ER first wins."

"But why not just go right away? I mean, how would he know if it took two or twenty bolts to twist your guts in a knot?"

He spared the game a moment and gawked at me as though I'd asked him to dress in a tux and go to the preppiest prom ever. "That'd be cheating." He shook his head and returned to killing trolls. "Rule is, you gotta be hurting before you can go. And then someone else has to suggest it. You can't ask to go." He *pffed* his amazement at my stupidity for not knowing basic bolt-eating game rules.

I had to wonder about the intelligence of today's kids, which only reinforced my lack of desire to have one. Like I needed another reason. "And that's winning? Getting to go to the hospital? Gee, how fun." *Not.*

"Yeah. 'Cuz whoever wins gets out of doing chores tomorrow."

Ah, the real prize was revealed. "I see. Well, good luck with that." I stood up, happy to have an easy solution for this assignment. Walking over to the grandmother, I pulled her aside to break the news. "Ma'am, I think you're right."

She sucked in a startled gasp. I guess she hadn't really expected me to agree with her. "I am? Oh my goodness. What are you going to do?"

"Not much. But if I were you, I'd fire up the old jalopy and take him to the ER."

Another gasp. "But won't they dissect him? I saw a movie where they did that to get the demons out of a little girl's body." One more teardrop slid down her face, making me feel lower than pond mud. Still, I knew this old girl was way too set on the demonic-possession theory to hear the truth. Occasionally, I have to bend the truth a little, especially when dealing with a geriatric fan of horror movies.

I gave her a conspiratorial wink. "Don't worry. I know a

couple of the docs there. I'll call ahead to make sure they take special care of him." The relief on her face twisted my guilt a little more. "You take him and tell them he ate bolts. Real steel-type bolts. They've seen worse cases. But don't mention the possession. We wouldn't want to start a panic." I didn't want to add that they might have to cut him open to get the bolts out. Hopefully, they could wait until they came out the other end. You know, the natural way.

"But how will they know how to help him if I don't mention the demon?"

Here was the best part of my plan. "Don't worry. It'll all work out. See, when demons possess a teenage boy, the boy's own soul battles back by eating the one thing demons don't like." I gestured to the diminishing pile of bolts on the floor. "Then, when the boy goes to the hospital and they get the bolts out of the body—" preferably through a poop-inducing procedure,"—the demon is released along with the bolts without anyone even knowing." I smiled and added the last part of my fabricated story. "Ma'am, I hate to say it, but his friend Josh is possessed, too. So if you wouldn't mind calling his parents..."

I could almost see a steel backbone sprout in the older woman as she prepared for a spiritual battle to save her grandson and his friend from the minions of Hell. "I understand. Thank you, Ms. Taylor, for your help. Please send me your bill for today."

Ya betcha I will. I nodded, feeling better about my lies, and left Mrs. T. and Emo Boy alone. Once outside, I pulled out the digital camera I carried in my purse and started taking exterior shots of the home. As part of each assignment, I take pictures of the places I'd debunked along with the surrounding area. Snapping off pictures one after the other, I shuffled in a circle, catching the best angle and light for each structure. With one last turn, however, I pointed the camera and suddenly wished I hadn't. Just as I aimed the lens at an architecturally unique building housing a boutique coffee shop across the street, Kaine and a beautiful red-haired woman stepped through the front door.

I clicked the picture and observed my husband with the woman. *Omigod. It's the woman in the photo Fitz showed me.* I almost snarled in jealous irritation. Figures she'd be even more beautiful in person. Long red hair streamed down her back to meet the rounded curves of her buttocks. Of course the red hair wasn't that awful orangey-red color most of us end up with, but the gorgeous five-hundred-dollar version only a stylist to the stars can bestow on a goddess. Yet somehow I knew hers was all natural. Her legs must've made up at least two-thirds of her height, never-ending in that sexy way very few women had. And of course her body was perfectly proportioned. Her breasts, bouncing freely unhindered by any bra, pointed at Kaine, begging him to touch them. Hell, even I wanted to touch them, and aside from a brief experiment with Judy Lassiter in high school, I was one-hundred-percent heterosexual. But it was her angelic yet mischievously sensual face that gave the green-eyed snake inside me extra venom. Her face was a cross between an angel and a devil, alluring and enticing, yet pure and innocent. In the tried-and-true tradition of every woman who'd ever lived, I instantly hated her.

Who the hell is she and what's Kaine doing with her? Nix that. I don't care who she is. I just want her away from my man.

I ducked behind one of the overgrown hedges in Mrs. T.'s front yard and clicked off three more photos. Calming my irrational urge to run across the street shouting, "He's mine, he's mine!" I pushed aside the branches and kept snapping away. Kaine and the woman continued to talk. The Plastic Pussy—because, come on, no one could look the way she did without some kind of nip and tuck—excitedly waved her arms.

Obviously, the conversation was getting a bit tense. *Good.*

Could they be arguing about a business deal? I studied Kaine, noting how he stood very straight, very stiff. Nonetheless, Miss PP kept moving closer to my hubby. Silently, I urged him to back away, but he held his ground. Was he holding his ground because he wanted to win their argument? Or because he wanted her to get closer? I tried to cage my green-eyed monster and barely managed to keep her on a short leash.

Kaine took the woman by the arms. Half expecting them to embrace, I rejoiced when he made her take a step back from him. I almost yelled to congratulate him. Instead, I took more photographs.

What the hell? I lowered my camera and squinted at Miss PP. *Did she just change color?* Not only her eyes as I'd imagined Kaine's had done, but her entire frickin' body. It was only a flash of purple, but I saw it. *Didn't I?* I studied her more intensely, wondering if Kaine had noticed what I had. I would've sworn I'd seen her fair skin turn a deep purple. And this time, I was definitely not dreaming.

"Chrissy, girl, you're starting to scare me." I don't usually talk to myself, but sometimes you gotta hear your own words to believe them—especially when you start doubting your own sanity. Letting the bush fall back into place, I knelt down and pushed the memory button on my camera. One after another, I zipped through the pictures until, at last, I found the one where she'd changed color. Or at least, I thought it was the right one. The screen of my camera was too small to really see the color clearly.

Slipping my camera into my purse, I stood and once again spied through the branches. Kaine and Miss PP were gone. *Where did they go? Did they leave together?*

"Ms. Taylor, are you all right?"

I jumped, swiveling around to find Mrs. T. and Emo Boy staring at me. "Uh, yeah. I'm fine." I scanned the ground around me. "I dropped my... Oh, there it is." Before they could notice that there was actually nothing on the ground, I bent, scooped up an imaginary pen and pretended to put it away. "Good deal. I, uh, would've hated to lose my favorite pen."

"But why were you in the garden, behind the bushes, in the first place?"

I opened my mouth to speak even before I had an answer. Sometimes ya just gotta go with the faith that the words will pop out on their own. Fortunately for me, Emo Boy came to my rescue.

"Gran, let's go. My stomach's really hurting." Emo guided Gran down the steps and started her along the path toward an old clunker of a car. He dropped her arm, *shoosh*ed her ahead of him and turned back to me. "Hey, thanks, lady."

"What for?"

"For getting her to take me to the ER. I'm totally gonna win this thing."

"Oh." I smiled, hoping he wouldn't recognize how I truly felt. "You're welcome."

He shot me one of the few grins he'd probably ever had and rushed to the car. "No, Gran, you can't drive. Remember they took away your license after you hit that policeman's car?"

Uh-oh. I should stay away from this neighborhood and Demolition Granny. I waved a quick goodbye to the odd couple and strode to my car. I slid into the driver's seat and waited for the two to get on the road and down the street. Way down the street.

I caught my reflection in the rearview mirror and had to wonder. I was in this particular driver's seat, but was I even riding in the car of my relationship with Kaine? Or, to put it in another way, when it came to my marriage, was I in a partnership? Or had one red-headed bimbo just carjacked it?

"Wow, when you start sounding like Carrie Bradshaw, you're watching way too much *Sex and the City*."

A blur dashed behind my car and I gasped, nearly sending my head in a Linda Blair twirl in my haste to see what it was. Yet, although my work as a supernatural debunker had prepared me for even the strangest of sights, I wasn't ready to see the Mouse Muncher standing behind my car.

"Fitz? What the hell are you doing here?"

"He is mine to protect."

"Possessive much, are we?" I opened the door and swung out of the car, hurried toward the rear—and found nothing. Searching the area around me, I couldn't find any indication that the MM had really been there.

What in hell is happening to me?

Kaine crushed his mouth to mine. Running his hands down my back, he claimed my buttocks and lifted me off my feet, banging us against the wall. Damn, but I loved it when he got rough. My mind swirled and desire raced through me, exciting me as only Kaine's touch could do.

"You were gone all day."

An exaggeration, but I liked the sentiment so I didn't correct him.

"I missed you." His words, murmured against my neck, thrilled me more than any ghost-busting could. In between words, he nibbled down my neck and along my shoulder. "I need you."

"I'm here now." I admit it. A jolt of power rushed through

me that I could command such emotion from my hunk, and I liked it. I liked it a lot. Did I want to ruin it by mentioning that I'd seen him and the Plastic Pussy together? Or that Fitz had a major stalking problem? Uh, nope. I promised myself I'd bring up those unpleasant subjects after we christened our bed.

With a moan borne of pure lust, Kaine picked me up, carrying me like Rhett carried Scarlett. I laid my head against his hard chest and watched the steps of the ornately carved mahogany staircase grow in number as he hurriedly swept me up to the second floor. Moving swiftly down numerous hallways, we finally arrived at our bedroom door. He bumped against it and the door flew open.

"Kaine?"

"Yes?"

"We need a bedroom that's closer to the front door."

He chuckled and threw me on our bed. I yelped, then giggled. With practiced ease, he removed my clothes almost before I realized what he was doing. He quickly dropped his clothes to stand gloriously naked above me. I gasped, stirred beyond words. Although I'd seen my hubby naked many times, his wonderful physique never failed to provoke a carnal reaction in me.

Above the ramrod pole, a six-pack—hell, an eight-pack—abdomen rippled with every breath he took. A trail of dark hair traveled over the hills, like a forest highlighting the beauty of the mountains, to find the peaks rising above them. His chest overwhelmed me with granite-like pecs. His muscles flexed, dominating the broad expanse, while taut brown nipples lay silently waiting for attention. Attention I would gladly give them.

Shoulders, wider than any man's I'd ever known, beckoned for hands to feather over them, taking time to enjoy the trip to the iron-like arms. He lifted one hand to track through his glorious mane and I studied the rippling movement of his biceps.

His eyes, so dark yet so brilliant, drew my gaze away from his arms. Piercing in their intensity, his eyes made me want to dive in and swim in their depths. He snaked his tongue out between his teeth, drawing my attention away from those alluring eyes, and I inhaled slowly, welcoming the rush of moisture spreading outward from my abdomen.

I paused, knowing I had saved the best for last. Slowly I slid my gaze downward. Textured with a few veins, smooth and crowned with a mushroom-shaped top, his dick was the eighth wonder of the world. And that wonder was all mine. With exactly the right amount of curvature, his penis pointed upward, waving its declaration of manhood.

Wow, oh, wow. Will I ever get used to seeing his shaft? One day I'm going to measure him. Seriously. Maybe I'll even enter him in the Guinness Book of Records for the Biggest, Longest Cock in the World. Now there's a record worth winning.

"Why do you always smile when you look at me? Especially when you look at me there?"

I tore my gaze away from *there* to find him watching me, curiosity with a little bit of nervousness etched on his features. "Because I love what I see." I scrunched up my face in a don't-you-get-it expression. "Duh."

"Oh." A grin filled with lecherous intent spread his lips wide and I wanted to spread wide something of my own.

"Why are you smiling?"

"Because *I* love what *I* see." He scanned his gaze down my body. "All of what I see."

To a woman with self-esteem issues like me, his words were pure poetry. *How the hell did I get so lucky? Eat your heart out, Miss PP, whoever you are.* Irritated that I'd allowed the mystery woman to infiltrate our private time, I ordered her out of my head. *Out, you skank, out!*

My voice came out all husky and majorly horny. "Damn it, Kaine, what are you waiting for?" I couldn't help myself. Running my tongue over my lips, I opened my legs, inviting him in.

"Chrissy-doll. My Chrissy-doll." His perusal settled on my snatch and a gleam lit his eyes. "I don't want to rush this. We'll take our time, all right?"

Unsure if I could trust my voice, I croaked out my answer. My crotch grew wet, my pulse quickened and my pelvic muscles tightened at the way he'd said my name. "I'll try, but I'd never knock a quickie either."

I reached out for him, wanting him, aching for him to touch me. His huge beautiful cock called to me, stronger even than the sound of him saying my name. Every woman's fantasy stood before me and I was the woman who could claim that fantasy. The dusting of dark hair covering his chest drew my gaze once more and I lifted my hand to comb my fingers through it. A sizzle that was all male zapped from my fingertips to my snatch.

He groaned, slid his body over mine, and cupped my breast in his big hand. Bending his head to my neck, he ran his tongue along my shoulder blade until he reached my ear. He nibbled at my lobe while rubbing his thumb over my tit. I arched my back, welcoming his mouth on my nub.

"I ache for you."

"Then don't stay away at night and maybe I won't stay away all day." Again, an exaggeration, but I needed to make a point. "I expect you in our bed no later than ten o'clock, Mr. Delcaluca."

His chuckle tickled my breast. "Yes, dear."

I envisioned Kaine as a hen-pecked husband and started to

laugh. No way would that ever happen. Yet when I started to tell him so, he slid his fingers between my folds to stroke my throbbing clit and laughter was the farthest thing from my mind. I threw my head to the side and opened my legs wider. Grasping his shoulders, I tried to pull him closer, to take his very essence inside me, to become a part of me below my skin.

Kaine moved quickly, leaving my breasts to find his way to the core of my heat. I watched, fascinated, as he feathered kisses down the side of one breast, then the other. Taking the direct route now, he licked the hollow between my breasts and followed the path down to my bellybutton. He flicked his tongue around the indentation, nipped at the skin and murmured soft words of desire. His hands flattened against the soft mound of my stomach, marking the boundary as though his tongue would get lost traveling between my bellybutton and the curly mass below. I squirmed, ready and aching for release.

"Kaine," I whined, putting all the frustration, all the anticipation I felt into my tone.

"Be patient. It's worth the wait."

"Don't I know it. Still...how about speeding it up a bit? You know. Before I explode?"

His answer came when he slid his tongue into the crease between leg and crotch. A myriad of sensations erupted within me. *Wow. And he hasn't even reached his goal yet.*

"Do you want me to eat you?"

Is he kidding me? I lifted my head to gape at him. *Yep, he's kidding.* "What do you think?" I reached out and popped him on the head.

"Ooh, violence." He wiggled his eyebrows at me. "I like it when you get rough."

"Back at ya, bub. Now hurry— Omigod!"

To say Kaine's quick move scared me—in a good way—was an understatement. Now face down on the bed, I was left gasping for air. "Kaine, what the hell are you doing?"

He grabbed me by the hips, pulled and tugged me to my knees. "I thought we'd try something new."

"Doggy style?" *Yes!* Had he read my mind? Hell, with his preoccupation on babies, I'd thought about suggesting anal sex, but I'd been squeamish about going into that unchartered area. In fact, I'd worried that he would realize I wanted sex in the ass to keep from getting preggers and would outright refuse me. So for him to suggest it was a victory.

Kaine surprised me yet again. Taking my ass, he spread my butt, opening the crack between my cheeks. Before I could think, he slipped his tongue from the top all the way down into my hole.

I gasped, "Omigod, Kaine." At first, I wasn't certain about this new technique. New to me, that is. But obviously Kaine had experience in this—*ahem!*—area. Trying to stay relaxed, I took deep breaths. But I needn't have worried. Kaine's tongue dipped into the crevice and my pussy creamed in ecstasy.

Laving his tongue all around, he dove and plunged, going deeper only to then swipe the tender muscles along the rim. My ass clenched and unclenched involuntarily. Letting my instincts take over, I lowered to my elbows and tucked my head between my knees. Just because my back was to him didn't mean I didn't want to see whatever I could.

Kaine kneaded my ass and plunged his tongue into me and I licked my lips, concentrating on the sight of his dick and balls hanging between my legs. *If only I could touch them. Hell, I am going to touch them.* Yet when I tried to rise, Kaine placed his palm in the small of my back, keeping me in my place.

Hey, I could think of worse places to stay in.

"Don't move." A slap on my rump accentuated his command.

Did he just hit me? Shock overwhelmed me. Or at least it might have if another emotion hadn't shoved its way into first place. Lust caught my breath and ricocheted throughout my body. I moaned and closed my eyes. "Oooh, I likey. Do it again, Kaine."

Another slap cracked the air and I squealed in painful joy. A third spank sent my desire even higher.

He continued his exploration of my never-explored-before territory, moving his mouth, his tongue over the dips and valleys—hopefully not mountains—of my ass. I kept my eyes on his prize bobbing around with his movements.

He played in that recess, pulling me apart in a tantalizing way. When he parted me again, he placed the thick head of his cock against my hole and held it there, swirling it round and round the tender rim. I mentally tried to suck him inside me. When that didn't work, I tried wiggling my ass, trying to lure him inside. Another smack to my rump echoed in the room.

"Uh-uh-uh."

"Damn it, Kaine, you're killing me."

"That's kind of the point."

What a way to die.

His tongue slipped upward to taste the dimples above my ass cheeks and I almost complained. Yet when he continued his journey, sliding over my hips and up my back, I kept my mouth shut, ready to let Kaine lead the way. He moved over me, kissing his way to the nape of my neck. Shivers of excitement at his soft touches shuddered through me and I stretched my legs farther apart, opening this part of me wider and hoped he'd take the hint.

I could feel his legs, strong and taut as he braced himself. Although I could no longer see his cock, I now felt it riding between my legs, so close, yet so far. I mewed, calling for him to hurry up. But did I really want him to move faster? Yes and no.

He clasped one breast, and I shifted my weight to the other hand and covered his hand with mine. Together, we fondled my tit, my fingers helping his to pinch it. He adjusted slightly and, slipping his other hand between my legs, he speared my pussy with two fingers. Oh, how I wished I had three hands so I could join him.

He moved his fingers in and out while brushing the pad of his thumb over my other opening. I didn't know which one felt better, and frankly, I didn't care. Bumping his hips against me, he teased me with his cock. I cried out as a huge release rocked through me.

"I can only take so much, Kaine." I panted and twisted around to stare at him. "Please. Now."

"In your ass?"

"Yes."

Slowly, gently, he pushed two lubricated fingers—when had he lubed them?—into my anal cave, loosening the muscles. I kept regular breaths, concentrating on relaxing my body. Little by little, he slipped his fingers deeper inside me. He worked me, loosening my tight cavity, preparing me for the real penetration. I sighed, little by little feeling the ringlets of muscles inside me giving way, opening for more.

Although I wouldn't have ever called myself promiscuous, I'd had my fair share of sexual relations. But anal sex had never attracted me. Until now. The sensation of his fingers inside my ass rippled a wave of lust through me in an entirely different way than I'd ever experienced. If I'd had to describe it, I couldn't have. Instead, I simply lowered my head to the bed and enjoyed.

"Kaine. Please."

He stilled. "Do you want me to stop?"

"Hell, no. I want the real thing, not two imposters."

His low chuckle accompanied the removal of his fingers and announced the arrival of his cock against my puckered hole. Slickened with lube, his dick entered me, pushing gently yet firmly into me. My muscles contracted, then released with his entry, and I smothered the need to cry out in joy.

That's right, everyone. I was now an ass girl.

"Tell me if I'm hurting you."

"You're fine." Okay, so I lied. The pain wasn't pleasant, but the sensations that followed were. No way did I want him to stop. "More than fine."

Once fully inside, filling me, the vibrations coming from his cock sliding in and out of my ass, reverberated to my vagina and into my clit. I reached down and massaged my clit, getting hotter in both places. I moaned and leaned backward, urging him to continue. Kaine held my hips, moving slowly, sliding in, sliding out. He groaned, the pleasure deepening his voice.

"Chrissy-doll."

Who knew so much could be said with only a name?

"Kaine."

Together, we moved, rocking back and forth, bonded together with more than mere skin.

"I don't know how much longer I can last."

"It's okay, Kaine, let go." I wanted his seed inside my ass. *Safely* inside my ass.

"No. Not this way."

His wicked laugh alerted me, and once again, the man surprised me. Landing on my back—*how strong is this guy anyway?*—I gaped at my hubby. “Hey, I thought you were going to come.”

“Don’t worry.” He peeled the condom off his dick—which looked even larger than before. Clearly he was still armed and dangerous. “We can do it that way again. After we do it the right way.”

The right *way? As in missionary style?* I studied his face, so determined, and a shudder ran through me. Had our making love suddenly changed into something else? “But I really wanted you to—”

“Chrissy-doll, you can’t get—” He clammed up, guilt flickering across his face and alerting my internal guards.

“I can’t get what?” *Please, don’t say pregnant. Is he fucking me for fun? Or to get me pregnant?* “What’s going on?”

He took my face between his hands, searched my eyes and bore his own gaze into me. I recognized the raw sexuality in his expression and felt an answering tug in my gut. “I never expected to love you as much as I do.”

“You say that like you regret it, but that’s a good thing, right?” *Is he trying to tell me something? And do I want to hear it?*

Something flashed in his eyes. “No. I’ll never regret loving you, Chrissy-doll. Never.”

I wanted to tell him how much I loved him, but I couldn’t speak. Instead, I simply watched and prepared for the invasion of his tongue on my clit.

Wrapping my legs over his shoulders, he slipped lower to bring the juice closer to him. His tongue lavished me, sending shudders of unlimited delight through me. Sucking, nipping, he tortured my already sensitive nub. With devilish fervor, he attacked my pussy, lapping up my wetness while pressing against my throbbing clit. Another orgasm racked through me and I thrashed against the sheets, forgetting my worries of pregnancy. The sounds he made, drinking up my release, sent me into a higher, longer-lasting climax. When my body finally stopped shaking, I took a deep breath and ran my hand through my hair.

"Wow, oh, wow."

Just when I thought my body couldn't get much hotter, a vibration rippled over my pulsing skin, growing hotter and hotter. Unfamiliar with the painful, yet exciting feeling, I looked down. What I saw took my breath away and almost stopped my heart.

Kaine's mouth was open, lips pursed and blowing on my nub. Not that I hadn't seen this before. But what threw me was the tiny flame flickering over the sides of my folds, over the tip of my clit, almost reaching my pubic hair.

Is that fire?

I blinked, trying to calm down long enough to make sense of what I'd seen. Or thought I'd seen. Attempting to rise up on my elbows to get a clearer look, the searing heat coursing through me sent my body into uncontrollable tremors. The only thing I could do was to throw my head back and scream in ecstasy. This was real heat, real flame, real searing passion to the infinite degree. Whatever Kaine was doing to me was scorching me from the inside out.

I love it!

With every climactic explosion, the warmth within grew. Warmth? Ha, I was burning hotter than a supernova flashing through the universe. I'd never experienced anything like this. Yet a girl can only take so much. My body felt like it would dissolve into molten lava if the fire didn't stop soon.

As though hearing my thoughts, he abruptly stopped, leaving me stunned and bereft. *No!* I opened my eyes to peer down at him and he lifted his head, his gaze telling me he knew exactly what he'd done to me.

"I don't believe what I saw." I knew the experience he'd given me deserved so much more, but I couldn't find more words to describe how I felt.

"I love you, Chrissy-doll." His words warmed my heart in a different way.

"I love you, too, Kaine. But you're going to have to explain what just happened."

"Later." Kaine lifted my legs higher, wider. "Now keep those beautiful legs spread, woman, because I need to be inside you." With a roar, he rammed his cock into me. Somehow, some way it felt different than usual. Better. Natural.

Just how wide could I go? I guess we're going to find out.

Damn, but he was great. Not just good, this man, my man was great. He knew exactly how to please me, exactly where to lick, exactly how long to bite. With every plunge, he increased his onslaught, attacking me with an unrivaled enthusiasm. Although I would've sworn the flame he'd given me had burned every bit of desire from my body, having him inside me sent me to another height of pleasure.

Without pausing, he rose and crushed my mouth with his. His tongue wrestled with mine and a small cry escaped me. I could taste my juices on his lips and reveled in sucking them off his tongue. Dizzy with desire, I laced my fingers behind his head and held on for dear life. He finally broke away.

"Arrgh!" His shout was harsh, loaded with lust. Tremors rippled through his frame, traveling into mine. He shouted his climax and fell on top of me. Sweat dripped from his body and met my perspiration where our bodies met.

Holding onto him, I couldn't help but enjoy the quivers still moving along his arms and back. I slid my hands down the rugged surface of his torso, stopping to rest at the curve of his back. Continuing my exploration, I skimmed my fingers back up his hard muscles, running over rough skin.

Rough? I stiffened. *What the hell is this? I don't remember Kaine having any scars, much less what feels like...like leather? Much like a thick leathery scale.*

My heart gained speed with what I knew couldn't be true, but I explored farther, discovering more patches of tough skin. Did Kaine have some kind of medical condition? "Kaine, what's this on your back?"

He immediately stiffened and rolled onto his back. "What are you talking about?" Contradicting his first reaction, he sent me a soft smile and palmed my cheek. "That was amazing. You are amazing."

"Don't try and change the subject." I rose up and tried to turn him over onto his stomach. "Flip over and let me take a look. You may need to see a dermatologist."

He gave me quick peck and finally did as I asked. "I don't know what you're talking about. There's nothing on my back."

I ran my hand over the smooth unblemished skin. "But I swear I felt something."

Laughing, he flipped onto his back again and pulled me closer, pressing my breasts to his chest. "You know what I think it is?"

I held my breath. Was he about to tell me he had a terrible disease? Shouldn't he have told me about it before we got married? Not that I wouldn't have married him anyway. "What? You can tell me." *I'll be here for you no matter what you tell me.*

He cocked an eyebrow at me along with an *I've-got-you* look. "I think you're trying to distract me."

"Huh? Distract you from what?" Kaine had thrown me a

punch and I hadn't had time to duck.

"I think you want to talk about anything other than what I want to discuss."

Huh? Yet I knew in an instant what he wanted to talk about. And he was right. I didn't want to discuss that topic. Not now, maybe not ever. Although I knew I needed to tell him everything. "Urgh, Kaine. Please don't ruin amazing sex by talking about having a baby."

"I'm sorry, but I must. I really need to have a child with you."

Yeah, I know. Most women would've loved to hear those words from the man of their dreams, but this gal was different. "Kaine, I've already told you. I don't want kids. At least not any time soon." I swallowed the guilt. I couldn't see myself ever wanting kids, but did I dare tell him that? But maybe if I explained... "Why can't the two of us be enough?"

An expression I'd never seen came over his face. Removing—because there was no better word for it—me from him, he jumped out of bed, then turned to confront me. How had our lovemaking changed into a confrontation?

"Kaine, come on. Don't be upset."

"This is important to me, Chrissy. I want a child." He exhaled and ran a hand through his hair. "I *need* an heir. And I need one soon. I want you to stop taking birth control. We're wasting precious time fucking without a purpose."

Fucking without a purpose? "Did you say what I think I heard? A purpose? I thought the purpose of our fucking—as you so delicately put it—is to show our love to each other. Not to procreate. Damn it, Kaine."

He sighed and regrouped. "Of course it is. I didn't mean it to sound that way. I love making love with you." As though there were two personalities within one man, his body language changed, stiffening. "But that doesn't change the fact that I want a child."

The thought of baring my soul to him, telling him why I didn't want a baby vanished with my growing frustration. "So it doesn't matter what I want? I'm just supposed to open wide and produce an heir to the throne? What century do you think this is, Kaine?"

His face softened for a moment, then hardened again. *Mr. Jekyll, meet Mr. Hyde?*

He took a deep breath, obviously trying to steady himself. "I'm sorry. I don't mean to force this on you. Not now."

Not now? As in "I'd planned on forcing you earlier but now I'd like your cooperation"?

"I love you, Chrissy-doll. Is it so wrong for me to want a baby with the woman I love?"

Okay, either he really felt that way or he was super-duper at laying on the guilt trip. "No, of course not." I realized the time had come for explanations. I only wished I'd told him before he'd married me. But would he have married me had he known my baby-making shop was closed? Could I have faced a life without Kaine? "Let me explain."

But Mr. Hyde had returned. "We must have a child."

Aw, crap. I am so not good with ultimatums. "Not if you're commanding me to."

With a final hard look at me, he marched out the door.

I sat, covers pulled up to my chin, bewildered by my husband's reaction. What the hell just happened? When had our lovemaking turned into battle?

The New Desperate Housewife

A woman can take only so much before she has to put her foot down. And I was putting mine down and through the ground. Sure we'd had sex during the day, but after spending yet another night alone in my marriage bed—as well as dining alone every day—I was more than ever positive that I needed to confront Kaine and get some answers. Not to mention let him in on why I feared having a child. But why was he so damned insistent on my producing a little Delcaluca? Then, of course, we had the lesser issues of the beautiful woman and Fitz's obsession. I hopped in the shower and dressed as quickly as I could, determined to catch him before he got busy doing...well, whatever he did.

I dashed down the hallway, intent on finding one of the three offices Kaine had told me existed in my home, and—"Oh!"—ran straight into the diminutive Missy. "I'm so sorry. I don't know what's wrong with me. I've never bumped into people as much as I have since coming to live here. Considering the size of this place, you'd think I'd have enough space to avoid poor innocent targets like you."

"No, no. I'm the one who should apologize, ma'am." She shot me a very pretty smile before adding, "I mean, Mrs. Delcaluca. I should've contacted you first thing this morning. Then perhaps you wouldn't have had to rush around trying to find your office."

Apparently unfazed by our collision, Missy executed a perfect curtsy. Her maid's uniform was gone, however, and she now looked the part of the über-professional personal assistant in an expensive tailored suit that had to have been handmade to fit her tiny frame. I doubted she'd wear even a size zero. Her hair had undergone a transformation, too, from white with a pink stripe to an all-over robin's-egg blue. A not-as-timid-as-before smile formed on her lips, highlighted by the twinkle in her bright brown eyes. Her pale, impossibly smooth skin fairly glowed with an indefinable radiance. She carried a clipboard with a pen in her other hand, ready for business.

"Wait. What did you say? *My* office?" Suddenly feeling huge, I slouched and clutched my camera over my breasts. *One of my breasts is at least twice the size of her teensy head.* "I have an office? Kaine, Mr. Delcaluca never mentioned this."

Her laugh tinkled. Yep, there was no other way to describe the sound. Her laugh sounded like a crystal bell swaying in the wind. *Sheesh. Since when are my thoughts so picturesque?*

"Yes, ma'am, Mrs. Delcaluca." She stuck out her doll-sized hand and shook my hand. I gingerly took it and prayed my big paws wouldn't break any of her dainty fingers. "Mr. Delcaluca made me your personal assistant."

"Along with quite a transformation."

She smoothed her hair behind her ear. "That was Mr. Delcaluca's idea too. He didn't want Fitz to forget I wasn't a...a maid any longer."

The man has a big heart, that's for sure. Maybe that's why he wants a baby so much? You know, a child to represent the love we share and not just a machismo need for offspring? The *ping* of want stabbing that sneaky maternal spot in my gut shocked me. Fortunately, years of squashing that unwanted side of me rose up and did its duty again.

But wait? A personal assistant for me? I struggled to appear businesslike and ignored the little voice in my head telling me I wanted to make the business succeed without Kaine's help. I mean, come on. Who could turn down a personal assistant? "Great. Lead the way to my office, please."

"Of course. If you'll kindly follow me..." She bestowed another beatific smile on me, turned on her heel and started down the hallway. The girl was definitely happier than when we'd first met.

For a little person—uh, petite woman—she sure could move. I hurried after her, managing to stay a few steps behind her, but never quite catching up. After heading down two more winding hallways I was sure I'd left out of my hastily drawn map, she stopped and nodded at one of the many dark mahogany doors lining the hall.

A polished bronze plaque with my name—*Christina Taylor-Delcaluca*—was attached to the door. "You're shitting me!" I reached out to run my fingers over the gleaming letters.

"Of course not, Mrs. Delcaluca. I would never, um, shit you."

"Oops, forgive my Dutch, but this is unreal."

She tinkled again—as in laughed, not as in going Number One—and swung the door wide. With another quick nod, she motioned for me to step inside my new digs.

My mouth fell open. My new office was twice the size of my former studio apartment. An enormous ornate desk dominated the room with smaller pieces of furniture such as a comfy couch, side chairs and coffee table filling the rest of the space. Lush beige carpet—*oh, please, let my shoes be clean*—beckoned me to run my toes through it, while a large flat-screen television decorated one wall. Beautiful paintings hung on the other walls, but it was the state-of-the-art computer system resting on the desk that caught my attention and held it prisoner.

"Wow." I forgot to maintain a professional attitude and dashed over to examine the machine. I clicked the mouse and the monitor instantly lit up, showing a woman's face.

"Good morning, Mrs. Delcaluca." The woman, an identical match for Missy, smiled at me. "How may I help you today?"

I jerked my head up to stare at the real Missy. "No freakin' way! Did my computer just speak to me?"

"I did, Mrs. Delcaluca. I'm your P.A.M. You may call me Pam, if you wish."

"My P.A.M.?" I sat down, immediately luxuriating in the rich leather. "I know I have P.M.S. sometimes, but I've never had P.A.M."

Missy and the computer laughed identical tinkling laughs. "P-A-M., Mrs. Delcaluca, is an acronym for Personal Assistant Machine."

"I'm your personal *live* assistant," added Missy.

"Excuse me, Missy, but I'm as alive as you are." Pam glared at Missy, who had moved to stand beside me.

"Of course you are. I was only trying to explain the difference to Mrs. Delcaluca." Missy inclined her head first to Pam, then to me. "Pam handles all cyber-related activities while I take care of hands-on duties. Think of us as two halves of one efficient assistant."

"Actually, we're two-thirds of one efficient assistant."

I checked around the room, looking for yet another version of Missy. "Three? There's three of you?"

If anyone could scoff in a sweet way, it was Missy. "In a way." She reached into the left-hand drawer of the desk and picked up a cell phone—or at least something resembling a cell phone. “This is a mini-version of P.A.M.”

I took the gadget and examined it. Another image of Missy-slash-Pam lit up the touch screen. This version spoke at the same time Pam did.

“We’re both a P.A.M. or Pam. One of us—” Pam waved from the monitor on the desk, “—is dedicated to your office, while the other—” the mini-Pam in the cell phone tipped her head at me, “—is the mobile unit. When you speak to one, you speak to both.”

I glanced at Missy. “But not to you? Because you’re real, right?”

“A-hem!” Duplicate glares assaulted me from both screens. “Both of us are just as real, Mrs. Delcaluca. Not being organic in nature does not make us any less real.”

Missy caught my eye and shot me an undeniable look. Obviously the flesh-and-blood assistant didn’t agree. I wasn’t, however, ready to start a war. “Okay. Got it.” I glanced around, wanting to get busy doing what I’d started out to do. “So, do I have a printer in here? One with photo quality paper?”

“Of course.”

Having all three assistants answer simultaneously was a bit overwhelming, but I tried not to let it show. I wasn’t used to having one assistant, much less three. Heck, the best I’d ever had was a twenty-five percent discount at Kinko’s. “Okey-dokey, then. How about I slip this card into the media slot and we get some pics uploaded and printed.” Before I had a chance to strike a key on the keyboard, however, the pictures I’d taken of Kaine and the #&#*@ lady were on Pam’s large screen. The printer hummed away.

“Who is the lovely woman with Mr. Delcaluca?”

I cringed at the same question being asked by three voices. *That’s what I’d like to know.* “Do you three share the same brain or something?"

All three images shook their head. "Yes and no. However, we do think alike. Would you like us to explain our programming to you?"

Missy interjected, "*Their* programming."

"No, thanks. I'm pretty sure it's beyond my grasp."

Missy studied the photo of Miss PP. "So who is—"

"Um, not to be rude, but that's for me to know." I caught the flash of irritation on Missy's face before it swiftly vanished. *Seems meek-and-mild Missy might have a mean side.* I figured I needed to set the tone of our business relationship before it got out of hand. "I think we need to have an understanding, ladies." Were cybernetic individuals considered ladies? "Anything you see, hear or download in and out of this office, as well as any correspondence from, to or by me is strictly confidential. Agreed?"

"Are you asking us to keep information from Mr. Delcaluca too?" Missy's all-too-knowing gaze bored into me.

I swallowed and took the leap. "I am."

The feeling that all three assistants had somehow silently communicated swept over me. My assumption turned out to be correct when they answered in unison. "I can live with that."

"And Fitz?" Pam chimed in.

"Especially from Fitz."

Their joint answers echoed cheery tones. "No problem."

I grinned at them, happy that I'd found three new friends, saluted them and darted out of the room. Clutching the photos of the woman, I darted down the hallway, making a beeline for Kaine's office. I'd made up my mind to confront him. I didn't care that I had absolutely no concrete proof that he'd done anything wrong—unless speaking with a dazzling woman could be considered a crime. (By the way, it can when you're a new and somewhat insecure bride.) At this point, however, I was ready to jump on the slightest indiscretion. Trust me. Hell hath no fury like a bride ignored.

I rounded the corner and slid to a stop outside his door. Gasping more from the sight of my hunk-o-hunks than from my quick trip, I paused to catch my breath and admire the scenery. I had to admit I'd snagged one delicious-looking male specimen. Even though he was fully clothed, I could see the outline of his hard form, the ripple of his arms as he held the phone to one ear and punched his computer keyboard with the other hand. His jaw, firmly set, let me know how irritated he was, but his irritation was also pretty damned sexy. I stood, letting my own vexation ooze out of me until, at last, he glanced up and met my stare.

Gold? Had his eyes been gold? I blinked. But the gold was gone and the green eyes I loved sparkled at me. Why did I keep seeing flashes of gold in his eyes? Seeing gold wasn't necessarily unusual—lots of people have flecks of gold in their eyes—but this was something different. I could've sworn the entire irises of his eyes had changed from green to gold. *Maybe I'm seeing his Midas touch.* I snorted at my less-than-humorous joke.

He ended the conversation with an abrupt command and placed the phone back in its cradle. "Chrissy-doll? Did you need to see me?"

His question, although sweet in tone, still made me feel like a shy secretary disturbing her intimidating boss with bad news. I shoved away the unnerving thought and warned myself to stay on track. "Yes, I did." It was difficult, but I barely managed to keep from waving the photos at him like some irate housewife confronting her cheating husband. "I'd like you to take a look at these."

"Oh? Photos from our honeymoon?" Kaine, a small smile forming on his face, reached over his desk for the photos.

I admit it. I was a bit thrown by his pleasant attitude. After all, he'd left our bedroom last night in a huff. I suddenly changed my mind about explaining why I didn't want a child and instead decided to focus on the present problem. I handed him the pictures and waited for his reaction. If I hadn't been watching closely, however, I would've missed it. A quick frown grazed his forehead before his expression became unreadable. *Damn. If Kaine ever wants to quit his entrepreneurial business, he'd make one helluva player on the World Poker circuit.*

"How did you take these?"

The barely concealed edge to his voice made my heart beat faster. "Well, duh. With my camera, of course." I had to give him credit. He tried for a grin, but fell short.

"You know what I mean." His gaze broke away from the snapshots to search my face. "Were you following me?"

Ah-ha! Me thinketh you soundeth a bit guilteth, er, guilty. I nearly laughed until I realized I shouldn't feel victorious that I'd accused him and found him lacking. Still, this old dog wasn't about to let this old rawhide go. "*Should* I be following you?" I could tell I'd caught him off-guard, but he quickly recovered.

"I don't know why you would want to." He visibly relaxed and moved around the desk to slide his arm around me. "If you'd wanted to follow me around all day, you could've simply asked. Although I think you'd probably have been bored out of your mind."

I leaned into him, a sucker for his touch. "Well, I, uh..."

"But what were you doing in that neighborhood?" He laid the pictures on his desk and pulled me into his embrace. He narrowed his eyes and zoned in. "Have you found another lover already?"

Already? Does he expect me to eventually cheat? Yeah, like that'll ever happen. I snuggled against him. "Not a chance, big boy. You're stuck with me, forever and ever." I sighed and fought to keep my mind on my original mission of finding out who Miss PP was. "I was in the area to de-demonize a teenage boy for his grandma. But you haven't explained why you were there. And who's the redhead, anyway?" I swallowed and grabbed at the opening he'd given me. "Have *you* found another lover already?"

Somehow his chuckle was both comforting and unsettling. "I have dealings all over the world, Chrissy-doll, including most of Atlanta and the surrounding area." He took me by my arms to move me back from him. If I could've held on without feeling like a clingy wife, I would have. "The woman is a business associate. Nothing more."

I'd never seen a businesswoman who looked like that. Except in the movies. But then, most of my business transactions dealt with average Joes, not ladies who could stand next to the biggest movie starlet and not feel inferior. I sighed and thought about pushing him down on his desk and having my way with him. As newlyweds went, we weren't getting nearly enough sex. "What kind of business is she in? What's her name?"

Kaine cupped his palm to my cheek and made my knees melt along with any coherent brain activity. "Chrissy-doll, I would love nothing more than to throw you on top of my desk and make wild passionate love to you."

Yes, please!

"After all, time is of the essence and—" At my glower, he rounded his eyes and held up a hand in supplication. "No. Not now. We'll continue that discussion later. Right now, I'm sorry, but I've got to run to another appointment."

He stepped away from me and I could swear I felt a black hole appear between us. Or at least a gaping hole in the fulfillment of my desire even if he had dampened the mood with his baby-making implication. "But, Kaine, I'd really like to talk more about her. Now."

He grinned at me. "Christina Taylor-Delcaluca, are you jealous?"

"Don't be silly." Of course I was. But I wasn't about to admit it.

He scoffed and let his grin grow wider. "Come here, my love." Taking my hand, he pulled me over to the ornate mirror hanging on the wall behind his desk. Turning me to face my image, he held my shoulders and caught my gaze in the reflection. "Look at yourself. You are the most gorgeous woman I have ever known. And I've known my fair share." Pointing at the image of me in the mirror, he commanded me to keep studying my features, then turned back to his desk, putting his back to me.

"Hey! TMI. I don't particularly want to know how many women you've known." *Or do I?* "But just for funsies, how many would that be? More than twenty? Fifty? A hundred?" I pivoted to place my hand on his shoulder before he could answer. "Never mind. Like I said, TMI. Way too much information."

He wrapped his arms around me again and pressed his lips on mine. After a doozy of a kiss, all swirls of yearning and Kaine's musky taste, he cupped my face and stared into my eyes. "Never ever doubt that you're the love of my life." With one more kiss that nearly dissolved me into a sexual puddle at his feet, he stalked out of the room.

An image of Kaine naked and waiting for me in our bed had me swallowing a hard lump. *But not as hard as the lump between his legs—the one I really wanted to swallow.* My knees buckled and I plopped into his chair. "Wow. I have got to get that man back in bed."

"I'll say."

Jolted out of my lust-filled thoughts, I peered down at Mini-Pam who I hadn't realized I'd slipped into my pocket. "Hey. What are you doing eavesdropping on us?"

"I'm sorry, Mrs. Delcaluca, but I'm not the one who forgot to turn me off."

I glared at the Missy face in the tiny monitor. "Oh, sure. Like you probably can't turn yourself off and on at will. Am I right or am I wrong?"

At least Mini-Pam had the decency to appear remorseful. "Well, that's true." At my angry expletive, she quickly added, "But you should be glad I was watching."

"Oh? And why is that, o-miniature-machine-o-mine?"

"Because otherwise, you might not have realized that Kainey—er, Mr. Delcaluca—took one of the photos with him."

What? I glanced at the pictures lying on the desk. *One, two, three, four... Didn't I print out five photos? Did he take the photo of the beautiful woman turning purple?* I tried to jog my memory, but my memory got stuck at the starting line. "Are you sure?"

"Positive."

"But why would Kaine take one of the photos without telling me?" I stared at the monitor as though staring into Mini-Pam's eyes would give me the answer.

"I'm sorry, but I don't know the answer to your question."

Grumbling, I scooped up the remaining photos and started for the door. Started, that is, until what I'd heard finally hit me. "Wait a sec." I held Mini-Pam closer to my face. "Kainey?" *Did Mini-Pam just use a pet name for my husband? Did my electronic assistant have a sweet spot for my husband?*

But Mini-Pam, I discovered, had suddenly discovered that her batteries were low and quickly shut down for an "emergency recharging". *Harrumph. Seems to me like she's doing more avoiding than recharging.* But I had bigger problems to solve than a possible cyber crush on my husband. So instead of finding out why she'd used the very familiar and slightly disturbing Kainey, I rushed through the house, hoping my memory would lead me to the garage. If Kaine wasn't going to give me any complete answers, I'd get them the old-fashioned way. I'd snoop on him. (Oh, hush. Like you wouldn't do the same.)

Following someone isn't as easy as it looks on television, especially when you're driving a cherry-red convertible Porsche. According to Kaine's on-site automobile mechanic, my dear old Honda had sputtered its last fume-clogged breath and driven off to Car Heaven the night before. Tears had threatened to spill when I'd heard the news, but when he ushered me to the sassy Porsche, I'd managed to regain my stiff upper lip. (Hey, seriously, though. It was tough.)

On hindsight, I should've asked for one of my hubby's other, less noticeable automobiles, but could I help it if the mechanic suggested the Porsche? Getting used to my new billionaire lifestyle would take some doing, but I decided that fighting to retain my noble-yet-poor image was counter-productive and I was now willing to give my new station in life my best shot. You know, for Kaine's sake.

I slid into traffic behind his limo—*I'll never understand why he owns so many cars when he always uses the limo and chauffeur*—and tried to keep one car between us. I doubted he would notice the Porsche following, but I wasn't sure about Gerald, the limo driver. Was he familiar with the rest of Kaine's cars? Or did his position as the limo driver keep him restricted to the Rolls? If so, I figured my not-so-little tail might just get away with my investigative tail job.

Questions I knew I should've asked Kaine before marrying him kept firing off in my head. What exactly did he do for a living? For a very, very good living, I might add. I'd accepted his earlier vague explanation and never really pressured him for details. I figured I wouldn't understand the complicated workings of his billion-dollar business. After all, I'd hired an accountant for my own small business—even though he took one look at my jumbled-up books and declared that I couldn't afford the time it'd take for him to unscramble my mess. Handling finances had never been one of my strong suits. Shoot, I could barely balance my personal checkbook so how could I possibly grasp the complicated dealings of Kaine's enterprises?

Still my new hubby's finances weren't what bugged me the most. I was more distressed because I'd never delved into his personal life. We'd clicked so fast that asking him about his past had never occurred to me. I hadn't watched before I'd leapt—or however the saying goes. Shoot, as far I knew, he could have four other wives with twelve children scattered in countries around the world. The beautiful redhead popped into my thoughts and I cringed. Was he having an affair with her? Was she a gold-digger in search of a rich sugar daddy?

I snarled, my churning anxiety making me utter curses under my breath. Better to rail than to wail, is what I always say. Pulling the car into a parking space a row down from where the limo had parked, I scrunched down into the seat—not an easy thing to do in a convertible Porsche—and watched the man of my dreams stride toward an outdoor café. He waved the protesting hostess away from him and joined a group of men seated at one of the larger tables. All four of them stood when he approached and, with a curt nod of acknowledgement, he pulled out the chair at the head of the table. The men waited for him to sit before they did and the meeting—if that's what it was—began. A waiter zipped in and out, keeping their drinks filled.

Twenty minutes later, I'd almost nodded off out of boredom when one of the men raised his voice and clutched the frightened waiter's arm. The boy's eyes grew wide and he tried to pull away from the shimmering horned man. *Shimmering? With horns? How the heck does anyone shimmer and grow horns?* But that was the only way I could describe the man. I rubbed my sleep-heavy eyes and squinted. Had the man actually shimmered? Were the horns real or an oddity of his hairstyle? Or, in a more logical explanation—because I'm all about logical explanations—was the combination of semi-sleep and the Hotlanta heat getting to me? Before I could decide, Kaine nodded farewell and slipped into the limo. I shook my head to clear the cobwebs and followed, determined to keep up my secret-agent act.

Ten minutes later, I watched in horror as my presumably loyal hubby waltzed into a strip joint. Granted, it was a very high-dollar establishment boasting the class of a gentleman's club but, let's face it. A strip joint is a strip joint no matter what you call it. The only difference was the neighborhood.

But what was my presumably devoted hubby doing in a place like that? Did Kaine have a fascination with ladies of the night? Was he already sexually bored with me? Perhaps even visiting a specific exotic woman? Again, the redhead invaded my mind, but I couldn't imagine her as a dancer. Maybe she was one of those incredibly well-dressed madams? Besides, who goes to a strip joint in the middle of the day? I glanced around the almost full parking lot. Apparently lots of people did.

My stomach grew more knotted and nauseous. *What should I do now?* Just as I'd decided to confront him, he came out. He'd almost gotten back into the limo when a very large skuzzy man dressed in a ratty jacket ran out, calling his name. Instantly, Fitz—a larger, bulkier, and definitely scarier-looking version—jumped from inside the limo, coming to stand at Kaine's side. Her stance, her vicious snarl boasting a row of shark-like teeth was an obvious deterrent to the man rapidly approaching her boss. I held my breath, alarm tightening my neck, and waited for the man to pull out a gun or knife. Fitz stepped in front of Kaine, protecting him. Instead of attacking, however, the man dropped to his knees and bowed his head. Kaine stepped around Fitz, waved his hand over the man's head, then slipped into the limo with Fitz following closely behind. I watched dumbfounded at the Godfather-like scenario. Yet when the man stood up, I knew it was me, not Kaine, who was in trouble.

Is that a tail? I rubbed my eyes, certain I couldn't have possibly seen a gray tail sticking out from under the man's jacket. *Omigod. I'm losing it. Call the men in white coats and tell my husband I'm sorry he married a nutcase.* Not only had I seen his skin-and-bones assistant turn into a muscled bodyguard with lethal teeth, but I'd seen a man sprout a tail. What the holy hell was happening to me?

Mini-Pam, recharged at last, decided to turn on and join my little escapade. "May I be of assistance, Mrs. Delcaluca?"

I jumped, startled by the device resting on the passenger seat. "Jesus, Mini-Pam, you scared the crap outta me." I looked back, but the man was gone. *Should I say anything to Mini-Pam?* Although my logical brain was apparently slipping away, I still had enough pride to keep my yap shut.

She smiled prettily. "Oh, I'm sorry. I'll try not to turn on again without warning you." Her dimples popped out. "But if you want me to warn you, I'll have to turn on."

I took a few moments to pull myself together. "Yeah, it's a

regular catch-forty-two."

Could a machine giggle? If so, she did one helluva job. "I believe the phrase is a catch-twenty-two. Not forty-two."

Had I just been put into my place by a bunch of metal and wires? "Whatever."

I mentally dismissed her. What should I do? I couldn't keep following Kaine around all day, and after what I'd seen, I wasn't sure I wanted to. Sooner or later, Gerald or Fitz—why didn't I notice her earlier?—was bound to notice the bright red car trailing them. Still, how else was I to find out what my hubby was up to? I had no choice but to continue my 007 routine.

Kaine's limo pulled out of the parking lot and sped down the street. The limo rounded the far corner and my gaze fell on the woman standing in the alley outside a trendy boutique. Miss PP slinked back into the shadows of the alley seconds before the limo whisked past her.

"Looks like someone's trying not to be seen."

"Who?"

I held Mini-Pam up and faced her screen toward the boutique and its skulking visitor. "See the woman in the shadows? Miss PP, that's who."

"Oh, you mean the beautiful woman with the long red hair? The one in your photos?"

Did she have to emphasize the beautiful part of the description? "Yeah. Her."

"Miss PP? Do you know her?"

Once Kaine's car was a dot on the horizon, she stepped back into the light, then entered the upscale boutique. "Yes and no. I don't know her know her, if you know what I mean. That's just the name I gave her." The limo disappeared from sight. *So much for tracking him now.*

“Oh, I see. I think.” Mini-Pam made a soft whirring noise. “Are we going home now? Forgive me for saying so, but you don’t seem quite…right.”

“Nope. I’m fine. In fact, I suddenly feel much better. I’m going to bite the gun and meet this mystery lady. Maybe she’ll tell me how she and Kaine know each other.”

“I believe the phrase is bite the—”

“Mini-Pam?”

“Yes, Mrs. Delcaluca?”

“Bite me.”

“Oh!”

I’d placed my hand on the car door handle when, out of the corner of my eye, I caught a familiar face.

“Holy crap, it’s Tuo Chow.”

Tuo skulked down the sidewalk, staying in the shadows of the canopies as though the sun would burn him. My thoughts immediately turned to vampires, but even after the day I’d had, I wasn’t about to go down that crazy path. When Tuo ducked into the boutique, however, I almost fainted away. Could this day get any weirder?

I zoomed across the street in ten seconds, all while keeping out of view of Miss PP and the odd Mr. Chow. I flattened my body beside the frosted door of the boutique, edged around and peeked inside.

At first, the boutique’s wonderful clothes and accessories dazzled me. I’d only seen merchandise like this on celebrities in the movies. *Are those Manolo Blahniks resting on the glass display shelf? Is that the bracelet I’ve seen Paris Hilton wear? One of her own designs?* For a moment, I felt like I’d walked into an alternate universe—the one where all the beautiful and famous people live. In fact, my first impulse—after my delighted shock wore off—was to cross my arms over my T-shirt and jeans, turn around and hightail it outta there. Damn, how I wished I'd worn one of the fabulous new outfits hanging in my huge walk-in closet at home. But those clothes were just too fancy for DeBunkers' work. For a moment, I forgot why I was there.

Or at least I did until I saw Tuo grab Miss PP's arms and yank her to the side of the room, out of view of the other customers. I, however, had a front row seat.

Tuo's face was a mask of anger and Miss PP's wasn't a delight of joy either. She whipped her arms around in a circle, using a breakaway move I recognized from defense class, and pushed the small man away. He flailed his arms, gesturing and literally spitting his words. Although they were obscured from view, the other patrons heard them arguing and turned toward the clothes rack the two had hidden behind. Not being able to read lips, but still wanting to hear everything, I had no choice except to crack open the door.

"Sabrina, you stupid bitch, do you really think I'm going to believe that load of crap?" Tuo flicked his hair over his shoulders in a gesture that would've made Cher proud. "I know for a fact that he's going insane looking for the scepter. The Dynasty is calling for him to step down if he doesn't find it. Don't insult me by telling me he still has it."

Sabrina. Damn. Even her name was beautiful. I filed the name away for future use. But what was this stuff about a scepter?

Sabrina crossed her arms and arched an imperious eyebrow. "I don't care a whit for what you believe. I tried and I failed. The Scepter of Fire remains with the Dragon Dynasty."

Scepter of Fire? And a dragon dynasty? Were Sabrina and Tuo sci-fi fans? Were Kaine and these two involved in some role-playing game? Their conversation was getting stranger by the second.

Tuo's scoff sounded more like he'd blown his nose. "Zeiwacians don't fail. That's why I hired you." His eyes narrowed. "But they do double-cross their clients. Tell me. Is someone paying you more than I am?"

Was Zeiwacia a minor third-world country? I crept closer.

Sabrina gave the Wicked Witch of the West a run for her money with her cackle. "Well, my dear Tuo, the only way to find out is to up your offer. Then, perhaps, I'll increase my efforts to procure the prize."

Tuo scrunched his features even tighter, meaner. "Why, you little whore-hound. I ought to—"

An employee, presumably the manager by her demeanor, worked her way over to the dueling clients but kept a safe distance. "I'm sorry if there's a problem, but I'm going to have to ask you to—"

Sabrina shot her hand out and pointed a finger at the woman. Immediately, the manager clutched her throat and gasped for air, her eyes bulging. Sabrina and Tuo, however, barely noticed as another worker pulled the manager away and shouted for someone to call for an ambulance. I gasped and went to my knees, trying to make myself smaller. *What the hell happened to the manager?*

"Tuo, you'd better stay away from me or I'll—"

"You'll what? Choke me? Please, I know your powers are in limited supply while you're here. You'd better save them for when you really need them. Like when you don't hand over my merchandise and I have to forcibly take it from you."

Powers? What kind of powers did she have? Wasn't being drop-dead gorgeous enough? I sniffed derisively. No way. She probably knew some kind of tricky mind-control thing. No one could actually choke someone by pointing at them.

If Sabrina got any redder in the face, I thought she'd explode. Instead, she screamed at Tuo, startling everyone except him, then turned and stormed toward the door. I fell backward onto my butt and quickly remembered how to do the crab walk. I made it around the edge of the building a split second before the door slammed open and she stomped out.

With my back as flat against the building as I could make it, I tried to breathe without making any noise. I could no longer see Sabrina, but I heard the sound of a car roaring off. Trying to slow my heart down, I decided to wait until I thought I could scurry away safely.

"Mrs. Delcaluca. How good to see you."

Instead of slowing down, my heart skipped a beat. I was surprised it hadn't stopped altogether. Bracing myself, I glanced up to find Tuo smiling down at me. "Oh, hi, Mr. Chow. Fancy seeing you here." I smothered a wince but, hey, it was the best I could do.

Fake concern replaced the smarmy smile. "Did you fall? Please, let me help you."

I stared at the hand inches from my face and resolved that there was no way in hell I would touch it. Instead, I continued my ungraceful maneuver on my own, bracing my hands against the brick wall and shimmying my way to a standing position. "Uh, no thanks. I'm fine. No fall. I, uh, simply decided to take a breather from all the walking. You know, I shopped 'til I plopped." Did that sound as lame as I thought it did? The expression on his face gave me the answer. *A-huh-a-huh, a-yup.* But, since I was already caught, I figured what the hell, I'd just plow on and hope for the best.

"So you were shopping? Is that your story?" His smirk grew.

"Story? I don't know what you mean." I tried, but I couldn't hold his gaze. Instead, I edged toward the sidewalk and into the sun. If he was a vampire, then he'd get one helluva sunburn if he followed me. "Well, gosh, it was good to see you. Goodbye, Mr. Chow."

Damn. He was by my side and walking me to my car. I glanced up at the sun and frowned. For once I'd wanted to believe in the supernatural and it had failed me. *Vampire, my ass.*

"Please, call me Tuo."

"Okay. Tuo." *Urgh.* I picked up speed, hustling toward my car. For a minute, I left him a few paces behind me. But only for a minute, damn it.

"If I were in your place, I would follow her too."

The man definitely knew how to get my attention. "What're you talking about?"

His beady gaze bored into me, but I stood strong. "I assume Kaine told you about his relationship with Sabrina?" He held up his palms, stopping me before I could challenge him. "Former relationship, of course." His smirk hit an even higher smirk level. "Or at least, she told me it's a former relationship. But one can never trust anything Sabrina says."

I wanted to snatch his hair right off his head. Instead, I put on my best poker face and hoped I could pull off the bluff. "Of course." I'd let him figure out if I meant the relationship or trusting her.

"Interesting."

The twinkle in his eyes nearly drove me to commit murder. "He is my husband, after all." *As if that explains everything. Ha!*

"Good. Then I'm sure I'll be congratulating you both soon."

I gritted my teeth, desperately trying not to ask. But damn

it, I had to. “Congratulating us?” Why didn’t I keep going, get in my car and get the hell away from this freak?

He feigned his surprise. “For the little one on the way, of course. For your pregnancy. After all, I’m sure you’ll be giving him the heir he so desperately wants. You wouldn’t want to suffer Sabrina’s fate.”

I’m sure the stun in my heart reflected on my face. “What are you talking about?”

All pretense of civility fell away. Instead a stone-cold mask covered his features, icing his words. “When she didn’t, wouldn’t bear his spawn, he kicked her out. Dumped her.” His lip hiked into a sneer. “Good luck, Mrs. Delcaluca. You’re going to need it.”

He pivoted quickly and walked away from me at a good clip. Hell, he couldn’t have made a grander exit if he’d had a cape to twirl.

Is That Your Torch Pressed Against Me? Or Are You Just Happy To See Me?

Okay, I chickened out again. Instead of barging into my hubby's office as I'd planned to do, I peeked around the doorframe. Kaine stood with his side to me, a frown on his face and obviously deep in thought. One look at him told me I'd better keep my yap closed and my questions quiet—at least for now. Besides, I didn't want to risk him not coming to our bed tonight. I wanted sex and I wanted it tonight. After all, a girl's gotta do what a girl's gotta fix.

So I tiptoed past his office and hurried to our bedroom. I took Mini-Pam out of my pocket, tossed my clothes on the bedspread and gazed forlornly at our bed. Sighing, I smoothed out Kaine's pillow and sent a quick plea heavenward that the sheets would end up rumpled before tomorrow morning came. For a guy wanting to make babies, he sure had a funny way of going about it.

Oh, damn. How had a baby thought popped into my head? *Girl, if you're thinking that the only way to get sex is to have a baby, you'd better knock some sense into your noggin. Unless...* I had to wonder. *Don't I love Kaine enough to give him what he so desperately wants? After all, the man gives me everything I want, a life filled with riches and love, and I won't give him the one thing he asks for?* Ah, but was that part of the problem? That he didn't actually ask for it? Instead, demanding I have a baby? Still, a part of me felt very bad—and yeah, even guilty—for refusing him.

Irritated at myself for even thinking about a baby—and at Kaine for insisting we have one—set up a knot of tension in my neck and I decided right then and there to get something useful out of this night. My conversation with Tuo, albeit definitely interesting, hadn't done anything except add to the growing number of questions I had about my hubby and one certain lady. I didn't want this night to end on such a sour note.

Gathering my determination like the robe I wrapped around me, I scooped up Mini-Pam and headed for my office. This time, I made it there without the help of a map or servant. *Score one for the lady of the house.* It was a small victory, but I was willing to take any encouragement I could get. I slipped into my leather chair and reached for the keyboard.

"Good evening, Mrs. Delcaluca."

I'm not sure which jumped higher, my heart or my body. "Damn, Pam, scare the hell outta me, why don't you?" Placing a hand over my chest, I leaned back in the chair and waited for my pulse to even out.

"I'm sorry. I didn't mean to frighten you." Pam's remorseful face glowed against the screen's dark background.

"That's all right. No harm done." Unless you count heart failure. I frowned. Come to think of it, I've had a lot of jolting moments since moving into Kaine's house. More than I've ever had handling debunking jobs. Between the offbeat business associates, the odd assortment of household servants, not to mention Fitz the Mouse Muncher and today's run-in with Tuo, I'd turned into a regular jumping bean.

I touched the mouse and clicked. Nothing happened.

"You don't need to use a mouse, Mrs. Delcaluca. I'm here to assist you."

Did I want Pam helping me? Could I trust her—it—to keep quiet? "Pam, do you remember what I said about whatever happens in my office?"

"Of course. You told me that anything I see, hear or download in this office is strictly confidential."

"Good memory, Pam."

"I enjoy one-hundred percent accuracy."

"Good to know. Just remember that one-hundred percent belongs to me and no one else. Not even Mr. Delcaluca." Guilt at hiding anything from my husband twisted my stomach, but I forged ahead. Sometimes a girl's gotta try what a girl's gotta do. Or however that damn thing goes.

"I remember."

"As do I."

I jumped again. "Sheesh. Will you guys stop doing that?" I glared at Mini-Pam in my robe pocket. I took her out and placed her on the desk. "I'm serious. Maybe you two could beep or something before you speak."

Mini-Pam tilted her head to the side at the same instant Pam did and answered in the same moment. "If you wish."

"I do. Oh, I definitely do." I nodded to emphasize my insistence.

"Should I do the same?"

Maybe it was the fact that it was a human voice or maybe I was simply all jumped out, but I wasn't startled to find Missy standing in the doorway. I grinned at the diminutive lady. "Nah, we'll put a cowbell on you."

She gawked at me, then imitated Pam and Mini-Pam's

quizzical tilt of the head.

"Missy, I'm joking." I glanced at the clock. "What are you doing working so late?"

"Late?" She followed my gaze to the clock on the wall. "Oh, you mean after five. I don't mind at all. Besides, mice are used to running around at all hours of the day."

That proved it. My heart must've jumped one too many times because now it wouldn't even beat. "I'm sorry, but did you say *mice*?" *Please say no.* After everything else I saw and went through today, now I was faced with a mentally ill assistant. When had I lost control of my practical and logical life?

She gave me a pitying look. "I'm sorry. I assumed Mr. Delcaluca or Fitz would have told you."

Told me what? That my assistant was wacko? "Uh, nope. I guess it slipped their minds." *Or, in actuality, you've slipped yours.*

She scurried into the room, coming to the edge of the desk. I tensed, ready to run for my life if this delusional doll of a woman went psycho-killer. She clasped her hands in front of her like a bad schoolgirl confessing to smoking in the bathroom. "It's true. I...am a mouse."

Both Mini-Pam and Pam supported her. "It's true. She is."

Their confirmation of Missy's claim made sense. After all, they were programmed to be like her, right?

I had to give it to her, though. She had me considering her incredible claim. She could pass as a cute little mouse with her lovable looks and small frame. And hadn't I thought of her as mousy? But I wasn't ready to let my mind slip all the way down the crazy slope. *Take it easy, Chrissy. Stay calm and she'll stay calm.*

"I see." I struggled to find words. "So you must've grown

really big? I mean, the mice in Cinderella were very small." I hoped she wouldn't bring up Mickey and Minnie for a comparison. But once I'd thought of them, I couldn't get them out of my head. I couldn't help it. I had to ask. "Are you any relation to Mickey?"

Cheese. I smell cheese.

I squinted, spying the bit of cheese sticking out of her pocket. *She carries cheese in her pocket.* I swallowed, unnerved by the discovery. *Get a grip, Chrissy. You're tired and you've had a rough day.* Besides, lots of people—*human, sane* people—liked cheese.

I glanced up quickly, noted the annoyed expression on her face and decided changing the subject might be the safest route. "Sorry." I had to fake a smile, but I managed it. *Remember to tell Kaine about the crazy lady he sent to work for me.*

"No problem." She pulled up a chair next to mine and waved at Pam. "Were you going to do some work? May I help you?"

Nutty assistant or not, I had things I needed to get done. Besides, changing the subject really appealed to me. "I'm going to do some research. If I can figure out how."

All three of my assistants came to my rescue. The hard drive running Pam whirred while Mini-Pam beeped, signaling she was ready to help. Missy edged closer, eager to help. But only Pam kept talking after their initial attempts to explain how things worked had died down. "If you'd like to access the Internet, documents, or whatever, all you have to do is ask. Remember, Mini-Pam and I are voice-activated."

"So am I," tinkled Missy.

"Great. Then how about helping me get some facts on a thing called the Scepter of Fire?"

The whirring ground to a stop, the beeping disappeared, and Missy turned to stone. All three assistants exchanged a telling glance. At last, Missy cleared her throat and asked, "Why do you want to know about the Scepter of Fire?"

My nerves prickled at her careful tone. All I asked for was a little help. If I had to put up with a cheese-loving assistant, then she could damn well do her job. "Not that it matters, but I heard someone mention it and it sounded interesting. Now, are you going to help me or not? If not, then you—" I pointed one finger at Missy, "—can clear out of my office. And you—" this time I pointed at Mini-Pam, "—can power down for good. Which leaves you." I aimed my human gun at Pam. "You can tell me where I can find a normal personality-free computer."

The sound of my ringtone jolted me out of the conversation. I shot a look at Mini-Pam indicating that I wasn't through with her, snatched my phone from my pocket and pushed the button. "DeBunkers, Inc. Your ghoul is my job." I frowned. When would I come up with a good slogan?

"Chrissy? Thad here."

"Oh, hi, Thad. Listen, now's not a good—"

I lifted my gaze to see Fitz hurrying into the room with a vacuum cleaner. Missy let out a squeak, hopped up and dashed from the room. Mini-Pam whirred an angry sound and blinked off.

"Hey! Come back here, Missy! No, no, no! Mini-Pam, don't you dare power down."

"But I haven't talked to you in such a long time. Have you forgotten your old friend?" Thad's voice held more than the usual whine, but I didn't have time to do my usual take-care-of-my-sensitive-friend thing right now.

I snarled at the Mouse-Muncher. "Can't you see I'm working, Fitz?" Mouse-Muncher. Pink-striped mice. Missy had a pink stripe once. Then, when she'd taken the job as my assistant, she'd changed her hair color to blue. *Is there a connection? If Missy is indeed a mouse, wouldn't it be natural for her to fear the Mouse-Muncher? Wait a sec. Am I actually starting to believe this looniness?*

Fitz's face remained calm and unnaturally void of expression. "What are *you* doing here?" With a dramatic flip of the switch, she started the vacuum and began sweeping the floor underneath my desk.

"This is my office, remember?" I glared at the woman. "I can think of a couple of better questions. Like what are you doing vacuuming? Isn't that the maid's job?" I bit my lip but it was of no use. I had to go there. "Have you been demoted, Fitz?"

Fitz kept sweeping, apparently not hearing me above the roar of the machine. *Damn. And it was such a good zinger, too.* I took a closer look at her. Or maybe she was ignoring me. I chose the latter when she glanced up, an evil leer lifting one corner of her thin lips. With a wicked gleam in her eyes, she pushed the vacuum farther underneath my desk.

Errrrrrrrrr, zrrrrrrr!

"Stop! Fitz, stop the vacuum!" But my warning came too late. Pam, my only assistant left standing (so to speak) died, her power cord cut in half by the vacuum. Pam's frightened image blinked into cyber-nothingness.

You know how sometimes you feel so mad you could kill? When Fitz cut the cable to Pam I was beyond that point. Hell, I was beyond-that-point, over-the-hill and on-the-way-to-the-other-side-of-the-universe mad. So, instead of doing what I wanted to do to her—and wind up on trial for murder—I clamped my mouth shut, stood up and stalked out of my office.

A chuckle had me whirling around, ready to storm back in. Thankfully for Fitz, that's when I heard Thad's voice calling out from the phone.

"Chrissy? Where'd you go? Chrissy?"

Wishing my phone was a gun I could use on a certain mouse abuser, I held it up and answered. "Yeah, Thad, I'm here." *Thank goodness for friends who inadvertently keep you from a life in prison.* "Can you come over? I need some help investigating...something. Oh, and bring your laptop. My computer is on the Fitz."

I crisscrossed my bedroom in a frustrated pace and listened to Thad run down the highlights of our investigation. He kept turning his laptop so I could see the screen and the photos there, but I merely glanced at it. I had enough to deal with and my brain was already teetering on the edge to a bottomless precipice.

"So from everything we've gathered, which isn't a great deal, the Scepter of Fire is a relic of indeterminable age and power. Myths say the scepter was created by Merlin and used to slay dragons in the days of King Arthur and the Round Table. Folklore tells of a fight between Sir Lancelot and a mighty dragon that tore the scepter out of the knight's hand. The dragon then flew off and hid it away, thus keeping all dragons safe."

Thad shook his head. "This is amazing stuff. I couldn't have written anything better." He swiveled the computer around. "In modern times, however, the scepter is said to be in the possession of an organization called the Dragon Dynasty, whose members are, supposedly, real dragons. Rumor has it that many have tried to steal it, but all have died in their attempts."

I stopped halfway across the room. *Kaine collects ancient artifacts.* Tuo's angry words to Sabrina came back to hit me in the gut. *I know for a fact that he's going insane looking for the scepter. The Dynasty is calling for him to step down if he doesn't find it. Don't insult me by telling me he still has it.*

Could Kaine have this mythical Scepter of Fire? And Sabrina tried to steal it? If so, no wonder he dumped her. Better for that reason than because she wouldn't get preggers. Or is this all coincidence matched with silly stories? Slumping onto a chair, I held my head in my hands and dismissed all the questions except the really important ones. *Did the scepter actually exist? And if so, did Kaine still possess it?*

But the revelations and the fun had just begun.

"Hey, didn't you once tell me that Kaine has a rather unique tattoo? But you never described it to me." He coughed, then spoke again. But this time his voice sounded weak, even frightened. "Chrissy, I think you'd better see this."

This time I did look and looked hard. My heart beat faster in weird contrast to my lack of breath. Centered in the middle of the screen was a photo of a man, eerily similar in appearance to my husband. But their dark looks weren't the only thing they had in common. I stepped closer even as my mind screamed for me to run far, far away. In the hollow of the man's throat was a tattoo. A sideways figure-eight tattoo exactly like Kaine's. "Oh, crap."

Thad shook his head. "Tell me he doesn't have a tattoo like that one."

I slid into the chair next to him. "I wish I could. But yeah, he does. Exactly like that one. What is it? Does it mean anything? Kaine told me it was a symbol for good luck." Did I really want to know anything different? I wasn't sure, especially since Mr. I-Love-To-Hear-Myself-Talk had suddenly clammed up. Talk about strange. I elbowed him in the ribcage. "Don't make me read it for myself. Spit it out."

He took a deep breath and checked to see if I'd meant what I'd said. "Okay, here goes. According to this site, the mark at the base of the throat isn't a tattoo."

"What?" I leaned in to better examine the marking. "Then what the heck is it?"

He huffed at my interrupting him and read the text verbatim. As if I couldn't have done that myself. "According to ancient legend, the figure-eight tattoo on its side is a birthmark designating a leader in the upper hierarchy of..." He paused and wouldn't read on until I'd made a face egging him on. "...the Dragon Dynasty."

Yep, the name was in caps and Thad had read the words like that. *The Dragon Dynasty?* A sick feeling twisted my gut. I gripped the arms of my chair, fighting to keep upright and not drop to the floor in a faint.

"Are you all right, girlfriend?"

"Is this some kind of Oriental club? Maybe an organization dealing with ancient artifacts?" Maybe even a crime ring? "Surely we're not seriously talking about bona fide dragons." I laughed but it came out sounding forced. "What is this? Harry Potter, Atlanta style?"

Thad's arms around me helped to keep me upright. Too bad they did nothing for the storm raging in my heart. "I know it's a shock, but give it time to sink in. I know you're a skeptic, but some of the things you call fantasy are real."

He stared at me and I swallowed a lump of nervousness. I knew Thad believed in the supernatural, but why did I get the feeling he was trying to tell me something important?

"Chrissy?"

Through the hazy fog surrounding me, I managed to lift my head and see Kaine in the doorway. His stern expression made my heart sink.

"Sweet sugar and molasses. Is that who I think it is?" Thad whispered in my ear. He quickly clicked the monitor off.

I was still a little out of it, but that didn't keep me from being pleased with Thad's impressed reaction. Or at least I assumed it was a good reaction. "Yep, that's him."

Thad let out a little groan—so much for good reactions—and returned his attention to my hubby. "Uh, you know what? I, uh, forgot about this meeting I have." He glanced at an imaginary wristwatch. "Oh shoot. Will you look at that? I'm already late."

"Are you kidding me?" My best Pal Gal was bailing on me? I locked onto him, determined not to let him get away. "Not a chance, Thad. I want my two favorite guys to meet." Yet when I tried to make him stay, he still resisted. We half-stood half-stumbled out of our chairs. "What's the matter with you? Why are you acting so freaky?" Was it the tattoo thing? I had to admit it threw me for a loop too. But still...this was Kaine, not some gangster-looking type on the Internet.

"Nothing's the matter. I simply need to be somewhere else. Like right now."

By this time, Kaine had stepped into the room. His former stoic demeanor had shifted until he was, once again, the likable man I knew and loved. "Chrissy, I was beginning to worry about you. We've missed each other a lot in the past few days. I was hoping we could have tonight to ourselves." He covered the last few yards between us in record time.

How did he do that? It's almost like he ran the distance—without actually running. In fact, they way he moved sometimes made me think of those superheroes with lightning-fast speed. One second he's in one place, then you blink and he's in another spot. The only difference was that I couldn't see the ripple trail behind him, showing the path he'd taken. "I'm sorry.

I didn't mean to worry you." I leaned in to kiss him. Not an easy task while keeping a hold on my struggling friend. "Thad stopped over to help me with a bit of research."

"For a DeBunkers' case?" He eyed Thad, his gaze raking over the smaller man.

The tension between them was so thick I could've cut it with a hatchet. But why? Had they met before? Or was it an instinctual dislike? Like the gut reaction I get when I meet a beautiful *single* woman. (Oh sure. Like you're never that shallow.)

My ego gave me another idea. Could the two men in my life be jealous of one another? I shook the ego back down to size and dismissed the preposterous idea. Thad certainly wasn't one of my ex-lovers and Kaine had never shown any signs of jealousy. I tried again to come up with a reason for their obvious aversion, but couldn't. After all, my normally reliable radar was way off lately.

Kaine thrust out his hand. "Thank you for helping my wife."

I frowned, surprised when Thad took too long to take his hand. "No problem." The two stood, hands locked together, and I almost expected them to start wrestling. What was with these guys? "Kaine, you've heard me talk about Thad. You know. The actor, director, etcetera, etcetera? Remember? He's the guy who had the birthday party at the lake?"

"Yes, I remember." Kaine's right eyebrow hooked higher. "Good to meet you, *Th*ad."

At last they dropped hands, yet I couldn't believe it when Thad wiped his palm on his slacks. Talk about rude.

"The name is pronounced Tad. T-a-d. The H is silent."

Uh! There was that brilliant flash of gold in my hubby's eyes! Had Thad seen it too? Is that why he sucked in air and took a step back from Kaine?

"Then why don't you spell it T-a-d?" Kaine's eyes, back to their glorious green, twinkled with mirth. Yet somehow I knew he wasn't at all amused.

"Why don't you spell your name C-a-n-e?" Thad, who had been ready to run a few seconds before, stepped closer, almost bumping chests with my husband. Or rather, Thad's head to Kaine's chest. "Or aren't you as sweet as sugar cane?

Kaine chuckled, although it sounded like more of a warning growl than a real laugh. "Because my friend, I am definitely not sweet." He flashed me a short (*and sweet?*) smile. "Except, of course, to my charming lady."

What the hell was going on? Did I need a white flag to call a truce? I half-expected Kaine to call for dueling pistols. "Wow, should I rent a boxing ring and let you two go at it? Or would you prefer to settle this with a pissing contest?" (Like Kaine said, sometimes I just ooze charm.)

Kaine made a real chuckle this time, placed his arm around my waist and pulled me against him. "Thad and I are simply getting to know each other." He over-exaggerated Thad's name and gave my friend something between a smirk and a true smile. *Would that be called a smirle?*

Thad winced and agreed. "That's right. We're good, aren't we?"

"Of course."

Uh-huh. Next he'll be trying to sell me the Brooklyn Bridge. "Why do I get the impression you guys know each other? Have you met before?"

"No."

"No."

Both of their negative replies came a little too quickly. Were they both lying? Thad, it seemed, had had enough.

"Okay, well, uh, I've got that meeting to get to." Thad took my hand and squeezed it. "You call me if you need me." He glanced at Kaine and back. "Anytime, day or night, okay?"

I fumbled with an answer, stunned at how my usually welcoming friend had treated my man. "Uh, yeah, okay."

Without another glance at Kaine, much less a goodbye, Thad hurried down the long hall toward the front door. I think.

"What the hell was that about?" I took Kaine's hand, holding him while I studied his tattoo. *Yep. It's definitely the same as the one on the man on the Internet.* Glancing down the hall, I couldn't see Thad any longer. *Does everyone move that fast? Or am I just a slowpoke?*

Kaine ushered me back inside our bedroom. "I don't know what you mean."

When I started to explain, he laid his fingers on my lips and shook his head. "Tell me about your friend later. Right now I have something else we need to attend to."

"Kaine, if you're going to bring up that subject about you-know-what, I am not in the mood." *Will I ever be in the mood? Maybe when they come up with a cure for cancer.* Suddenly, an image of Kaine holding a baby blindsided me. Yet more amazing than the image, however, was the overwhelming need I had to see that image become real. *Omigod.* "I'm sorry. Maybe we could—" But I never had a chance to finish my sentence with *have that talk.*

"All I have on my mind is pleasure."

The word *pleasure* zapped the rest of my sentence from my mind. (Okay, let's be honest. I still wasn't ready to spill my guts so it didn't take much to change my mind about having the discussion.) "Oh, really." My libido instantly revved into high gear, telling my brain all my questions—and surprising ideas—

could wait. Sex first, questions later, I always say. Besides, didn't people say more secrets are revealed in pillow talk than anywhere else? As far as I was concerned, it was time to test the theory. If my new husband had any deep dark secrets, I wanted to find them out now. I put my invisible sleuth cap on my head and let him lead me toward the bathroom.

I walked through the door and my lover-wife bonnet knocked the sleuth cap right off my head. I gazed around the room in awe. Six vases of red roses adorned the spacious room while rose petals artfully decorated the floor. Steaming water filled the spa-sized jet tub, the water glistening in the dim light of dozens of candles. The flicker of the flames made rainbows in the two champagne flutes sitting on the tile ledge.

"Wow." I'd barely whispered, but Kaine heard me.

He cupped his hand under my chin and lifted my face to his. My heart fluttered at the tender expression on his face and in his eyes. "I hope you like it. I wanted to do something special for you." He tilted his head in an apologetic manner. "I wanted to try and make up for my not paying you enough attention of late. As you know, an urgent business matter has kept me—" He waved his hand, dismissing what he'd been about to say. "No. No more excuses. You are more important than any business problem." He caressed my lips, brushing lightly over them with his own. "You are more important than anything."

Okay, I'm not one who generally swoons at the sweet nothings, but I challenge any woman not to melt at those words. If she doesn't, she's either a bitch or dead. "This is amazing."

"No. You're amazing. *We're* amazing."

"Ah, there's my guy. The epitome of modesty." I leaned against his hard body, but he wouldn't let me stay that way. Instead, he unbuttoned the top button of my blouse and marched his fingers down the row of them. Not being a slouch in the getting-your-lover-undressed category, I tugged at his slacks, eager to expose what lay in wait underneath.

He bent to place a tender kiss on my neck and moved the blouse off my shoulders. The blouse joined the rose petals at my feet. Taking my breasts in his hands, he traveled his kisses along my shoulder to my ear where he nibbled at the sensitive spot behind my earlobe. His thumbs circled my already taut nipples. A shiver slid through me and I pushed his slacks to the floor.

"I want you, Chrissy-doll." Slipping his hands along the material of my bra, he unclasped it in record time. The warm mist of the heated bathroom drifted across my naked breasts, stimulating them, readying them for his mouth.

"Kaine Delcaluca, you do have a way with words." I forgot about trying to unbutton his shirt in a sexy way, and nearly ripped the buttons off getting the damn thing off his hard body. "Don't you think we'd better get in the water before it cools off?" We hadn't had sex in a tub yet—how had we missed doing that in Vegas?—and I was ready to get wet in more than one way. Finally undressed, he stepped closer to the edge of the tub and reached out his hand. "M'lady?"

Ooh, I so liked being the lady of the manor. But hopefully that didn't mean we'd have seventeenth-century sex. I'm sure that kind of boring bed antics was all well and good back then, but I wanted hot, lusty, carnal sex of the twenty-first century. Hell, I'd even explore further into the next millennium if possible. But I figured there was no harm in playing along. I delicately laid my hand in his, tipped my head in acknowledgment and let him help me into the water. I tried not to gasp and failed.

"Is it too hot?"

Although I was sure my foot was probably scalded red, I wasn't about to put a kibosh on this lovely evening. Besides, I was already getting used to the heat—kind of. Keeping my gaze on his, I did my best to act alluring and sexy as hell when I lowered my generous self into the waiting warmth.

Kaine smothered a smile. "Seriously, Chrissy-doll, if it's too hot I can cool it down."

I ran my gaze from the tip of his head to his feet and back up to stop at his fully erect cock. "Don't you dare, Kaine Delcaluca. I want it—and you—as hot as possible."

"You, my dear, are incorrigible and I love it." He stepped into the tub, sat across from me, then handed me a glass of champagne. "I flew this bubbly in from my vineyard in France. I hope you'll approve of the vintage."

I sipped the drink and the champagne lived up to its reputation as a nose-tickler. The smooth liquid ran down my throat and into my empty stomach. From the bath water, to the drink, to my hunky hubby, everything was perfect tonight. "Well, to be honest, I've never been much of a drinker. Much less champagne. Even the cheap stuff was way beyond my budget. But don't get me wrong. I like it. A lot."

This time I basically gulped the lovely liquid down before I realized how uncouth I probably appeared. I wasn't ready for Kaine to realize what a bumpkin he'd married, so I forced myself to sip when I wanted to chug.

"Chrissy-doll, I know what you're thinking."

I'm thinking how much I want you to go down on me right now. Trying to act cool and calm, I kept the thought to myself and hoped the glimpses I sent toward his nether regions would tell the tale. "Are you saying you can read minds?" Sure. Why not? Seemed like everyone else could. *Kaine, are you hearing my thoughts right now? If so, say ooba-dooba.*

"Only those whose minds I know well." He finished his drink, lifted the bottle from the sterling silver bucket and refilled both our glasses. "Like yours."

When did I empty my flute? I frowned at the glass, then shook the question away. *Who cares anyway?*

"Okay, swami, what am I thinking?" I grinned, ready for the punch line.

Kaine motioned for me to turn around. "Come here first, then I'll tell you. I want to wash your back."

I know it's hard to believe, but I'd never had any man wash my back before this. The closest I'd ever gotten was having Uncle Luther scrub me down when I could still fit in the kitchen sink. *So* not the same thing. I floated—yes, I said floated because that's how terrific I felt—over to him and tried not to slosh water onto the floor. Scooting backward, I placed my ass against his front and sighed when his dick slipped perfectly against the crease between my buttocks.

"You're thinking you have to act all proper and sophisticated with me."

The sip I'd taken spurted from my mouth and I hastily wiped it off my chin, hoping he hadn't seen. He hadn't said "ooba-dooba" but now I had to wonder again. Could my hubby really read my mind?

"Honey, you never have to worry about acting a certain way around me. I love you exactly the way you are."

If the hot water hadn't already nearly melted me, his words did the trick. I literally *hummed* with delight.

Kaine reached for the large sponge on the edge of the tub, dipped it into the water and poured a generous amount of soap on it. Using one hand to hold up my hair, he urged me to lean forward and started rubbing the sponge on my skin, circling and circling outward in slow, blissfully agonizing movements. I closed my eyes, enjoying the pampering and swore right then and there I'd never take another bath alone.

"Mmm. That feels so good. All that's missing is music," I murmured.

I heard a snap of his fingers and soft instrumental music filled the air. "How did you do that?" Giggling, I tried to turn to see him, but he held me in position. "What's your trick?"

"Oh, I have lots of tricks."

"I'll just bet you do." I smiled and leaned forward more, letting him run the sponge along my spine to meet his eager shaft. He paused, then resumed bathing me, gliding the sponge to each hip and back to the center.

"You're going to lull me to sleep if you don't watch out." Yeah, right. Fat chance of that happening with his gloriously huge appendage teasing my ass.

"Oh, really. Trust me. Sleep will be the farthest thing from your mind."

The touch of his lips, his tongue against the nape of my neck, woke me from my trance and I straightened my back, ready for action. "Oh, Kaine."

Keeping the sponge in one hand, he skimmed both hands around my torso and tugged me closer. His breath tickled my neck, sending shivers through me and he rested his chin on my shoulder. He worked his hand slowly, sinfully over my breasts. Although the water was still warm, I felt a different kind of warmth—an even hotter one—rush between my legs. My first climax broke free unexpectedly, shaking me.

"Easy, Chrissy-doll. I have so much more I want to do to you."

Hot damn. "Then do it to me, Kaine. Do whatever you want to me."

He dropped the sponge and cupped my breasts. Rubbing my tits, he bounced them, making them jiggle.

"Having fun, big guy?" I laid my head back to rest on his collarbone.

"Actually, yes, I am. Are you?" He blew into my ear, then raked his teeth down my neck to bite the curve between my neck and shoulder.

I placed my hands over his and pressed, encouraging him to be rougher. "Harder, Kaine. I want you to squeeze them hard. You won't hurt me."

"I don't want to cause you any pain."

"You mean with your supernatural strength?"

Suddenly, he went rigid, stopped his fondling.

"Kaine?" I tried to turn around, but once again, he held me firmly in place. "Did I say something wrong?"

He relaxed, hugging me to him. "No. It's nothing. Ignore me."

"Are you kidding me? How can I ignore...this?" With a lecherous smile he couldn't see, I reached behind and wrapped my hand around his dick. He and it jerked in surprise. Although it was a bit awkward to do, I managed to glide my hand along the length of him until the side of my hand bumped against his mushroomed cap. Pushing him against my ass slit, I moved my hand back and forth, rubbing him against each cheek.

With a groan filled with frustrated desire, he let go of my breasts and walked his fingers over my stomach—*suck it in, girl!*—to the mound below. His arms fully enveloped me, making me feel safe and diminutive. A very good trick, by the way.

Kaine fingered his way through my hair and parted my folds. I sat up a little straighter, wanting to make it easier for him to reach me.

"I'm going to make you come, Chrissy-doll."

"Uh, in case you didn't notice, you already have."

He chuckled. "Then again. With my hands."

Oh, hell, yes! Just telling me what he planned to do was enough to trigger another small *O.* I spread my legs, opening wide to his unspoken command.

It's incredible, but even though I knew what to expect, I was still unprepared for his touch on my clit. If I hadn't known better, I would've sworn a flame, like the flame of a match, danced on each of his fingertips. Heat flowed over my clit, over my pussy, spreading into my abdomen. I cried out from the amazement and the sensation of it, and gripped his legs straddling my body.

"Omigod. What— I mean, how the hell— Omigod, what are you doing to me?"

The fire kept moving upward, moving through me until it reached my nipples. Stunned and overwhelmed, I looked down and saw sparks spitting out of my nipples. "Holy crap!"

"Close your eyes, Chrissy-doll. Just close them and enjoy."

"But—omigod—there's fire. I saw—"

"Close them." His forceful tone calmed me as nothing else could have. Instantly, the panic starting to take hold of me fled, leaving behind only the lust. I moaned, raising my hand to grab him by the neck. Pulling me against him, he nipped my skin and continued the fiery exploration below. My hand around his cock matched his quickened pace on my clit. The stroke of his tongue over my ear, the tender bites on my neck stoked the fire inside and, I swear, the one outside me. At this point, I went beyond thinking.

Orgasm after orgasm racked my body and I shuddered,

making small waves in the water. I shouted, grasping his dick harder than I should have, than any normal man could've endured. But he didn't say a word.

When he finally lifted his hand from me, I found I had no strength and I slowly melted against him. "That was amazing, Kaine. What did you do?"

"Nothing compared to what I'm about to do. Turn around."

I opened my eyes, and with his help, managed to squirm around to face him. Taking his face in my hands, I assumed we'd be sharing a post-coitus kiss. You know, a little cuddling after the loving. Boy, did I have that wrong.

Instead, Kaine met my kiss with a force of his own, his tongue diving into my mouth, licking up every taste I could give him. I moaned and, incredibly, felt the tug of desire again. Still, after what I'd just gone through, I figured he'd have to do most of the work. This Georgia girl was plain tuckered out.

When I thought I couldn't hold on any longer, he broke the kiss and I took a much needed breath. Moving from my mouth, he trailed his kisses along my shoulder, then dipped to take a nipple into his mouth. Slowly, repeatedly, he tugged my tit, using first his sucking and then his teeth to keep it in his mouth. The man knew how to work my body, churning my desire.

I arched up and held the breast higher for him. "Bite me, Kaine. A little pain is always good."

He answered by bringing up the other breast, then moving back and forth between them, sucking, nipping, biting. I braced my hands on his shoulders and dug my fingernails into his skin. Urgency slithered through me, slowly bringing my strength back to life. But still Kaine had to do most of the work.

Grabbing my ass with his hands, he lifted me, spreading my legs to straddle his as his legs had done mine. "Kaine, seriously, I'm not sure I have it in me."

The corners of his mouth tipped upward. "Oh, yes, you do."

For a moment, I wondered about the lack of a condom, but figured my pill would be enough this time.

He plunged into me, driving deeper than he'd ever gone before. I gasped, unable to do anything more. He pressed my breasts against his chest and rocked against me. Hot water sloshed around us, making waves high enough to splash over the edge. My core spread wider, opening to allow him to go deeper, harder.

He drove his cock home like a rigger drilling for oil. I gushed over him, my juices mixing with the fire burning between my legs. I was wild, free, and strong.

"You feel so tight." He gritted his teeth and panted against my shoulder. "So very tight."

"I want to see your dick coming out of my mouth. Harder, Kaine, harder."

He kept rocking against me, but took my face in his hands to question me. "I don't want to hurt you."

My nails dug in more. "You'd never hurt me. I know that with everything I am." *Screw Sabrina and every other woman who lusts after my man. He's all mine.*

He slid down into the water until only the tops of his shoulders were above the splashing waves. Impossibly, I took him deeper inside me.

I wanted him more than ever. Without thinking about what I was saying, I begged him. "Make the fire again, Kaine. Make me burn."

My plea unleashed the beast inside him and he roared his answer. His cry echoed around the bathroom, reverberating off the walls. I closed my eyes and shouted after him, connecting with him in our cries of love.

"Chrissy-doll, open your eyes. I want you to see what we can make together."

I did as he asked. Steam billowed around us, cloaking our bodies in the fog. I laughed, no longer afraid of what might happen. The steam thickened, becoming a tangible entity. I reached out with my tongue and licked it, tasted it, enjoying the texture.

When I finally glanced down, I saw what I knew couldn't be real.

The water we moved in boiled around us. Bubbles popped with the sound of sizzling moisture. And yet, nothing scorched us, no blisters reddened our skins. The water churned around us, sending more steam to cover us, but all I felt was my lover's shaft pushing into me, his hands moving to my hips to keep me on top of him, his mouth on my taut nipples.

Kaine continued to plunge into me time after time, relentless in his quest to have all of me.

My body tightened, readying for yet another release. How many had it been? I had no idea, but that didn't matter. All that mattered was Kaine.

"Don't be afraid."

Why would I be afraid? Needing to see his face, to seek the answer in his eyes, I opened mine and inhaled a sharp breath. Astounded, I stared at the wonder around us.

Fire burned. On top of the water. At the edge of the tub. Around Kaine's shoulders and face. Dancing over my arms up to my head and into my hair. Flames licked our bodies, and yet nothing burned.

"Kaine?" I should've been terrified. Logically, I knew I should have. I should've jumped away from fire, away from the tub, away from him. But I wasn't afraid. Somehow, some way I knew nothing could harm me while Kaine held me.

I looked to him for an explanation, my gaze locking to his. Brilliant golden eyes sparkled back at me, tiny orange-red flames playing against the gold. Instead of the answer I sought, I found more questions.

"Chrissy-doll, don't think. Just feel. Just see what can be."

The trance that held me kept me firm in its grip. I nodded, panting as I moved with my husband. I watched, mesmerized, and clenched the walls of my cave around his cock. Slowly, an image appeared in the smoke around us, swirling to form a shape of something familiar yet unknown. I held my breath, squinting at it, until it finally grew solid enough to see. What I saw rocked me more than Kaine's powerful thrusts. My husband, a wide smile covering his face, stood holding a baby, his other arm wrapped protectively around me. Yet even though the vision was startling enough, it was my reaction that blew my mind.

Forgetting the fear that had always lived in my heart, I knew with absolute certainty that I wanted that vision to be real.

"Kaine?" I whispered, afraid to speak too loudly and ruin the moment.

"You see it, don't you? You see what can be." He ran his hands along my back, reassuring me that what I saw could be our truth. "You see what will be."

Yet as much as I wanted to believe at that moment, the snake of my terror began winding its way through me again. I shook my head, fighting the invisible snake and closing my eyes against the impossible smoke-image.

"I love you, Chrissy-doll. Let me love you."

At his words, I opened my eyes and concentrated on his

face. “I love you too, Kaine.”

Grasping my back, he threw back his head and yelled his release.

I had no choice. Connected to him physically, mentally, emotionally, I had no choice but to answer his call. I cried out, matching his sound and climax with my own.

Honey, About Your Friends…

I woke up in bed the next morning with a smile on my face. Who wouldn't? I hadn't gotten any answers for all the questions plaguing me, but I'd sure gotten a whole lot of something else wonderful. I snuggled into the comforter and wrapped my arms around myself. Damn, but the man was great in the sack *and* in the tub.

But what about what I'd seen? I tugged the comforter under my chin and suddenly pictured Kaine holding the baby—our baby—in his arms. Last night, I'd actually wanted the vision to be real—at least at first. Now, however, I knew better than to focus on something that was an impossibility. I ran the idea out of my head, instead focusing on the pleasant sensations still quivering inside me. *For once, girl, don't try to analyze everything. For once, just enjoy.*

However, the gloriously sated feeling soon left me. The empty side of the bed taunted me, forcing me to throw back the covers and swing my feet over the side way before I wanted to. Kaine had obviously started his morning without bothering to wake me. But that could simply mean he was being considerate, right? Then why couldn't I shake the idea that he'd snuck out before I could question him about last night's heated romance? Had my hubby actually lit a fire under me?

Heated was right. My body started getting hot again just

thinking about the sex we'd shared. But seriously. What about the flames? Had I drunk too much champagne? Possibly. But that much? Or was it all a trick of Kaine's? Maybe my hubby really was a closet magician. I grumbled, unwilling yet unable to keep my thoughts from going the other way. *Maybe I'm delusional? It isn't the first time I've seen or thought something off-the-wall lately.* But go figure, I was less inclined to believe I was losing my sanity.

Questions from the start of my marriage sent chills that iced the warmth out of me. Swiftly the questions came, but my mind couldn't keep up with them much less put answers to them. Purposely, I strode over to the writing desk and did what I always did whenever I was stumped. I wrote a list, noting one curiosity (Yeah, I'm sugar-coating it) at a time.

1. Fish-monster at the lake. What had my soon-to-be husband killed at Lake Lanier the night we'd met? I hadn't been prepared, had been startled in fact, and I hadn't gotten a good look at the thing. But I did remember this much. I'd never seen anything like it. Of course, I wasn't an expert regarding fish and the like, so maybe if I did a thorough Internet search I could find something resembling it. After all, every time I visited the Georgia Aquarium I saw new and odd-looking creatures. I resolved to get going on the research as soon as possible and blew out a relieved sigh. *Makes sense.* I placed a check mark beside number one. Good. One nagging incident down, more to go.

2. Kaine's appearance. I frowned. Damn, I wished I'd paid better attention that night at the lake. Had Kaine's features really changed or not? Or had I celebrated Thad's birthday a little too much? That had to be it. After all, how can a man change into a dragon?

A dragon? As in Dragon Dynasty? My stomach did a sickening flop. *I told Jenn that I thought I'd seen his face change.*

Oh shit. This can not be real. My hand poised over the paper, wanting desperately to make a check mark next to number two. But I couldn't. *Move on, girl. Keep going.* I took heart and decided to sort Number Two out once the list was complete.

3. Kaine's skin. I gnawed on the end of the pencil. His skin had felt rough in the shower. Almost like...scales. But scales like on the back of a dragon? People had dry skin, right? Maybe he had psoriasis or some other skin problem. Yet I'd seen his entire body naked many wonderful times and had never noticed anything unusual. Still, a skin condition hardly made anyone a fire-breathing lizard. *Damn. There's that dragon thing again.*

I couldn't shake the feeling that I was missing—or ignoring—the answer. I broke the pencil into two pieces and tossed it in the wastebasket next to the desk. When had I started having irrational flights of fancy? Had my business finally started driving me wacko? No. I'd find a logical explanation if I continued. I was sure of it. I took another pencil out of the drawer and persevered with the list.

4. Kaine's eyes. People's eyes sometimes changed colors. Like when I wore green, my eyes added flecks of yellow. But I'd never seen anyone whose eyes changed color as much as Kaine's—or as quickly. His eyes could zap from green to brilliant gold in a flash. Too quickly and too fleeting to be contacts. Comparatively speaking, the color change didn't seem that big a deal, so I decided to move on and tackle the fourth problem later.

Later. When had I started pushing away problems instead of attacking them head-on? I gritted my teeth, vowed to return to the unchecked items and moved on.

5. The Mouse Muncher. Fitz's preoccupation with rodents along with my husband's other strange friends and associates didn't help matters any. Missy the assistant who claimed she was a mouse and the very strange Tuo Chow were at the top of the list right after Fitz. Sure, everyone has a weird relative, one the family would rather not claim, but no one knew as many oddballs as my husband. *Just because Kaine has a wacky assistant who may or may not eat mice—yuck!—doesn't mean there's anything wrong with him, right? It means the assistant's got a few bolts loose. And the way she's always around him only means she takes her job seriously, right?* I put a check next to the number. As far as I was concerned, I'd nixed this one in the bud as irrelevant. (Yeah, I know now that my ostrich gene had definitely kicked in.)

6. *Sabrina.* Had I actually seen her change color in the photograph? I quickly dismissed the idea as a fluke of light. But what about her weird choke-'em-till-they-drop finger trick? I considered what I'd written and quickly scratched out the problem. I'd stick to the relevant facts surrounding Kaine. After all, I didn't know what had caused the manager to choke. She could've swallowed a piece of gum for all I knew.

7. *Kaine's tattoo.* I doodled a figure eight next to the words. Was it such a big deal that my husband had a tattoo? Or even that the location of the tattoo was a bit different? More and more people were getting tats these days and in much stranger, not to mention more painful, places. But what about the information Thad found on the Internet? I shook my head, determined not to go down that slippery slope. *Nope. It means nothing. Nada. It's just a silly tat. Nothing more.* The fact that it looked like one related to some dragon group was a coincidence. (My denial was taking hold of my spine and turning it into jelly big time.)

8. *The tub fire and vision.* Even with my pitiful spine and the gnawing in my stomach, I still had to smile. However my hubby had pulled it off, the flames—and, yeah, even the image—had made for one blazing sexual encounter. If ever there

was a time to shut up and let things be, that was it.

However, the investigator in me wouldn't lie down and die entirely. I scanned the list again and tried to come up with reasonable explanations for the unchecked ones and failed miserably. Sometimes a girl can't ignore her gut. And my gut was telling me things were not as they seemed. The real question was...would I accept my lame explanations and stay blissfully ignorant? Or would I investigate until I found out the truth?

"Damn it. I wish I'd learn how to let things go."

I stomped toward the massive walk-in closet, fussing at myself as I went. Minutes later, I trudged down the hallway headed toward my hubby's office. This time I wouldn't let him seduce me out of asking questions. I needed answers and I'd get them—before sex.

Gripping the door frame, I wheeled around and took a step into Kaine's office. I took a second to watch him, unaware of my presence, his back to me with a phone tucked to his ear.

He is such a hunk. He wore a black silk shirt with the sleeves rolled up, black slacks that hugged his body and no belt. I skimmed my gaze from his wide shoulders—shoulders that had more than once supported my legs—and glided down to his trim waist. His waist was the perfect size. Not too lean and not so wide I couldn't wrap my legs around it. I bit my lower lip and tilted my head. *Um, those slacks hug his squeezable butt nicely. Any woman would appreciate that Armani behind. Rounded and firm, just like I like.* Although it was difficult to do so, I broke away from his butt and examined his thighs and legs. *The man has thighs like a bodybuilder and legs like a wild stallion.* My mouth filled with saliva and I wanted so badly to moisten the part of his anatomy hidden from my view.

I remembered last night and licked my lips. Maybe having sex before the questioning began would be better. Then I'd be able to weaken his defenses and concentrate on my interrogation. I considered my plan's revision. Plans, however, are made to go awry.

"Calm down, Muras. I know who took the scepter."

Eerrrrk! Bam!

My meanderings over Kaine's body and what I wanted to do with it slammed to a stop, along with my scheme for sex before questions. Had I heard what I thought I'd heard? Did he say *scepter*? I gawked at my hubby. *This is so not happening.*

"Yes, I'm sure. From the information I've gathered, Tuo hired Sabrina to steal the scepter." He growled, a sound familiar, yet much more menacing than the growls I'd heard in bed. "He didn't, however, expect her to double-cross him."

The argument between Tuo and Sabrina came back to hit me in the face. Stunned, I backed out of the office and pressed my spine against the outside wall. Sabrina had swindled Tuo just as Tuo had accused her inside the boutique. She'd stolen the scepter from Kaine and then double-crossed Tuo. I started to step back inside to tell him about Sabrina when Tuo's words stopped me cold.

"When she didn't, wouldn't mother his spawn, he kicked her out. Dumped her."

Since Tuo had told the truth about Sabrina stealing, did that mean he'd told the truth about why Kaine and she had split? I swallowed to dislodge the lump in my throat. But that didn't mean he'd do the same to me, did it? No. Kaine loved me. I was certain of it. Wasn't I? The lump grew bigger and I fought against the weakness in my legs.

Nonetheless, I had an obligation to tell Kaine about Sabrina and Tuo's altercation. Again, I started to go to him and got knocked in the gut before he saw me.

"Patience, my friend. I'm almost ready to make a move on Sabrina and recover the scepter. This is a delicate matter and I would rather not antagonize Chow's Eastern Dragons if I don't have to. Plus, we don't want Sabrina doing something rash with it before then. You know how those people can get. Then, with the scepter in the dynasty's possession again and Christina impregnated with my heir, no one will dare question my leadership. Trust me. Things will soon return to normal."

Normal? As in without me? I knew then that I'd underestimated Kaine's desire for a child. I could almost hear my confidence in his love cracking into a thousand pieces.

"Until then, I remain as your leader. Call the families together for a special meeting. I want this traitorous talk of my resignation thwarted before it has a chance to take root."

I valiantly pushed the word *heir* from my mind and concentrated on listening to his conversation. Later, somewhere safe, I'd deal with the implications of what I'd overheard.

"Good. Tonight is fine. Tell them to arrive at eight sharp."

The click of the earpiece striking the phone's base sent me scurrying down the hall. I passed by several of the household staff, ignoring their words of greeting, and choked back the tears threatening to fall. I knew if I let even one of them free, I wouldn't be able to stop the rest.

For the first time in my career, I cancelled appointments. Hunting down a saber-tooth tiger in Underground Atlanta dropped way down on my list of priorities. (Sorry, all you tourists.) Not that I actually thought a prehistoric cat was loose among the restaurants and bars of that unique shopping area. In fact, having gone hunting for gigantic alligators—reported by the same person, mind you—in Underground last year, I was sure I'd find a nasty-tempered, oversized alley cat making a cozy home somewhere in the storage area of one of the shops. The cat problem would have to chill for now.

Then I rescheduled an appointment dealing with fairies inhabiting Mrs. Webber's rose garden and buzz-bombing her so much she couldn't tend to her blooms. Considering this time of the year usually brought out the large carpenter bees, I was in no hurry to wage my own War of the Roses. Oh, sure, they were generally harmless—until you pestered them too much.

Instead, I paced my office trying to make sense of everything I'd seen and heard. Missy was glaringly unattainable while Pam and Mini-Pam had suspiciously come down with two terrible cases of a computer virus. Uh-huh. Riiight. Obviously, when push came to tug, they weren't about to cross Kaine for little ol' me. By that afternoon, however, I'd decided that this southern girl had no alternative but to listen in on his meeting.

I opted for flat shoes, telling myself that my choice was made out of a nod to style and not because I could run faster in flats than in higher heels. Smoothing my hair into place, I took one final glance in the mirror and left the bedroom. *Ready or not, people, here I come.*

The guests for the meeting congregated in the same conference room where I'd met Kaine's associates. I peeked around the edge of the door I was hiding behind, an entrance used mainly for servants to enter the room from the kitchen, and watched everyone enter.

To say they were a striking group of people would be like saying the Empire State Building was a modest structure. A tall woman, her raven hair slicked away from her face, walked over to Kaine standing at the head of the table, stopped and stared at him. They regarded each other for several minutes without speaking. She finally nodded and took her seat. A short round man came after her, his skin the color of a copper penny with frizzy orange hair framing his face. He shook Kaine's hand, leaned in to whisper in his ear, then roared with laughter. Kaine's expression, however, never changed.

One by one the visitors came, some shaking his hand while others bowed their heads. One by one they took their seats. A soft murmur filled the room and I waited, wishing I could take a load off too.

All at once, a hush fell over them and they swiveled to the doorway to see Tuo, hands fisted on his hips and a smirk on his face. The others expectantly glanced at Kaine who merely nodded at Tuo and waved him to a chair at the opposite end of the table.

Kaine cleared his throat and talking ceased. A heavy silence filled the air until, at last, he spoke. "Thank you for coming. I see each of the dynasties has sent a representative. May I introduce our newest members? Joining us are Lyeis Switai of the European Dynasty, Mylan D'anrd representing the Northern Dynasty, Zulo Zane of the Fairie Dynasty, Cherry Somers for the Southern Dynasty and, of course, Tuo Chow, an officer of the Eastern Dynasty. Welcome to you all."

Some tipped their heads while others murmured a greeting.

Dynasties? As in more than just the Dragon Dynasty? Why does this dynasty stuff keep coming up when I want nothing more than to forget I ever heard the word dynasty*?* My world tilted and I gripped the edge of the door to stay upright. If everything I'd learned was true—and part of me could no longer deny it—then the Dragon Dynasty was real too. I looked at my husband and tried to see him through unemotional eyes.

"Good. Let's get right to business. As some of you know, the Scepter of Fire is missing." He shifted slightly to gaze at Tuo.

Gasps showed which of the group hadn't known about the theft, while the hard stares of the rest highlighted their anger.

"Why didn't you tell us when it first went missing, Delcaluca?" The man with the copper-colored hair squinted at my husband, a challenge written on his face and heard in his tone. His eyes sparkled with animosity.

Kaine studied him, his lips curved in a tolerant smile. "Am I to tell you everything, Chaus? Since when do I report to you?" He scanned the people at the table. "To any of you?"

An angry grumble erupted from them, many of whom stood to face him. "Since when have we given you complete power with no one able to question your actions?" The striking woman glared at my husband, her finger pointed at his chest. Flashes of Sabrina pointing at the boutique's manager had my heart skipping a beat.

I had to admit it. I was pretty darn proud of my man. He stood straight and tall, unruffled by all the discontent swirling around him.

"Of course you may ask questions, Mylan. However, I can not and will not seek your advice for every matter that arises. Now sit." He narrowed his eyes at them. "Please."

Although he'd added the *please*, they heard the command and did as they were told. Chaus, however, wasn't ready to give up. "Losing the scepter is not an ordinary matter. Instead of threatening us, tell us you've located it."

"I'm hardly threatening you, my dear friend." My husband's features changed. "Trust me. If I were, you would have no doubt."

I blinked, thinking my eyes must have played tricks on me. But I would've sworn I saw his face shift, extend and—*can this be real?*—a pointed tongue flick out from between his lips. I closed my eyes, picturing in my head what I had to admit I'd seen with my eyes. For a split second, my husband looked like a dragon.

Omigod. My husband is *a dragon.* My breath hitched in my throat and all the unchecked items on my list came back to haunt me. I had to think it again. *My husband is a dragon.*

"What are you doing here? Are you spying?"

The furious whisper in my ear startled me and I yelped. Slapping a hand over my mouth, I turned to try and run away through the kitchen, but Fitz blocked my way.

"What do you think Kaine would think if he knew you spied on him? Do you think his love for you would be enough? You've changed him, made him weak, but he is still a powerful dragon."

"Fitz, I, uh..."

"Let's show him what a sneak you are, shall we?"

With a wicked grin, she pushed me against the door. The door flew open and I fell into the conference room face first, landing with a *thud* on the hardwood floor. With my hair in my face and lying flat on my stomach, I cringed at the commotion going on around me. I hurriedly ran through my options. I could either 1) stay on the floor and pretend I'd passed out, 2) run like hell and never come home again or 3) stand up and demand what the hell was going on. I was still trying to choose which option when someone grabbed me by the collar and literally hurled me to my feet.

Gasping, I stared into Tuo's bemused face. I struggled against his hold, but I couldn't shake free.

"Well, well, who do we have here? Mrs. Delcaluca, were you sticking your nose in where it doesn't belong?"

Fitz, the traitorous bitch, had apparently exited after tossing me to the dogs, er, dragons. I glanced around, hoping to find the others more curious than furious at my abrupt entry. However, judging from their expressions, I was shit out of fortune.

"Oh, hello, everyone. I'm sorry to, uh, barge in on you. I, er, kind of tripped." *Yeah, tripped as in pushed.* Gathering my courage, I placed my hands on Tuo's wrists and tugged. "Thank you for helping me up, but I'm okay. If you'll just let go, everyone can get back to the meeting."

"Christina."

Christina? Since when had my husband ever called me by my proper name? Suddenly, I felt like a school kid standing before the principal. Tuo released me and I shuffled to face Kaine. "Hi, honey." I tried to keep one eye on him and one on the guests. Not an easy task, mind you. "I'm sorry, I didn't mean to interrupt your meeting. I wanted to ask you what you wanted for dinner." *Lie like a dog, girl.*

Fitz pushed through the door, an oh-so-fake look of surprise on her face. "Mrs. Delcaluca, what are you doing here?" Syrup would've seemed bitter compared to the sickly sweet of her tone. She sidled to the other side of my hubby, a smirk on her face.

When Kaine wrapped his hand around my arm, I wasn't sure if he meant to help me or hurt me. Yet, ever the gentleman, he pulled me against him. "Everyone, I'd like to introduce my wife, Christina Delcaluca." He didn't, however, wait for pleasantries, and instead, herded me back the way I'd come.

Unfortunately, Tuo had a different idea. "Stop!"

Kaine and I exchanged a look, then faced him and the rest of the group. "What do you want, Tuo?" His tone was low and menacing.

Fitz growled, dipping her head to narrow her beady eyes at

Tuo.

Tuo's face hardened, yet he kept his smile. "We can't have her simply walking away. We must know what she heard."

Agreement swept through the others, some nodding their heads while others simply waited. A chill like none I'd ever experienced while working a DeBunkers case swept through me. "Me? I didn't hear a thing. I tripped over the carpet or something on my mad dash in from the kitchen."

Tuo was a persistent man-dragon. "Neither of these rooms have carpet."

Little snit! "I said or something."

Kaine held me closer. "She stays. I give you my word that you can trust my wife completely."

Fitz's expression morphed into genuine surprise. Confusion followed and she glanced from Kaine to me and back again as though trying to figure out if he meant what he'd said.

Mylan came to my rescue. Sort of. "Who cares what she heard? Let the woman listen. She is, after all, Delcaluca's wife and the soon-to-be mother of his heir."

Damn. Does everyone know Kaine's out to knock me up? I slowly tilted my head up and arched my eyebrows to silently question him.

"Mylan is right. We have to discuss the scepter." The one called Zulo waved, gesturing at them to take their seats. "I want to know what you've done about the missing scepter, Kaine. If it should fall into the wrong hands, the consequences to dragons everywhere could be devastating. Our enemies could destroy us."

Kaine moved me and not-so-gently sat me in a chair off to the side. Although his actions raised my hackles, I knew when to keep my trap shut. I figured I was getting off easy with the added bonus of getting to listen in.

Mylan took her seat. “Zulo is correct. What do you intend to do, Delcaluca?”

Kaine glanced at me, then addressed the members. “I have information that we have more to fear from one of our own than from our enemies.” His announcement left them speechless, waiting for him to explain. “I believe one of our own has tried to possess the scepter in hopes of ruling the rest of us.”

“Who, Kaine?” Chaus was on his feet.

“You’re insane. What dragon would dare take the scepter out of hiding and risk our enemies getting their hands on it?” Mylan shook her head, yet fear masked her wrinkle-free face.

Kaine strode toward Tuo and pointed at him. “Tuo Chow hired the alien Sabrina Stellina to steal the Scepter of Fire.”

Alien? Are you frickin’ kidding me?

Reaction was swift and, frankly, very loud. I covered my ears at the roars echoing around the room. Tuo shouted something in a language I didn’t recognize and hurled his body at Kaine.

If I hadn’t seen it, I wouldn’t have believed it. Both men altered, their faces growing length-wise, scales covering their skin, and tongues whipping out of their mouths. When they opened their mouths wider, long, deadly fangs glistened with saliva. Claws replaced fingers and eyes changed color, both of their eyes glowing a brilliant amber. I jumped to my feet, but couldn’t make myself run. *Am I really seeing this?* For one of the first times since meeting Kaine, the answer came back a resounding and undeniable...yes! *Holy crap, I am not crazy. Dragons really do exist.*

The two half-men half-dragons slammed against each other, their chests bumping like two fraternity brothers in greeting. Slashing out, Tuo raked his claws across Kaine’s chest, ripping open his shirt and leaving an angry trail of blood from his pecs to his abdomen. They landed at the same time, but this time Kaine was the first to strike.

He opened his jaws wider than I thought possible and blew. A dark cloud of smoke billowed out from his mouth, aimed straight at Tuo. Suddenly, Fitz changed, morphing into a cross between the mythical creatures Cyclops and Medusa. Her skin melted together, gathering around one centrally-located eye while tentacles sprang from every part of her body not covered in clothing. Long, saliva-dripping fangs contorted her already homely face, transforming it into an even uglier version of the troll under the bridge. She roared a hideous sound and lashed out several of her tentacles at Tuo.

The other dragons (*Dragons!*) threw back their chairs and hastened out of the room. Mylan and Chaus paused a moment at the door, shouted at Kaine to kill that disgusting traitor, then dashed away.

"Chrissy-doll, run!

Kaine's words mobilized me and I took off. Part of me wanted to stay and help him, but another part of me knew he'd fight better without me there. Besides, Fitz fought with him, putting her body in front of his and I'd learned early in life that when someone tells you to run, you'd better run. I slammed through the kitchen door and made tracks.

I prayed Kaine would soon follow me. With dragons—*dragons!*—fighting in my home, there was a high possibility of my home going up in flames. I hit the back door, banging it against the wall, and virtually flung my body over the patio, clearing the steps by a good two feet in the air.

Harrumph!

What the hell?

Whatever I'd hit broke my forward motion and I struck the

ground butt first. At least this time my landing was padded—if you get my drift. Nonetheless, shockwaves rattled my body and head, making lights flash behind my eyelids. When my vision finally cleared and I looked up, I couldn't believe my eyes. Sabrina lay in front of me, holding her head in much the same way as I was.

She glared at me. "Watch where you're going, you animal."

I'm an animal? I let the confusing dig pass. Sabrina was up and ready for action seconds after I pushed myself off the ground and wobbled onto my shaky feet. "What the hell are you doing here?" I gritted my jarred teeth and refrained from adding *bitch* to my question. Was she here to see Kaine? But if she'd stolen the scepter, why would she return to the scene of the crime?

"None of your damn business." She stumbled a few feet away from me, craning her neck to peek through a window. "What's going on in there? Is Tuo inside?"

"Are you seriously asking me to tell you anything? After you stole the scepter?"

I gloated at the surprised expression on her face. However, she quickly recovered. "So Kaine has told you about the Scepter of Fire?" Her eyes narrowed. "Or did you find out from someone else?"

Not wanting her to have the pleasure of knowing I'd found out by snooping instead of having my husband tell me, I shrugged off her question. "That's for me to know and you to guess."

She tilted her head at me. "Stupid woman. That's not how the saying goes."

I stuck out my chin. "Whatever. Now get your ass off my property before I call the cops." I crossed my arms and struck a pose. "And that, *stupid woman,* is exactly how that saying goes."

"Do not threaten me, human."

Human? Does that mean she's an alien and *a dragon?* I started to ask, but clammed up when she raised a pointed finger at me. *Are you frickin' kidding me? She's giving me the finger.* Although I'd been thinking of the manager at the boutique, the implication of what I'd thought made me giggle. "You're giving me the finger." I copied her gesture. "Get it? Finger." I adopted a fairly good imitation of a gangster and spouted, "Are youse fingering me, Bugsy?"

She dropped her hand and gawked at me. "Why are you calling me Bugsy? Who's Bugsy?"

"Sabrina!"

I whirled to find Tuo standing at the top of the steps. His clothes were in tatters and singed in several places. Black soot covered his cheeks and forehead. "What happened to you?"

He snarled at me. "Your husband happened to me." Hurrying down the steps, he stomped over to Sabrina, his nose a couple of inches from hers. "Where is the scepter?"

"I don't have it." Her snarl matched his and she held her ground.

"Bullshit. You stole it and everyone knows. At this point I don't even care why you didn't hold up your end of our bargain. I just want the scepter."

"I didn't say I didn't steal it."

"Ah-ha! So you finally admit it." I stuck my finger in the air again, this time in victory. But when Tuo and Sabrina both glowered at me, I dropped it quickly enough. *Where is Kaine anyway?*

The two brought their stares back to each other. Tuo lowered his tone, menacingly. "Take me to it and I'll still honor our deal. You'll have the prunes."

Prunes? I glanced from one to the other. *Sabrina wants prunes? Is she so constipated that she'd trade a valuable artifact for prunes? Or are prunes an alien delicacy? Eeww.*

"I admit I stole it." She blinked several times and backed away from Tuo. "But I don't have it any longer." Clearing her throat, she lifted her head defiantly. "Someone else took it from me."

"You lie! Give it to me." Tuo grabbed her arm and she struggled to get away.

I wasn't sure what to do so I let my instincts take over. I clutched both their arms and tugged, trying to break them apart.

"Hey, let her go!"

Thad rushed toward us. Although I wasn't in any real danger—or at least I didn't think so—Thad apparently thought I needed rescuing. He wasn't the hero I would've liked to have shown up, but at least he was on my side. *Speaking of heroes, where is mine?*

Thad launched his body at our little group. I yelped and raised my hands, bracing for impact. Tuo froze, surprise written on his face and Sabrina scampered out of the line of fire. Thad landed on Tuo, knocking him to the ground. The two men wrestled with Thad managing to stay on top of the smaller man. "Chrissy, don't let her get away!"

I chased after Sabrina but only made it a few feet. She whirled back at me and pointed her Fabulous Finger directly at my chest. "The scepter is mine and Kaine will never find it." She twirled her finger in a circle. "Or me."

In the instant an invisible *something* slammed into me, I heard a loud crack. I ended up lying next to Thad, both us of flat on our backs. Together, we lifted our heads to see Tuo grab

Sabrina. They struggled, but before Thad and I could gather our wits and our feet, they both shifted, revealing a dragon (Tuo) and a two-headed creature (Sabrina).

"Omigod."

Thad shook his head in wonder. "You can say that again."

"Omigod."

Saved By My Uterus

After what I'd seen, I could no longer deny the existence of dragons and other supernatural beings. The woman who had vowed to bring all the scary things that go bump in the night into the light of day was now a Grade-A believer in everything paranormal. I sat on the steps of my home, trying to let all that had happened, all that I'd discovered, seep in. I'd gone from not believing in anything except what the rational world told me existed to being married to a dragon and immersed in the theft of a powerful artifact, the Scepter of Fire. I'm not certain how much time passed before I determined what I needed to do. My eyes had told me the truth, but I still needed to hear it from my husband. My brain was set in stone and I needed that last little push.

I found Kaine in his office, slightly battered but definitely in better shape than Tuo had been. Unfortunately for me, he was not alone. "Kaine?" I recognized the two men with him as being members of the fun group who'd witnessed my earlier "fall". Fitz, back to her icky human form, stood by his side. *Does this bitch ever leave my man alone? You'd think she's his bodyguard or protector. Wow, oh, wow.* Realization of Fitz's true role hit me. *She* is *his bodyguard. She's his mouse-eating, tentacle-waving bodyguard.*

"Could I speak with you, Kaine? Privately?" I pulled my

body straighter and gathered my nerve. "No, forget the asking part. We need to talk. Right now."

The men's—or should I say *dragons'*—amber eyes glowed with rage. I suddenly and desperately wanted to backpedal right out of the room. Hell, maybe even clear out of the house again.

The first man—*Chaus?*—was by my side and holding my arms behind my back even before I saw him move. "How can you allow this female to speak to you that way?"

Sheesh, the way he'd said female, *you'd think it was a four-letter word.* "Kaine, I know what you are. You're a dragon."

His soft smile met my own.

Chaus's nails dug into my arm. "Ow!"

Kaine's eyes flashed, the amber color intensifying until I had no choice but to look away. "Take your hands off her."

The other man moved to join his friend on my other side. "He's right, Delcaluca. She has crossed the line in many ways. First spying on our meeting and now disrespecting you. It's bad enough that she has refused to give you an heir."

I couldn't believe my ears. Had Kaine spilled his guts about our baby discussions? What else had he told them? How I liked kinky sex? What next? Videos of us in bed on YouTube?

"Liam," Kaine's tone vibrated with power, "you gamble with your life."

"She's too much trouble, Delcaluca. It's time to get rid of her and find another. After all, she's nothing special."

Of course my number-one fan had to chime in. "They're right. She hasn't fulfilled her purpose." I couldn't help but notice the gleam in Fitz's eyes. "I will help you find a more suitable and willing mate."

I scowled at them. It wasn't the first time anyone had called me trouble or useless, but that didn't make me feel any better.

Plus, I was pretty sure that getting rid of me was more involved than simply dumping me as he'd dumped Sabrina.

Kaine's gaze fell on me and his eyes sparkled with flecks of jade. "I've waited a long time for her. She is the one—the only one to bear my child." He turned his attention back to Liam and his eyes grew solid gold again.

The only one to bear his child? He only wants a child with me? No one else? I melted under the warmth of his words. *Sheesh. Could he have said anything more romantic?*

Liam snarled at him. "Then force her if you have to, but you must produce an heir before it's too late."

"Mind you own business, asshole."

Liam inhaled sharply and raised his hand to strike me. Kaine, however, had other ideas. He reached out, taking the man's wrist and bent his arm in an impossible angle. I heard the *snap* of bone breaking and winced. Amazingly, the dragon didn't cry out.

"Don't ever raise your hand to my wife again." He leaned closer to the cringing man. "If you do, I'll break your neck instead of your arm."

I hate like hell to admit it, but watching my man in action made me wet with desire. If I could've stripped naked and ridden him right then and there—with Fitz and the two dragons watching—I would have. Too bad I wasn't free to act on my impulse.

"Be reasonable. If you do not produce an heir soon, our kind will slowly cease to exist. The other clans will take our property, our women, our lives. Our survival depends on you."

I watched Kaine's face, trying to gauge his reaction. He remained, however, stone-faced.

"What's he talking about? Why will—" I glanced at Liam,

hoping to get the words just right, "—your kind die out?"

At Kaine's nod, Chaus finally let me go. I scurried to my husband, who pulled me to face him. "It's true. I belong to the rarest of dragons, the Golden Dragons. In order to keep our breed alive, the leader must mate and produce an heir or the Time of Death will come."

The Time of Death? What is this? A bad sci-fi movie? I couldn't help it. I cocked my head at him and grinned. "You're joking, right?"

The intense glow in his eyes faded, morphing back to their usual green color. "I would never joke about something this important. I need an heir and you can give me one."

"I'm still not understanding. Golden Dragons. Heir. Time of Death." I searched my hubby's eyes, hoping to find meaning in their depths. "This is all so unbelievable."

"Every dragon dynasty is led by one true leader. That leader must have an heir to carry on his clan. Since I am the leader of the Golden Dragons, that responsibility falls to me. But I only have a limited time to fulfill my duty. Once I reach a certain age, if I haven't produced an heir, I will no longer be physically able to do so."

I shook my head, trying to absorb all he'd told me. But his explanation seemed like a fantasy from a storybook. "Are you saying that if you don't get me preggers soon, you'll be too old to get the job done?"

"Essentially, yes." Kaine straightened his shoulders. "I am, after all, not getting any younger."

Could my virile young husband really think he was too old? "But, Kaine, you're an adult man in your prime. After all, you're only thirty-six—"

"Actually, I'm one thousand, five hundred and twenty-two years old."

My mouth gaped open like a fish hanging from a hook. "Say what? How in the world can you be that old?"

Kaine arched one eyebrow, sending me a telling look. "Dragons do not age the same as humans."

"Wow. You really are old." The words were out of my mouth before I knew it and I immediately regretted it. Kaine's proud expression fell, transforming into a mixture of hurt and irritation. "Oh, my, I'm sorry. I didn't mean it like that. But seriously, over fifteen hundred years old is quite a lifespan."

"The point—" Kaine regained his ruffled composure, "—is that I only have a few days before I lose the ability to impregnate you. And once that time has passed, my life will soon end, along with the future of the Golden Dragon clan."

Kaine will die if I don't give him an heir? Shock rattled through me while a slow burn started in my gut. Why hadn't he told me the truth from the beginning? And if he had, would I have still married him?

I took a step away from him. "So that's what all the baby talk is about? An heir to save your people?" I searched his face, afraid of what I might find. "Is that the only reason, the real reason you married me? So I can give you a child?" Granted, saving his people was a heck of a reason, but it wasn't the one I needed to hear.

"Delcaluca, none of this matters. The Time of Death grows closer. You must mate and impregnate a female. If not her—" Liam threw me a sneer, "—then another."

"Let us take care of her for you. You should start the hunt for a replacement now." Claus moved menacingly toward me.

"Kaine?" I gaped at the man slowly advancing toward me, then at the man I loved. Realization of what I truly meant to him broke my heart and I tucked my face away to hide the tears in my eyes. Yet even though I was only a baby mamma for him,

I still loved him. In fact, I loved him so much I wanted to give him the child he needed, especially now that I knew why he so desperately had to have one.

After all, what choices did I have? Either I could give him a child or I could leave Kaine now and live an unhappy life without him. The heartache of a future without Kaine overwhelmed my fear. Could I live with myself if I let Kaine die and his dynasty die along with him? I wiped the tears away and stood tall. "Just hold up, Claus." I held up the palm of my hand, stopping the big lug in his tracks. "Kaine, please, I need to talk to you alone." Taking his hand in mine, I lifted my head and led my husband out of the room, leaving the two thugs behind.

Hurrying through the house, I focused on one goal: getting to our bedroom before I changed my mind. I had to boink his head off and get myself knocked up. I had no clue what I planned to do after that. The hole in my heart wouldn't let me think beyond the present moment.

"Chrissy-doll?"

I whipped around and poked him. "Shut up." *Damn it. He should've told me earlier. I would've said yes even then.* "It's your turn to listen." I scanned the hallway, thankful that no servants were around. "If you'd told me the truth before we got married, I would have..." I stopped, fighting the lump in my throat.

"If I had told you then, you would have what, Chrissy-doll? Tell me."

I allowed Kaine to tug me close, needing the firm reassurance of his chest to battle the ache building inside my heart. "I would have understood. I would have found a way to give you a child." I gazed into his beautiful eyes. "Even though I would've been scared shitless, I would have tried."

"Now I'm the one who doesn't understand. Why would you have been scared?" He inhaled, an idea coming to him. "Because I'm a dragon? Chrissy-doll, your child would be conceived and born human. It's only later, as he grows older, that he would become a dragon. You'd be perfectly safe giving birth."

"No, that's not it." I wrapped my hands around his neck. "Although if I'd had time to think about it, that would've frightened me big time. But no, I've always been afraid of having a child."

"But why? Is there something wrong? Please, I need to know."

"The reason doesn't matter any longer. I want to give you a child. I can't imagine watching you die and knowing I could've prevented it. Not to mention putting all your people in danger. How could I live with the guilt?" Tension turned my neck into a steel rod.

"That doesn't answer my question. If it's not because I'm a dragon, then tell me why you're afraid of having my baby." He scanned me, digging for the secret I could barely admit to myself. I braced myself against his invisible attack. "If there's something wrong, if there's any way you could be hurt by giving me an heir, then I need to know. Or is it about the baby? Do you think our baby would be...unhealthy?"

I did some searching of my own, gazing into his eyes, trying to detect any sign that he cared for me. Or was he only interested in finding out about any possible defects I might pass on to the infant? "No, that's not it. Not exactly."

"Not exactly?" A low growl escaped him. "Chrissy-doll, tell me what's going on with you? Now."

I opened my mouth to speak, but suddenly all my words dried up. Although my brain wanted to tell him everything, my heart had squeezed tight, keeping the truth hidden. *Let it go, Kaine. Please, don't make me say it.*

He grabbed me by the arms. I gasped, too stunned to pull away. Yet I knew Kaine would never hurt me. At least not physically.

"Chrissy, I'm a patient man, but you are pushing me to my limits. What do I have to do to make you tell me?"

Just love me. Surprised at my silent admission, I dropped my gaze, fearful that he could see those words in my eyes. Instead, I gathered my composure and placed my hands on his arms. He let go of me but didn't step back. A tear rolled down my cheek and I quickly wiped it away. *Hang tough. This isn't even the hardest part.*

"I'm sorry. I didn't mean to upset you. I'm worried, is all." His face softened, yet grew sadder. "Chrissy-doll, trust me."

I wondered if I could do as he asked. His expression—so forlorn, so vulnerable—finally did what his words, his command had failed to do. That look shot through the barricades surrounding my heart, burst into the pain living there and opened the way for my secret to escape. *He may not love me as I love him, but I do trust him. Not only with my life, but with my child's.*

"I've never wanted a child because..." Almost as though the words had been building up inside me for decades, the truth burst out of me. I shuddered from the avalanche of emotions rolling through me. "Because I'm afraid of leaving her alone like my parents left me."

Kaine silently waited for me to go on. I swallowed, afraid to say anything more, yet afraid not to. Had I made the wrong decision to tell him? "I couldn't stand it if my child had to go through what I did. So I decided to never have a child."

"But, Chrissy-doll, what happened to you parents isn't

going to happen to you."

My dear old friend Logic told me he was right. But he didn't know the whole story, hadn't experienced the heartache I had. "Accidents happen all the time."

"Yes, of course they do, but to think you're going to die like your parents did is just plain wrong."

I wanted to tell him, then hear him tell me I wouldn't be affected by the same disease my parents suffered, but my heart's defenses closed ranks, refusing to let any more ache get out. Instead, I took a big breath and resolved once more to give him what he needed. "Maybe you're right, but that doesn't matter any longer. I'd rather fight my fear than risk losing you. That is, if you still want me."

Kaine's placed his palms on my face. With an expression showering me with love, he spoke quietly, reverently. "Chrissy-doll, I love you. And yes, I still want you. I will always want you. No matter what."

With his declaration, Kaine wiped away every ounce of dread. I blinked back more tears, struggling between crying about leaving my child alone and rejoicing because my husband cared for me. *I should tell him everything. He deserves to know the whole truth.* But, once again, uncertainty took hold. *Later. I promise I'll tell him later.*

"Come on. Let's make a baby." Spinning around, I surged down the hall like Patton charging onto the battlefield. Taking prisoners wasn't an option with me either and I was bound and determined to win this battle. However, I hadn't planned on getting lost. *Damn this huge mansion.*

"Chrissy-doll, are you lost?"

"Of course not." I darted my gaze around, trying to get my bearings. "Why would I get lost in my own home?"

"Well, you did say that sometimes you needed a map to get

around."

I could see how he bit the inside of his mouth to keep from laughing. *Oh, he thinks he's so funny!* Okay, maybe he was a little funny, but I wasn't about to let on. "This is exactly where I intended us to be."

He looked around him. "It is? But this isn't anywhere near our bedroom."

"Who said I was headed toward the bedroom?" With what I hoped was a lecherous leer, I grabbed him by the shirt sleeve and yanked him along with me through the closest door. Once inside, I paused and thanked my lucky stars. "See? It's my office."

"Yes, I see."

Can the doubt in his tone be any clearer? Taking a big breath, I faced him, clutched his shoulders and crammed my mouth to his. He kissed me back, forcefully, matching my anger with heated emotion of his own. Wrapping his arms around me, he lifted me and carried me toward my desk.

"I hope you don't have any important papers on your desk."

I studied his expression, trying to decipher what he meant. "Uh, no."

With one brush of his hand, he swept papers, folders and even my favorite ghost paperweight off my desk and onto the floor. The only thing left on the desk was my computer, which sat off to one side.

He planted my butt on top of the cold wood and pushed me backward, knocking the breath out of me. But that was the last thing on my mind. Instead, I hung on to him as he tore my shirt away from my chest. Buttons and bra went flying, landing on the paperwork scattered on the carpet. With a groan, he stopped, looked at my breasts, then grabbed them and pushed them together. I tensed, waiting for him to take them into his mouth. Thankfully, I didn't have to wait long.

Kaine tugged on my nipples, biting, sucking, licking them. I squirmed under the pleasurable assault, arching my back to urge him on. Using his forearm and chest to hold both my breasts with one hand, he slid the fingers of his other hand down the front of my slacks and yanked. I heard the material tear and I lifted my hips to help him pull slacks and thong down my legs.

The darker side of me wanted to demand he get me knocked up and get it over with. If Kaine's only purpose for marrying me was to produce an heir, then I wanted it over and done. I loved him enough to give him what he needed. "Come on and take me. Shut up and get busy."

He let go of my tit and paused to stare at me. "No, my love, it's your turn to shut up." He ran his gaze down my body, stopping to rest on my mound. When he looked back at my face, I knew what to expect. The man was thirsty and wanted to drink.

He knelt on the floor. "I'm going to eat you up." Hungrily he attacked my pussy, spreading me wide to lap at the juices already running freely from me.

Omigod, but the man is good at sucking me dry. "Spread my lips. Show me what that tongue of yours can do."

Kaine used his thumbs and opened me to him, sliding his tongue from the bottom of my slit up to my throbbing nub. Moaning, he ran his tongue around, over and into me. I clutched at the smooth surface of my desk, finding nothing to hold on to. Instead, I grabbed my breasts and squeezed them.

Hey, if my mission was to give him an heir, then I figured I might as well enjoy myself in the process.

"Spread your legs farther apart." His husky tone spiraled the whirlwind in me faster.

I followed his command, happy to do so. “Eat me, Kaine. Lick me dry.”

With a wild growl, he crushed his mouth against my wetness again. Nipping at me, he moaned with pleasure, yet I was willing to bet I was getting more out of the deal than he was. At least, so far.

“Omigod.” The more he sucked on me, the hotter I grew. I wanted him inside me, deep inside me. “Do it to me. Make me hot, Kaine. Stoke my fire.”

Suddenly he stopped and I almost died. “No!”

“Don’t worry. I’m just coming up for air. And to do this.” Taking my ass cheeks in his hands, he lifted and drove his tongue far inside my cave.

Hot heat—fire—spread from my clit into my abdomen and I bucked, wanting to push him farther inside me, yet needing to get away from the torturous ecstasy. He moaned again, the sound at once tickling and stimulating me.

He nipped and pulled at my clit, pressing his tongue flat against my sensitive nub. Panting, I clutched my breasts, closed my eyes and marveled at the swirl of colors behind my eyelids. A climax tore through me, racking my body, making me unable to do more than mew my relief. And still he didn’t let go of my snatch.

Incredibly, the tension grew again and I couldn’t help but admire the man’s stamina. Was it because he was a dragon? Not wanting to think about my husband’s alternate identity, I swept the question from my mind. Another rush of wetness burst from my body and I jerked as the orgasm throbbed in me. Yet, still, I wanted more.

“Let me see my juices on your face.” Obeying, Kaine glanced up. A grin spread his wet lips. “Good. My come looks good on you.”

His tongue, longer than I remembered, swept over his lips, taking in the remnants of my juices. "I bet mine would look good on you too."

I laughed at his turnabout on my words and lifted up on my elbows. "I guess we'll have to test that theory."

"Theory, huh?" He stood, quickly disrobed and crawled over me, kissing my still trembling body. "No theory; just facts."

He traced his lips along the curve of my belly, pausing to dive his tongue into my bellybutton. I giggled and reached for his arms, urging him to keep moving. But he wasn't a man to be rushed. Moving his oh-so-talented tongue, he kept on his journey, sliding over my ribcage to run into the road stop of my tits. He circled lazily around the bottom of one to the hollow between them and over the top of the other.

"I swear, Kaine, if you don't get your ass moving, I'm going go crazy." I didn't bother telling him he was already driving my crazy.

"Crazy wild, I hope."

I narrowed my eyes at him. "Just plain crazy."

"Ooh, sounds dangerous."

"You have no idea."

I inhaled a deep breath, amazed at how his smile could excite me as much as his tongue between my legs. But that wasn't his tongue lying against my mound. I returned his smile and glanced down, trying to get a glimpse of his package.

"Looking for something?" He quirked an eyebrow at me.

"Yeah. I want that hot dog you've got pressed against me." I licked my lips, hoping to seduce him into complying. "And I want it now."

"Why, Mrs. Delcaluca, are you saying what I think you're saying?" He lowered his body, moving his hips up and down in a slow rhythmic motion.

I growled at him. Hey, I liked games as much as the next girl, but I was ready for the real sport to begin. "Kaine." I drew out his name, twisted my upper body and tried to reach for his cock. He pretended to play Keep Away, but in the end, lost on purpose. My hand wrapped victoriously around his dick. "Gotcha."

He gasped, but kept up his rhythm with me providing the friction. "Sure feels like you did."

I held on, working my hand from his pulsing root to the wet tip of his cap. I tugged when he pulled away. I twisted, adding another dimension to his pleasure. I ran my thumb over the tip, gathering his juices to lubricate my palm. The feel of his pre-come on my hand was too much for me to resist. Slowly, I slid my tongue from the base of his shaft upward, over the slight ridges of blue veins until, at last, I flicked the tip of my tongue over the top of weeping cock. He groaned and I fought back a satisfied smile. I teased him a little while longer, running my tongue around him, pausing to kiss and nibble at his sensitive skin. Another, deeper moan escaped him.

I pumped him a few more times with my hand, letting him think I'd stopped using my mouth, and enjoying his growing frustration as he tried to push my head toward his dick. His shaft grew thicker, longer and I had a hard—pun intended—time keeping up with his ever-increasing pace. Suddenly I deep-throated him, taking his cock all the way inside. Sucking, pressing my lips tightly around him, I pulled away, sliding over his shaft until his mushroomed cap popped out of my mouth. He closed his eyes, concentrating on the enjoyment I gave him.

"Damn but that feels great."

I flexed my grip, squeezing and releasing, and kept pumping him. "For me too." The heat in my abdomen had grown with the heat in my hand. "You're so big. So long. So hard." I wanted to give him everything. Physically, emotionally, verbally.

Yet when he tensed and stopped moving, I thought I'd gone too far. "Hold on, Kaine. Don't let go yet."

"I'm trying." He gritted his teeth and started pumping again. "But I'm only human." Opening his eyes, he caught mine and I saw the mirth there. "So to speak."

Oh, I am so not going there. Not right now. Later.

Thankful for all those grueling crunches I'd done in the past months, I lifted up so I could catch his balls with my other hand. He twitched, blinking at me in surprise. "Try warning a guy, will ya?"

"I don't think so. I like it when I can catch you off guard."

He started to say something, but I could tell he had to use all his determination to keep from climaxing. His breathing grew heavier and I had to watch his face, wanting to see the climax nearing its edge.

My heart raced at the amber in his eyes. *Is he changing into his other self? If so, what would that mean for sex?* My mind flashed back to the other night, the flames in the water and how I'd burned alive in more than one way. Now I wanted to embrace his inner dragon. "So you're really..."

He paused just long enough to check my expression. "Yes."

"Then, Kaine, make me burn." At first he didn't understand. As realization dawned, he smiled and the amber grew brighter.

"Like the other night?"

"Yes. Like the other night."

My heart pounded. For some reason, he acted like he didn't want to do it. I let go of him and slipped my hands over his shoulders. He grumbled at my releasing him.

"You have to understand. Doing that—" he tipped his head, indicating what that meant, "—can be tricky. Even harmful, when we're not in water."

I saw the concern in his eyes and knew that, although he may have married me to give him a child, he did care about me. I just wasn't sure how much. Would he still care after I gave him an heir? Or treat me as a friend? But I didn't want to examine the future that closely. *First things now.* "I don't care. I want heat, baby, heat."

He frowned and studied my face, irritating me.

"Kaine, you think way too much for your own good. Just fuck me."

I swear his features shifted, morphing until I saw two faces, the underlying one the face of the man I loved and the other, barely visible above the other like tracing paper over a picture. The other one shook me, frightening me. Yet with my pulse racing, I saw the strange image and recognized its beauty.

Kaine pushed my legs apart and slammed against me, driving his cock hard and fast into me. His balls bumped against the crack of my ass, swaying with his pumping motions. Rocking me back and forth, he worked his hips, ramming against me. With every thrust, the temperature between us rose, friction sparking the flame within.

Kaine may have married me for the wrong reason, a reason he hadn't told me until now, but I no longer cared. I wanted, craved him and I would do anything to help him. At that moment, I realized something more shocking than the knowledge that my husband was a dragon. I realized I *wanted* his child, my child, our child. Not only for him, but for me. Damn the future and what might be. Together with Kaine, *we'd* determine what would be.

Pulling his upper body to me, I locked my fingers behind his neck. I gazed at him, compelling him to know what I was thinking, how I wanted to please him. Not only in this moment, but forever. "Kaine, I need—"

He misinterpreted my meaning. "I need you too."

He nipped at my lower lip, breathing hard, and I inhaled, wanting to soak in the scent of him. And the simmer inside me, between us, started to boil.

My core throbbed, clenching and unclenching him to drag every ounce of sweet delight. I closed my eyes, wanting to heighten the sensation of his body against mine, sliding against my skin. I held him to me, wanting him closer than was humanly possible. He raked his tongue along the bottom of my ear and the fever inside me burned.

I cradled him between my legs and rocked, matching his moves, pushing him farther inside. Just when I thought I'd managed to keep up with him, he changed, rolling his hips in a small circle. The simple act made his shaft rub against my inner muscles in a different, excruciatingly wonderful way. I cried out, wave after wave of climax striking home.

"Flames, Kaine. I want flames."

He lifted away from me to examine me, question me. "Are you sure?"

"Haven't we gone over this? Don't hold back. Flame on, big guy."

Throwing back his head, he roared and plunged again. I gasped and looked at my arms. Tiny flames raced along my arms in both directions, to my hands and up my shoulders. Fear tightened my body for a moment and I searched his face.

It's all right.

I knew his words without hearing them and I believed

them. I believed in him.

No longer did he move slowly. Now he dove into me again and again. I opened wider, needing him to spread the fire. Bright red flames with an inner golden glow covered my body, striking a match to my hair.

Holy crap. I'm on fire.

But I wasn't afraid. Instead, I quickened my pace to keep up with his, turning my head to watch the inferno sparking more bonfires between us.

Red. Everything's red.

The entire room, the walls, the framed photos, even the desk underneath me was lit up in the fiery color, changing the logical world I'd known all my life into a fantasy land. A land of incredible creatures, amazing sights and incredible sex.

Yet the fire outside was only a spark compared to the fire burning inside. Reeling with the ache for him, the combustion in my abdomen burst free and I screamed. Kaine pressed his mouth to my throat, murmuring reassuring words, but I didn't have the strength to tell him they were unneeded.

He gripped my ass tighter, and for once I was glad I had an ample-sized butt. Lifting me higher still, he slipped my burning legs over his flaming shoulders and sank down into me. His panted breaths came out in small puffs of smoke and I watched, mesmerized by the sight. "Show me." Pointedly, I stared at his mouth.

The corners of his lips curved upward and he transformed, the once gauzy view of his dragon body growing more solid, more real. I reached out, wanting to touch him, needing to feel the scales I saw spreading over him. He lashed out his tongue and flicked the tips of my fingers. I gasped, then laughed.

Wow.

The flames stroked my skin, firing more than mere heat between us. My laughter died, replaced by lust, pure and undiluted. Although I'd been gasping before now, my breaths grew shorter, faster, even more shallow. The blaze of my desire went white-hot, swirling a tornado of heat between my legs. "Kaine." I wanted to say more, but simply couldn't.

Instead, I reached up to pull his face to mine. I licked and sucked at the rough flesh under his chin, noting the change in his skin and loving it. The steamroller of the forest fire raging from my clit to my head sped up and I knew I couldn't last much longer.

I clutched him to me, burying my face against his chest and closed my eyes. I listened, hearing his heart beat as quickly as mine, beating against his chest, against my face just as hard as he pounded below. *Kaine. Kaine.* I focused all my energy, all my thoughts on silently calling his name.

My release exploded and wetness, blissfully warm on my skin, spread over my butt cheeks. My body shuddered, roll after roll raging over me.

Kaine roared, this time louder than I'd ever heard him. I opened my eyes, stunned and thrilled at the intensity of his cry and gasped.

A burst of fire spewed out of him, from every inch of his body, flaming upward to lick at the ten-foot ceiling above us. For the first time, I feared we would burn the house down and us along with it. Still, I held on and trusted Kaine.

His magnificent body hardened in the throes of painful ecstasy. Eyes closed, he jerked, his climax battering his body, shaking him. As his shout finally ebbed, he stilled, tensed, then finally released.

I cried out, feeling his seed shoot into me. At that moment, I wanted every drop he could give me, every bit of the man—the dragon—I loved. With my sweat flowing over me, my come soaking the skin between my legs, I rubbed my hands over my breasts, my stomach and watched the flames flicker away.

"Chrissy?" Kaine, his features restored to fully human, gazed at me.

I tugged him down and he rolled to my side. "Yeah?"

"Your birth control pills…" He studied me, waited for me to answer.

"Oh, wow, that's right. I'm on the pill. I forgot about that." *Although I'd missed the last couple of days.* Had I subconsciously stopped taking them to get pregnant? Perhaps my heart had already known what my head needed to learn; that I'd do anything for Kaine, including getting pregnant. "Although I've kind of messed up on taking them lately."

"It doesn't matter."

"It doesn't?" Sure, women got pregnant sometimes by missing even one pill, but usually it took a month or so after getting your body off them for a pregnancy to happen, right?

"No form of birth control can protect against my flames."

"Oh. I see." *I think.* "So in the tub the other night…?" *Wait. That means I could already be preggers!* And he'd known. I choked, then coughed, anxiety closing my throat up. He'd known the fire would cancel out the pills. I should've been angry, but I wasn't. How could I be when I'd already decided to give him a baby? Still, thinking about getting pregnant was definitely different than actually already being pregnant. I couldn't get my mind around the idea. So, true to form, I pushed the possibility away. *Think about it tomorrow, Ms. Scarlett.*

"Exactly." Kaine skimmed his fingertips along the curve of my jaw, down my throat to my breasts. Taking a breast possessively in the palm of his hand, he sighed. "Good thing I bought you the biggest desk I could find."

I laughed, stretching my hands above my head. "Yeah, good thing."

"Um, excuse me. Mr. and Mrs. Delcaluca?"

Kaine and I gaped at each other. *This is so not happening.* I grimaced and made a face at him. "Is that you, Pam?" *Please, oh, please, tell me that's not who I think it is.* I tried, but I couldn't get my denial to stick. "Pam, were you turned on?" I inhaled, stunned at my own stupid words. "Uh, you know what I meant, right? Were you, the computer, up and running this whole time?"

Kaine slid off the desk, tossed my clothes to me and retrieved his own. He grinned and I sent him a mean look.

"Yes, Mrs. Delcaluca, I was."

I hurried to join my husband behind the computer monitor. "And you didn't think to say something? You know, like before things got heated?" *Heated, my ass. Hotter than hell.*

"Well, I started to, but Mini-Pam suggested we stay quiet. We didn't want to interrupt."

I glanced around and saw Mini-Pam lying on the credenza behind my desk. "Great. Just great." I checked the room, fearing the worst. "I suppose Missy is hiding under my desk?" Didn't mice like to hide under furniture?

"Of course not. That would be rude."

I snorted and fell into Kaine's arms. What else could I do? After all, the deed—ahem!—was done and nothing I could do or say could change that fact. "Oh, sure. That would be rude. But, Pam?"

"Yes, Mrs. Delcaluca?"

"Say something next time."

Kaine took my chin and tilted my face upward, a snarky

look on his face. "Next time?"

I woke up the next morning feeling conflicted. I was committed to Kaine and had decided to have his baby, no matter what the cost to me. But that didn't mean the idea still didn't scare the bejesus out of me. Plus, ending up alone in bed again didn't help. Reaching over to run my hand over his pillow, I frowned and tried not to let his early morning departures upset me. After all, my life had changed yesterday after discovering that supernatural beings existed—and Kaine saving my life from two of his nastier dragon associates. Not to mention (seriously, not a word!) playing porn star for my computerized assistant. And I'd thought my life before Kaine had been exciting.

I stretched and sat up, reflecting on the day ahead. Bad move on my part. *Uh-oh.* Now that I knew, how could I continue running DeBunkers, Inc.? Since dragons existed, why not ghosts and demons? What if I debunked a house only to leave the ghost, demon, boogie-man, you-fill-in-the-blank still around to pester the inhabitants? Suddenly my life's work, along with my stomach, turned upside down. Slinging my legs over the bed, I reached for my robe and hurried to the writing table. I pulled open the drawer, picked up Mini-Pam, and punched her *On* switch with my thumb. Yeah, that's right. My mamma didn't raise no idiot. Once burned, twice embarrassed—not. No way would I ever leave her on and out in plain sight again. Plain sight of whatever Kaine and I might, uh, get into.

"Yes, Mrs. Delcaluca?"

The memory of yesterday and Mini-Pam's voyeuristic activity swept through me, but I somehow managed not to blush. "Could you display my calendar for the day?" I half-imagined she'd bring up the schedule with an added note *Do Hubby On Top of Desk* added to the agenda. However, Mini-Pam was a smart little tool and my calendar—without any references to sex of any kind—popped onto her screen.

Damn. I'd hoped that I didn't have any DeBunkers assignments for the day. Recently I'd gotten a bit lax on setting up work. You know, what with learning my way around the mansion and finding out the paranormals of the world really do exist. Besides, I needed time off after such an exhausting honeymoon. (Not buying it? Bite me.)

I frowned at the appointment listed an hour from now. *Demon debunking.* Great. Just what I needed. I was set to visit an older home in the Little Five Points area of Atlanta. The owner supposedly thought her hubby was a demon. Before the last few days, I would've known in my gut that the woman was either off her rocker or trying to pull a scam. Now, however, I wasn't sure what I'd be getting myself into. Would I meet a real demon today? And if so, would I know what to do?

This is so not good. Yet, until I figured out what I would do with my business, if anything, I had to keep my professional reputation going. Although I wished I could crawl back into bed, I knew I wouldn't.

Thirty-five minutes later, I stood in front of the small home of Mr. and Mrs. Andrews. Pots on the wraparound porch boasted colorful flowers and a cat stretched out across the top step. No place looked less like a demon's home. But then again, what did I know? I certainly hadn't known dragons hung out at local lakes and took extravagant trips to Vegas. Summoning my courage, I stepped over the cat and walked to the front door. The door swung open before I could knock.

"Who are you?" A woman looking remarkably like Marge Simpson raked her gaze over my body before scanning the yard behind me, her eyes darting back and forth.

So much for first impressions. "Hi, I'm Christina Taylor from DeBunkers, Inc." I presented a card to her with my left hand and extended my right hand although I had a feeling she wouldn't take it. I was right.

The woman's fearful eyes locked onto me. "No you're not."

This was a first. I'd never had anyone challenge my identity before. "Yes, ma'am, I am. Are you Mrs. Brenda Andrews?"

"That's right."

"Mrs. Andrews, don't you remember making an appointment for today? To find out if your husband is a demon?"

Why couldn't I have taken a job picking fleas off stray dogs? Or maybe learned to scrape bunions off old people's feet? Right now, any profession other than my own sounded really good.

Brenda huffed. "Of course I remember. But you're not that Taylor woman." A loud crash from upstairs had us both looking toward the stairs.

The knot in my gut grew harder and bigger. I'd kept my maiden name for business purposes, but I briefly considered telling her my name was Delcaluca. Then I could whirl on my heels and run away. Too bad my parents had drilled responsibility into me. *Damn them.* "Um, I don't mean to sound difficult, but I know my own name. And I am that Taylor woman."

She cocked an eyebrow at me, frowned, then glanced at the ceiling. A scream broke the air, making us both jump. "Okay, so if you're Taylor with DeBunkers, Inc.—" she paused until I nodded to confirm my identity again, "—then who the hell is upstairs fighting my husband?"

And I thought things were strange before. I studied her

closely and came to a frightening conclusion. *She's not crazy. She's a sensible woman in a bad situation with one too many Christina Taylors and a possible demon in her home.* "I don't have a clue, but I'd love to find out."

She moved aside and waved me in. "Be my guest. As long as that thing is out of my house, I don't care what your name is."

I tried to give her a reassuring smile, but that's a tall order when you feel anything but assured. I scooted past her and took the stairs two steps at a time to reach the landing above. Another shout and curse sent me whirling to the left, toward the door at the end of the short hallway.

I grabbed the doorknob just as the door shuddered violently. Curses flew from a deep voice inside and I knew without a doubt I was about to face my first real honest-to-Satan demon.

Choking back the urge to cry for my mommy, I turned the knob and stepped over the threshold into my own reality TV show called, *Will the Real Chrissy Please Stand Up?*

Wanna Play?

"Jenn?"

I gawked and tried to make sense of the chaos around me. My friend, Jennifer Randall-Barrington, sat on the chest of a thirty-something-year-old man. But this man wasn't any ordinary man. His eyes glowed a fiery red, and spittle shot from his distorted, fang-encrusted mouth. His face, although recognizable as human, had grotesque ruts dug into his skin, boils popping up over his cheeks and hanging flesh breaking off to float to the floor. Aside from seeing Fitz eating her gourmet mouse lunch, I'd never seen anything as horrific as this.

Jenn, her copper-colored locks in disarray and dressed in black jeans and T-shirt, glanced up. Her usually pleasant face was set in hard determination with teeth gritted, eyes blazing. She kept one hand in a death-grip around the man's neck and pressed a knitting needle against his throat with the other. "Hey, C."

I wiggled my fingers at her. "Hi there."

The twinkle flickered in her eye at my casual greeting, but was gone a second later. Cold resolve slammed back into place. "I'm a bit busy killing a demon right now."

Taking advantage of our odd reunion, the demon-man bucked upward, nearly tossing off my friend. Jenn yelped but never let go of him. With a scream of rage, he spewed out a huge wad of spit. Jenn ducked to the side, dodging the missile that landed with a *splat* on the overhead fan. Thankfully, the fan was turned off or we'd have gotten covered with the mustard-colored gook. I slapped a hand over my stomach and hoped I'd keep my on-the-go breakfast bagel down.

"C."

Although Jenn struggled against the demon's frantic attempts to get free, she managed to shoot me a grin. Nodding toward the side of the room, she asked, "If you're not too busy enjoying the show, would you mind getting my knife for me? This needle just isn't cutting it." Her grin grew wider. "If you know what I mean."

Actually, I wasn't sure what she meant or that I wanted to find out. But when a friend calls, I answer. I hurried around the pieces of broken furniture littering the floor and searched while trying to keep one eye on Jenn and the demon.

I briefly marveled at how easily the word *demon* now fit into my vocabulary. At last, I saw the knife—more of a short sword really—and bent to pick it up. "Ouch." I studied the plain silver handle and sucked my thumb where I'd nicked it.

"Careful, C. That blade's very sharp."

No kidding. Sharp and very deadly looking. And pretty damn cool too.

"C, would ya mind speeding it up a bit?"

"Oh! Sure." Carefully taking the blade by the handle with both hands, I stood and retraced my steps to Jenn.

"Quick. Toss it to me. I need to finish this fast."

Didn't anyone ever tell Jenn not to run with knives, much less throw one? Or was it scissors? I shrugged and gently tossed it across to her. Jenn dropped the needle and snatched the blade out of the air in one seamless motion.

"I'll get some rope—"

"Don't bother." Jenn whipped her arm across her body, slinging the blade like a machete. The knife sliced neatly through the man's neck, severing his head.

Horrified, I froze, gaping as the head rolled to stop an inch away from my feet. "Omigod." *I have a severed head at my feet. I so didn't know this was how my day was going to go.* But my time to reflect was quickly cut short.

A screech filled the air, pulling me out of my daze. Brenda Andrews stood in the doorway, shock evident in the whiteness of her face, stared at her husband's detached head, then at his body. At last she glanced up at me and I saw the Vacant Sign planted in her eyes. Her eyes rolled backward in her head and I rushed, hurtling over the human hacky-sack at my feet, and caught her before she hit the floor. We crumpled together. Brenda collapsed on top of me and my butt banged against the hardwood.

"Argh!" Jarred, I clung onto the woman sitting on my lap and waited for the pain in my ass to subside. *My backside's taking a lot of abuse lately.*

"Good save, C."

I started to answer my friend and, instead, held my breath. Like something from a B horror film, Mr. Andrews' body and head slowly disintegrated until Jenn was left sitting in a pile of dust. Of course, I did what any former skeptic would do when faced with grisly physical evidence that demons are real. I laughed my ass off.

Jenn hopped to her feet, brushed the demon dust off her clothes and walked over to me. With a bemused expression on her face, she crouched down, pried my hands off Brenda and lowered the still-out-of-it woman gently to the floor. "C, are you okay?"

Her question only made me laugh harder. Tears streamed down my cheeks and I held my stomach, the stitch from my hilarity stabbing me in my side. "Yeah." (More giggling.) "I'm okay." (Giggle, giggle.)

"Are you sure? You seem kind of freaked out."

"Nope." (Hysterical giggling now.) "I'm good."

"O-kay. If you say so." Obviously not buying it, she shifted to sit cross-legged. "But I'm here if you need me."

"Uh-huh." I nodded and laughed at the same time which surprisingly is more difficult than you would imagine. "I've never seen a real demon before." Then again, I'd never known a real human-mouse—and mouse-eater—or dragon before. I'd experienced a lot of firsts lately.

"Yeah, it can throw ya for a loop. Although I don't remember anyone ever finding anything funny about it."

"What are you doing here anyway?" I pointed at the demon dust, giving renewed life to my giggle fit.

"I meant to call you, but things got hectic." Jenn glanced at the woman, then at the demon-dust hubby.

"But Brenda—" I gasped, "—said I was already up here. She didn't believe I was me." I wiped the tear streaks away and sucked in more air. Then I scrunched up my face and held my breath, trying to keep another round of laughter from hitting me.

"Yeah, sorry about that. When she came to the door, she assumed I was you and called me by your name. I figured it was the easiest way to get into the house without a lot of questions." Jenn reached for the bottom of Brenda's shirt and cleaned the gunky mess of blackish blood and dust off her blade.

Now that I could finally speak without breaking into hysterics, I had to ask. "Jenn, I don't understand. I know you always believed in these things—"

"And you didn't."

I ignored the triumphant gleam in her eye and hurried on. "—but how did you know he was a demon? And how did you end up killing him?" My gaze fell on the huge knife she still held. "With such a big knife?"

"The better to kill them with, my dear." Jenn twirled the blade in her hand and stuck it—hopefully in a sheath—behind her back. "Good thing you came along after he knocked it out of my hand. A knitting needle just doesn't do the job."

"I gotta say, I'm pretty impressed. You killed a demon." I looked at my friend, really seeing her for the first time. "You've done this kind of thing before, haven't you?"

She smiled her answer and pulled out a very unique-looking phone. "First things first. Right now I need to get reinforcements in here to clean up the mess." She looked at the screen. "Partner, I need a team for a demon cleanup. You've got the address." She glanced at the still prone Mrs. Andrews. "Oh, and the Psych Squad."

"Really, Jenn. Can't you ever do your job without witnesses?" the voice from the phone quipped.

Funny. I hadn't seen her dial anything. Was her phone voice-activated?

"Partner, don't give me grief. I only did this job because I was already in Atlanta and the local Protectors were busy. Now do your job and contact the area HQ."

"Partner? Since when do realtors have partners? And what's a protector?"

"Yeah, about all that." She obviously took a moment to reconsider opening up to me. "I'm not really a real estate agent. Well, I am, sort of." She held out her phone so I could see the screen. “And Partner doesn’t help me sell houses. In fact, he barely helps me with my real job.”

“Hey!” The image of a man dressed in a space suit huffed at Jenn. “I’ll have you know, Miss Taylor, that I am a valuable asset to the Society. Whether Jenn wants to admit it or not.”

“The Society?” I took Jenn’s offered hand and awkwardly rose. “I’m so confused.” Another glimpse at the scene around me didn’t help my turmoil. “About everything.”

Jenn slipped her arm around me, taking me along with her to the door. “I bet. Let me explain downstairs, okay? I’ve got some associates who should arrive any minute now.”

I let her lead me downstairs and onto the couch in the lovely—and very normal-looking—living room. Jenn took a seat on the massive coffee table. “Okay, here goes. Try to open your mind and know that everything I’m about to tell you is the truth.”

Alarm rushed through me. *More truth?* My stomach did a sickening flip-flop. “Frankly, I’m not sure I can handle anything else.” Yet Jenn’s chuckle reassured me that I could.

“Dear friend of mine, I’m not what I seem to be.”

“I kind of gathered that. Then what are you? Some kind of demon duster? A super agent with a super-secret organization that eliminates the nasties of the world?” I waited for her to laugh. She didn’t and the alarm I’d felt earlier shot up five levels above Code Orange. “Oh, come on, Jenn. I was kidding.”

“Kidding or not, it’s a good guess. You nailed it big time. The super-secret organization is called the Society and I’m called a Protector. That’s someone who protects—”

“Or tries to.” Partner let out a series of beeps that sounded amazingly like laughter.

Jenn rolled her eyes at me, letting out an exasperated sigh.

"Did you call HQ, Partner?"

"Of course I did. I always do my job whether on Earth or in space."

Jenn turned the screen away from herself and winked at me. "Great, then I don't need your help any longer, so off you go." She pushed a button on the gadget, sending the squawking space man into cyber exile.

I wondered if her partner was related to Mini-Pam.

"As I was saying, I protect innocent people from supernatural bad guys. You know, like our friend upstairs. Demons, ghouls, ghosts, were-animals and..." She took my hand. "...dragons."

My heart hit the floor and took my ability to breathe along with it. Suddenly, I didn't know if I could trust my friend. I swallowed and decided to play it cool. Or at least as cool as I could. "Wow. So all those times you insisted these beings were real, you were telling the truth. Were you a Protector way back then?"

"Yep, way back even in college. Demon dusting, as you called it, was kind of my real major instead of Business Management."

I shook my head, partly to rid my brain of confusion and partly to buy myself time. Did she know about Kaine? "This is a lot to take in. But tell me, why are you here?" I couldn't help but glance upward. "To get rid of Mr. Andrews, right?" I cringed. Calling that thing Mr. Andrews after what I'd seen seemed wrong.

"Not at first. Actually, I came to see you, C."

I met her gaze and knew. *She's here for Kaine. Please, oh, please, don't make me choose between my husband and my friend.* I steeled myself and asked the question I didn't want to ask, but had to. "You came to see me? For a quick visit?" *Please say it's only a visit and not a dragon-slaying.*

Her eyes glittered, scaring me. "I came to warn you about your husband. He's not what he appears to be."

How does she know Kaine and I are already married?

She took my hands. "Yeah, I know you're married. I did my research and found out more than that little tidbit. C, Kaine Delcaluca is a dragon."

So tell me something I don't know. Anger flashed through me and I yanked my hands away. If Jenn was here to hurt the love of my life, she'd have to go through me first. "Don't be ridiculous. My husband's no more a dragon than you are." *Lie, girl, lie.* I hated telling my friend a lie, but it wasn't as though she hadn't been lying to me all these years. (I'm really good at justifying things when I want to be.)

"Come on. You know what he is. You even said you saw him change the first night you met him. And the tattoo you described cinched it."

The doorbell rang and she reluctantly left to open it. Four men, looking every inch like accountants in their boring gray suits and ties, murmured something to her and headed upstairs. She returned to the coffee table. "Look, I understand you want to protect him and that you're probably mad at me for hiding my real job from you all these years. C, believe me. I'm not here to hurt him. I'm only here to warn you. So you'll know who—and what—you're married to."

"Seriously? You won't do to Kaine what you did to Mr. Andrews?" I studied her, hoping I could catch any insincerity in her expression. I didn't, but then she was probably a pro at hiding her feelings.

"Ah, so you do know. Good. From what I've gathered from my sources, Kaine Delcaluca isn't a bad dragon. Most of them aren't. Besides, killing a dragon is a whole lot harder than taking out a demon."

Yay! I breathed a little easier. "He's not bad. I know he isn't." Okay, marrying me only to get an heir was kind of a bad thing to do, but underneath he's a softie.

"So how about letting me meet Kaine?"

Oh, hell, no! Surprised at my first instinct, I was glad I hadn't said anything out loud. But that didn't mean my first reaction wasn't the right one. Could I trust Jenn not to hurt Kaine? And once he found out who she was, why she was here, how would he react?

"C?" Jenn crossed her arms and urged me on. "What's it going to be? Do I get to meet the man who won your heart or not?"

Not. But sometimes my mouth doesn't listen to my head. "Sure you do." Not giving myself time to change my mind, I hurried to the door. "And on the way, I can give you the lowdown on some other, uh, people in my life."

Maybe if I distracted her by outing Fitz, I could save my hot-in-more-than-one-way hubby.

I ushered Jenn into the foyer of the mansion. "Well, what do you think?" Maybe it wasn't the nicest thing I'd ever done, but I admit I enjoyed showing off my new home. From the moment we'd opened the ornate iron gates to the second I'd swung open the door, I could see that Jenn was duly impressed and, for one of the few times since I'd met her, speechless. "Jenn?"

She slowly turned in a circle, taking in the rare artwork, the enormous chandelier and the beautiful furniture. I had to fight not to gloat. "Hell's bells, C. I knew the guy was rich, but not Bill Gates rich. Hell, I think this surpasses even Bill."

I tried to act casual and blew it. "Yeah, I know. Wild, huh?"

"Very." She locked an arm through mine. "But I bet not half as wild as Kaine."

"You got that right." For a moment, we grinned at each other, once again two college girls talking about our handsome boyfriends.

"Did I hear my name?"

I'd never seen anyone—except Kaine—move as fast as Jenn did. Blade at the ready, she whirled around to face my husband, who stood at the entrance to the first parlor. Or whatever the hell that room was called. *Damn, I need my map with the names of the rooms listed on it.*

"Kaine, I want you to meet someone." I wanted to say more, but his expression left me without words.

He glared at Jenn and took a step backward. "I know what she is."

Jenn, who had at first appeared congenial to Kaine, sneered. "Back at 'cha, bub."

"Why are you here, Protector?"

I gaped at the two of them, both with feet spread apart, ready for battle. "Does everyone know all the supernatural stuff except me?" How stupid did I feel? I was the so-called paranormal expert, and yet, apparently I was the last to find out about that other world.

"Don't stir your embers, dragon. I'm not your enemy." Jenn held up the knife, then very deliberately slipped it out of sight. "Unless you want me to be."

I peered at the back of her shirt and jeans, but didn't see where she could've put the huge knife. *How does she do that?* "Kaine, this is the friend I told you about. Jennifer Randall. I mean Jennifer Randall-Barrington."

Kaine blinked a couple of times as though processing the information. "I see. You, however, neglected to mention that your friend is a Protector."

"You mean like you neglected to mention that you married her to get an heir to the Dragon Dynasty?"

Crap! Everyone does *know about our baby business.* "Hey, you two, come on. Let's have a seat in the parlor, or whatever this room is called, and get to know each other." Taking Jenn's arm, I tugged her along with me. She complied but came with me in an awkward sidestep, keeping her eyes on my disgruntled husband following several paces behind.

Once seated with Kaine and me on one couch and Jenn in the chair directly across from us, I folded my hands in my lap and dove in. "So here's the deal. Jenn came here to take care of a demon problem and decided to drop in on the happy newlyweds. Right, Jenn?" I shot her a look, urging her to play nice.

"Oh, uh, yeah. That's right." She darted her gaze between Kaine and me, but always lingered a second or two longer on him.

"A demon problem?" He sat ramrod straight as though ready to jump into action.

"Nothing much. A husband didn't tell his wife what he truly was. She found out when he ate her best friend."

Wow, oh, wow. Why didn't you tell me that part, Jenn? I pursed my lips, unhappy that she'd left that information out. Unhappy, yet at the same time grateful. "But that's done and over with. Now it's fun time. You know, just a friend visiting a friend." The tension between them could've been cut with a fork. I blew out a breath, quickly losing my patience.

"Have you shown your wife what you really look like?"

I didn't know whether to slink away or agree with her. Since finding out Kaine was a dragon, I'd been curious to see him in his full dragony form. Sure, I'd glimpsed his other half once in awhile in limited form, but never in his full glory. I have to admit I was ready. Deciding to follow her lead, I decided now was as good a time as any. "Yeah, Kaine, show me. I want to see you. All of you."

Kaine scowled at Jenn and, if glares could burn, Jenn would be toast. A golden flame sparked in his eyes. "Don't you think this should be a private matter between my wife and me?"

I'd always known Jenn was strong, but the woman before me had nerves of steel. "I think the time for privacy has passed. Show her, Kaine. Unless you're afraid you might lose your baby-maker."

Oh, tell me she didn't just say that. Wincing, I held my breath and hoped Kaine didn't spontaneously combust from hot fury. Instead, his posture changed, relaxed, a small smile forming on his lips. *Is this a good sign? Or should I run and get the fire extinguisher?*

"First of all, I've explained my need for a child. Not that it's any of your business. I admit that I married her for an heir, but I love her as any man loves his woman. If we never have a child, she will still be my wife and my love."

"Aw, Kaine. That's so sweet." A tear sprang to my eyes and I leaned over to hug him. "Believe it or not, I really want to have your child. Knowing what I do—" I paused, letting the knowledge of his imminent death pass silently between us, "—how could I not?" I swallowed back a happy sob. *I'd do anything for him.*

He pressed a kiss to my forehead. "I'm sorry I deceived you. But I'm not sorry that you're my wife. With or without a child."

"Don't worry. We'll have a child." I'd give him anything and

I wanted him to know it. "I want a child with you. For you. For us."

"Even if you don't survive either the childbirth or...later?"

A wrecking ball couldn't have hit me any harder. Why the hell did she have to say that? The familiar terror that always gripped me when I thought of how my parents had really died charged outward from the pain in my gut. Now that I'd planned on having a child with Kaine, I'd pushed the awful idea of cancer deeper into the recesses of my head. Come hell or high tide, I'd give my hubby what he needed. "Jenn," I warned, but she blatantly ignored me.

"Chrissy and I have discussed her fears. I've done my best to convince her that she will not die in a car accident." Kaine wrapped his arm protectively around me. "Trust me. I'll keep her safe."

Jenn scoffed and narrowed her eyes first at Kaine, then at me. "Oh, really? I've spent years trying to get her to believe she won't die like her parents. Not that anyone can predict the future, but there are tests now to see if a person has a genetic predisposition."

"Jenn." This warning was meaner, lower in tone, but just as ineffective as the first one. "I think we need to change the topic."

"No, Chrissy, let her speak." Kaine dropped his arm, yet remained close to me. "What does a genetic predisposition have to do with predicting if she'll be in a car accident?"

The chill—from the air conditioner or from the tension—skimmed over my arm and I had to resist the urge to grab his arm and make him hug me again. "I think she's said enough." *Please, Jenn, shut the hell up. Don't make me say anything. Don't make me go through that pain again. And don't make Kaine have to go through it with me.*

I scowled at Jenn although I knew she only had my best interests at heart. She was one of the few people who knew of my fear. I'd confessed one night in our dorm room over three bottles of Boone's Farm wine and a greasy pizza. Trust me. The secret wasn't the only thing I'd upchucked later. Even now my already churning stomach flipped over sickeningly just thinking about it.

"The accident isn't the whole story." Jenn waved her hand at me. "Look at her. She's still afraid she won't live to raise her own child. And yet, she's willing to run that risk for you."

Damn her for knowing me so well. I plastered on what I hoped was a serene expression and fought to keep from trembling. A flash of my parents lying in their coffins blindsided me and I had to clutch Kaine's arm to remain steady.

Kaine checked Jenn, then studied me. "I don't understand. Why wouldn't she survive? What am I missing?" He held me again, this time so he could urge me to answer him.

"Are you frickin' kidding me, C? You haven't told him about the cancer?"

I cringed at her use of the C-word. Why would she think I'd ever want to tell him? Had she totally missed my warnings? A flash of irritation mixed with the fear twisting me up inside, slightly easing my panic. "I was going to. It's just that we've both been so busy. You know, what with the impromptu marriage, moving..." My lame-ass excuses trailed off at her stop-shitting-me expression.

"Chrissy-doll, what are you talking about? What cancer?"

Damn! There's that damn C-word again. Someone, please make them stop saying it. I closed my eyes, taking the time I needed to gather my courage. *No, no, no. I don't want to do this. Why couldn't Jenn leave well enough alone? I've kept this my secret all this time, why can't it just stay mine?*

I clasped my hands together to stop them from shaking and desperately tried to come up with a way out. *Will they believe me if I faint? No. Can I simply refuse to continue, then walk away?* But I knew Kaine would get the truth out of me no matter how long it took him. Had my hope of sparing him finally come to an end?

"Chrissy-doll, it's all right."

Kaine put both arms around me, but I kept my eyes closed. *What if I tell him everything and he no longer wants me to have his baby? What if he suddenly realizes how much of a problem a sickly wife could become?* A new fear unleashed its wrath on me and I couldn't keep a small sob from slipping out. *Did I decide at last to give him what he needs only to have him turn me down? Please, please, don't let him leave me.*

His hand on my chin brought my head up and my eyes opened. His concerned gaze met mine. A soft encouraging smile lifted the corners of his mouth. "Chrissy-doll, please hear me." His face grew determined. "No matter what fear you hold inside you, no matter what horror you think you may face, understand this. I will always be by your side. Together, we can face anything, even the worst you can possibly imagine."

I couldn't breathe. Yet my breath wasn't stolen from the crush of the rising panic. No, this time my husband had taken my breath away. I stared at him, surprise and hope washing over my dark ache, wanting what he'd said to be real. *Wow. The man really does love me. I'm no longer alone in this nightmare.* In the instant the realization struck me, became one with me, I released a large breath, then inhaled. I could breathe again because of Kaine. I inhaled another deep breath and exhaled slowly, releasing the pain, the fear, the blackness that had been with me, locked away for safekeeping for so many years. I swallowed, cleared my throat to test my voice, and finally gave in.

"Cancer runs in my family. On both sides of my family." I blurted the words out, then waited, certain he'd understand without my having to actually explain further. But no such luck.

"But don't all human families have some kind of health problem? Why would this affect the way you think about having children?" He glanced at Jenn, who had suddenly and conveniently gone mute.

Breathe, Chrissy, breathe. You can do this. You have to do this. There's no going back now. I kept watching him, drawing power from the strength, the love I saw in his face. "Both my parents died of cancer."

If I hadn't lost him before that, I had now. "But I thought your parents died in a car wreck."

My breathing grew easier and, slowly, the tension holding my body ramrod straight lessened its hold on me. *I can do this.* "They did. But what you don't understand is how they were basically already dead. They'd been ill with terminal cancer for years and had given up on life." I choked back a sob, tucked my head down, and fought to stay strong.

"It's okay. You're okay. Go on."

Kaine's strong voice and soft touch gave me the energy I needed to go on. I forced myself to continue. "Sometimes I wonder if the accident was really an accident."

I heard Jenn's gasp. That was one part of the horrible story I'd never told her—or anyone. Hell, I'd always tried not to even think about it. I pulled my head up and bit my lip to stop the tears threatening to fall. "After their deaths, I spent most of my teen years with an aunt who didn't want me. It was the same as being all alone. Do you understand? The cancer killed them long before their wreck."

Nothing had ever felt as good as Kaine's comforting tones

enveloping me with his love. “Oh, Chrissy-doll. My poor Chrissy-doll.”

I clung to him, unashamed to need his support. “The cancer is why I fear I’ll leave my child alone. But then I found out how much you wanted one, needed one... I want to give you that child, Kaine. No matter what happens later.”

“I wish you’d told me everything earlier. I could’ve spared you all this torment.”

I smiled, feeling better, freer than I had in years. “Hey, you weren’t exactly Mr. The-Whole-Truth-And-Nothing-But-The-Truth Delcaluca, you know. I tried to tell you, but I was afraid. And when I found out that’s why you married me, I didn’t know what to do.”

He cupped my chin, bringing my gaze to his. “We’re a couple of fools, you and I.”

Okay, not exactly the reaction I’d hoped for. But after everything he’d just given me, I wasn’t about to complain. “Excuse me?”

“Chrissy-doll, it’s true. I married you because the moment I saw you I knew you’d give me a strong, healthy heir.”

My heart ripped apart and yet I couldn’t pull away from him. Had I misunderstood what he’d said? Or had he only said those things to get me to open up? Jenn, on the other hand, had no problem standing up for my vital muscle’s bleeding corpse. “Damn, Kaine, don’t sugarcoat it. Tell her straight out, you lousy son-of-a-bitch.”

His growl rumbled low in his chest. “*If* you’ll let me continue...” At Jenn’s curt nod, he did. “But what I never expected to happen did. I fell in love with you as we sat by the lake talking about unimportant things. I knew I’d love you even if you never gave me a child.”

Relief quickly spread through me. “Seriously?” I let a few

tears of happiness slide down my face. "But I love you, too, and want you to have your child. I just hope I'll be around to help you raise him."

"You will be, Chrissy-doll. I can promise you that."

I smiled at him, appreciating the sentiment and letting him off the hook. "Don't make promises you can't keep, Kaine."

"But I can." His fingers traced my lips. "When a dragon mates with a human, his essence transfers to the human."

I looked to Jenn to see if she understood, but she only shrugged. "I don't get it."

"My essence will stay with you, even after the child is born. And with that inside you, all your illnesses will be cured. You can't get cancer or any other disease, Chrissy-doll, after you get pregnant with a dragon's child. With my child."

I'm not a dummy by any means, but it took awhile for that little jewel to sink in. "Holy shit. Are you saying I can have a child and not have to worry about getting cancer? I won't die and leave him?"

"No, my love, you won't."

Resting my head on his shoulder, I wiped another happy tear away and caught Jenn doing the same.

Her features hardened, however, returning to the tough Protector she was. "C, that's the best news ever. But before she gets pregnant, Kaine, you owe it to her to show her what you are. She has a right to know what her child will become."

I pushed away from him. *Oh, wow. I never thought about the child in that way. Am I prepared to have a dragon baby?* For a second, I imagined a child inside me not kicking me, but blowing a flame inside my belly. *Omigod!*

"Fine, I will." He laid his hand on top of mine. "But only because Chrissy-doll asked."

A zap of excitement raced from my head to my toes. *I'm going to see Kaine in his dragon form.*

He stood up and crossed the room. Jenn, ever vigilant, rose and paced to the other side. *Great. Why are they putting me in the middle? Literally this time?* And then it hit me. Jenn knew Kaine wouldn't hurt me. But if he wanted to shoot a gust of fire at her, then he'd have to burn me too. I didn't blame her, though.

His eyes were the first to change. The gold I'd seen on previous occasions spread like wildfire from his pupils, then outward, filling every part of his eye. A second later, my husband's beautiful jade eyes transformed into balls of golden fire.

I'd barely had time to let that change register when his face morphed, elongating, spreading his mouth wider. Lips disappeared as the face kept transforming. His eyes, glowing brilliant yellow, grew bigger, more oval in shape, losing the eyebrows above them. His ears, one of the cutest parts of him, fell off, disappearing before they hit the floor, and I struggled not to cry out. In their place, pointed ears grew, ears longer and narrower than any human's. Fangs, long and sharp, edged over the huge mouth, saliva dripping from the two longest ones.

His body shimmered as though his human body fought to retain control. But the dragon side of him continued its dominance. I gasped to see his skin separate, letting scales slide out to cover him. His clothes strained under the pressure, tearing when muscled animal replaced muscled human. His slacks ripped apart in the rear, exposing a scaly lizard-like tail that whipped around, knocking knick-knacks off the side tables.

I knew I'd felt something rough on him. But how could I have known it was scales?

Unable to take my eyes off him, I clapped a hand over my mouth. Then he stuck out his tongue. Thin, long and pointed at the end, his tongue thrust out, lashing around in the air. Mesmerized, I stared and knew I'd seen it before—between my legs. *No wonder the man can make me come with one lick.*

A roar—one very familiar to those he'd made in bed—filled the room, shattering one of the priceless vases on the table beside him.

Sensing the transformation was over, I stepped closer and timidly reached out my hand. "Kaine?" *You're my husband. But just to be sure, please answer me, Kaine. Let me know you're inside this new body.*

The expression—cold, hard, ready to wage war—I saw on his face rapidly faded away. I looked into his eyes and recognized my husband. "Kaine." Tilting his head to the side, he sent me what I thought was a dragon smile, and at that moment, I knew what I had to do.

Turning away from my husband, I beseeched Jenn. "I bet you know about the Scepter of Fire, don't you?"

Her features flickered with surprise for a second. "Yes. But I'm surprised you do."

"Then you know that it means a great deal to my husband and to the dragons."

Jenn's eyes narrowed, but I saw understanding dawning in them. "And to the Society. Yeah. So?"

I moved closer, wanting her to see how earnest I was. "Someone—and we think we know who that someone is—stole it from Kaine. We have to get it back. Will you help us?"

Jennifer Randall-Barrington, my old friend, grinned and nodded. "Sure, why not? Consider it my wedding present to the happy couple." Her grin quickly faded. "But once it's in our hot hands, we have to turn it over to the Society for safekeeping."

"No way. Not a—" Kaine bristled and Jenn matched him glare for glare.

I used my position between them. "Let's worry about getting it back first, okay?"

If All the World's a Stage, Where's My Applause?

Jenn, Kaine and I sat huddled in my office. While Jenn worked the phones calling the Atlanta Protectors, enlisting their help in locating Sabrina, and hopefully, the Scepter of Fire, Kaine finally filled me in on his activities since we'd returned from our honeymoon.

"Let me see if I have this straight. The Scepter of Fire went missing the night before we returned home."

He thumbed through the contact file on his iPhone. "Right."

I frowned and typed another phrase in the search engine on Pam's screen. "Okay, this is where I get confused. Why didn't you tell me you were staying up all night, staying away from our bed, trying to find out what had happened?"

I knew he'd gone over this several times already, but I still didn't appreciate his heavy sigh. "I told you. I didn't want to burden my new wife with this problem. You were having a hard enough time adjusting to our rather unique household."

"You mean the fact that Fitz eats mice and that one of the mice is now my personal assistant? Sheesh, Kaine, I thought I was going crazy." I slapped him on the arm. Fairly hard too because I was kind of angry at him. "What the hell is she, anyway? Another type of dragon?"

"No. Fitz is a special creature, er, individual."

I snorted at his attempt to cover his mistake. "Pff. I think you had it right the first time."

"Fitz is a witziwilder."

"A what's-a-what?"

"Seriously?" Jenn spun around in her chair to gape at Kaine. "Get outta here! I've heard the rumors, the stories, but I never believed they actually existed."

"*You* didn't believe?" I was getting used to being the last to know, but that didn't make me any happier about it. "Never mind. Fill the poor schmuck of a paranormal investigator in."

"As I said, she's a witziwilder. They're very rare and only a few people know of their existence. Fitz is very old—"

Ha, I knew she was a cranky old hag.

"—and has worked for the Delcaluca family for two centuries. Although she makes a wonderful personal assistant, her main duty is to protect me from harm. Her mother gave her life for my father."

"So that's why she's hangs around you so much. She's your bodyguard and Girl Friday." *I knew it!* I was elated to have gotten at least one thing right.

"Correct. Unfortunately, she subsists on a diet comprised primarily of mice, which, of course, makes hiring servants—especially mice, who make the best servants—next to impossible."

Ya think? Getting eaten had to be a hard sell on the job description. "Missy was going to be one of her dinners, wasn't she?" I pictured a screaming Missy locked inside Fitz's mousetrap. No way would I let that happen to any of the other poor animals in her clutches. "We can not allow her to keep eating the mice, Kaine. They're people like us. Or at least they can be if you change them into people, right?"

"Correct. However, not all mice make good servants. It's a very difficult process and I only do so when I'm sure the mouse in question can handle the transformation."

"But, Kaine, if you changed them all into people, they wouldn't end up as dinner for Fitz. Or for a cat."

Kaine tossed me a wicked grin. "Even dragons have their limits. I do what I can. Besides, changing too many mice into people would disrupt the natural order of things."

Although his answer made sense, I still didn't like the idea of poor little creatures being gobbled up by a larger, less likable one—namely Fitz. "Can't she eat anything else?"

"Well, she can survive on another source of food. But she doesn't like it much."

Jenn and I had the same thought and spoke at the same time. "Too damn bad for her."

"Well, boo-hoo for her."

We high-fived. "What's the other source?" As long as it wasn't dragon's wives, I was okay with it. Maybe.

"Spam."

I paused, unsure that I'd heard him correctly. "Did you say spam? As in the canned ham-type spam?"

"That's right."

I couldn't help it. I roared with laughter. "Then spam she eats from now on."

"Now, Chrissy-doll, I can't ask Fitz to never eat a mouse again. It's her natural diet."

Talk about organic diets! But maybe he was right. Although witziwilder eating rodent wasn't listed on any Circle of Life diagram I'd ever seen, I guess he did have a point. "Fine. We'll compromise. She can eat any mouse she wants—as long as she catches and eats it outside our home. *And* it isn't one of our servants."

"Fine, if you insist."

"So if she's your bodyguard, where is she right now?" *Figures.* The one time she wasn't around was the one time I'd like her nearby. I'd love to get another load of her true bad self. I'd been too busy running to get a good look last time.

"She's following another lead." He sent me a knowing look and I diverted my gaze. "Now, let's get back to the more pressing business at hand."

"But why didn't you trust me with the truth about everything? I mean, I was bound to find out eventually."

Kaine ran his palm down my arm. "Think about it, Chrissy-doll. You make your living debunking the existence of people like me. I didn't want to take that away from you until I had no other choice."

We both turned at Jenn's snicker. "Did we say something funny?" As far as I was concerned, she wasn't totally off the hook for not telling me that she was a Protector when we were in college.

"He's feeding you a load of crap."

Kaine's eyes flashed gold and I reached out to touch his arm. "Easy, boy."

"Get real, bub. You didn't tell her because you were afraid she'd freak out and leave you. Or just think you were nuts and leave you. Either way, you were afraid of losing her."

He grumbled and I took that as confirmation. "So? How about you? You haven't exactly been forthcoming with me."

Now it was Jenn's turn to look contrite. "No-o-o. But let's not forget that I work for a secret organization. Telling people is kind of frowned on."

The tune of "Puff the Magic Dragon" interrupted us, turning our attention to Kaine's iPhone.

"Seriously?" Jenn said. "*Puff*?"

Kaine managed to look both offended and embarrassed. "I like the song, okay?" He punched a button and turned his chair away from the mocking Jenn, placing his back to us. "Delcaluca here." A few mumbled words later, he turned back and handed the phone to Jenn. "It's for you."

"Uh, thanks." Jenn took the phone and morphed into Protector mode. "Jennifer Randall-Barrington here." She listened for a few moments, exhilaration glowing on her face. "Great work. No, no. My, uh, associates and I will take it from here." Her calm movement belied the excitement on her face as she handed the phone back to Kaine.

"I wish you hadn't given my phone number to the Society."

Jenn motioned toward Partner, who was busy communicating with Mini-Pam through a special cable Kaine had given her. The two devices had been virtually and often literally inseparable for the past hour. "Can I help it if your Mini-Pam seduced Partner and made him worthless? Besides, shouldn't you be more interested in the fact that we know where Sabrina is?"

Kaine gripped the arms of his chair. "Where is she?" He jumped up, ready to spring into action.

"Does she have the scepter with her?" I followed my hubby's lead.

"One of the Atlanta's Protectors said his source told him that Sabrina is at a downtown theatre."

Huh? "A theatre? You mean instead of getting the hell out of Dodge, she's out for a night on the town? That doesn't make any sense." I could see by Kaine's expression that the news had thrown him too.

"If I remember anything at all about Sabrina, it's this. She doesn't always do what makes sense, and she'll lie whenever she can. Even when lying doesn't make sense." Kaine slipped his phone into his pocket and headed to the door.

Thirty minutes later we were in downtown Atlanta and standing outside a small neighborhood theatre. The name of the play on the marquee caught my attention. "I do not believe this."

"What is it, Chrissy-doll?" Kaine scanned the area around us, trying to see what I saw.

"I know this play." I still couldn't believe it.

"*Magical Mayhem*." Jenn shrugged her shoulders. "So?"

I motioned for them to follow me to the ticket office. "This is Thad's new play."

"Does your pal know Sabrina?" Kaine handed the ticket taker the money and took the stubs.

"Not that I know of. Besides, just because she's attending the play doesn't mean she knows Thad." Once inside, I could hear the voices coming from the stage. "Your source said he saw her outside the theatre, right before she went inside?"

Kaine nodded. "That's right."

"Then we'd better get in there." Fortunately for us, it being a small theatre meant no ushers or doormen to stop us from entering while the play was going on. Leading the charge—*why the hell am I leading the charge anyway?*—I pushed the door open, sending a shaft of light stabbing into the darkened theatre. Several patrons turned to glare and Jenn quickly shut the door behind us.

The stage, drenched in dim lighting, boasted a medieval

scene. Three actors, two men and one woman, were center stage. The two men, dressed in knights' costumes, were battling each other to win the fair lady's heart. The knight in black, who I assumed was the villain of the story, thrust an extremely fake-looking sword against the chest of the good knight wearing white. The white knight fell to the ground and the lady screamed. Unfortunately for my friend, Thad's new production wouldn't win any awards. *Gees, Thad, how corny. I guess I'll have to play the ever-supportive friend and say the play was terrific. Sometimes ya just gotta lie to spare feelings.*

"Whew. Thank goodness we didn't find out about Sabrina being here earlier. I'd hate to have sat through the entire play."

I elbowed Jenn in the ribs. "Shush. My friend wrote this play. Oh, and there he is." Thad, dressed in a flowing white robe, stepped from behind a cardboard rock.

"He has the Scepter of Fire."

I heard Kaine's whisper and followed his gaze. Thad may have skimped on the set decorations and props for everything else, but the scepter he held was magnificent. Towering well over Thad's five foot five inches, the golden staff was encrusted with elaborate ornamentation. Glowing at the top of the staff was a fierce dragon, his claws extended to strike his prey. His wings were spread, ready to lift him skyward.

I know sometimes I'm not the brightest bulb in the fireplace (yeah, whatever!) but I had to look at the scepter several times before Kaine's words finally settled into place. "No way. Are you telling me that that's *the* Scepter of Fire?"

His tense body language and hardened features said it all. Could Sabrina have told the truth when she said someone had taken it from her? Did Thad steal it from her? But then she'd reversed herself, acting as though she had it and Kaine would never be able to find her or the artifact. To say I was a bit puzzled was an understatement.

"How the hell did Thad get the scepter?" No way would my friend steal something. At least I didn't think he would.

"That question and its answer can wait until later." Kaine pointed toward the right side of the theatre. "I think the important question right now is...how do we keep the scepter out of Sabrina's and Tuo's hands?"

Jenn and I followed his direction. Tuo and Sabrina rose from their seats, both of them enraged to see us.

"I do believe we better get our butts in high gear." Jenn was off and running toward the stage with Kaine dead on her heels before I had time to register what she'd said. I was, however, quick enough to notice that Tuo and Sabrina had started their own mad dash for the stage.

"Hey, wait up!" I sprinted down the aisle.

Onstage, the actors continued with the scene unaware that five people rapidly approached them. The audience, thinking our appearance was part of the production, darted their attention between the stage and the race in the aisles.

Have I mentioned how fast Kaine is? The man, using his dragony powers, makes an Olympian sprinter look like an octogenarian with a walker. He passed Jenn in no time. Had he gotten an equal start with Sabrina I have no doubt he would've made it to the steps leading onstage before her. But life isn't just. Or whatever they say.

Sabrina hit the stairs running, taking two steps at a time, making it to the top seconds before Kaine did on the other side. Unfortunately for our team, Thad and the Scepter of Fire were closer to Sabrina.

I slammed to a stop, waiting to see what my hubby and his ex would do. Kaine glared at Sabrina, opened his mouth and let out the loudest bellow I'd ever heard. Audience members clapped their hands over their ears but kept their mesmerized stares on the action.

The black knight, showing his true colors, let out a girlish scream and fell to the floor. The white knight, using his part as the wounded hero to full advantage, huddled next to him. The actress was the only performer with any real balls. She stomped her foot and shouted for all the non-union actors to get the fuck off the stage.

I couldn't help but admire her spunk. Or at least I did until Kaine jumped—flew?—across the stage, aiming directly for Sabrina with the fair lady directly in the line of fire. She squealed and joined her fellow thespians on the floor. Poor Thad, standing stock still with a horrified expression on his face, was the only actor left in a vertical position. But not for long.

Sabrina's lips curled into a snarl and she hurled her body toward Thad. She struck him, grabbing for the scepter at the same time. Thad, never one to let anyone upstage him for long, regained motor function and grappled with Sabrina for possession of the scepter. By this time, Tuo had made it to the first step of the stairs and stood scowling at Jenn who was at the top of the other steps. They paused, waiting for the other to make the first move.

Call me a coward if you will, but I didn't see any reason to join the others on the stage. Besides, obviously being the slowpoke in the bunch, I wouldn't have made it there in time anyway. (That's my story and I'm sticking to it.) Still, I wish I would have tried. Maybe then I could've saved Kaine from what happened next.

Kaine, seeing Thad wrestling with Sabrina, landed a few feet away from them. "Sabrina, let go of the scepter or suffer the consequences."

Yep, that's my guy. Even when he isn't in a position to shout orders, he'll do it anyway. I know it's so not women's lib, but I rather liked his machismo.

Sabrina, however, had her own set of cojones. With one hand wrapped around the scepter, she lashed out with the other, striking Thad in the head. He fell backward, letting go of the staff and demolishing the cardboard rock.

"Hey, you can't get away with hurting my friend!" I pushed through the crowd of people who had finally figured out that the chaos on the stage was real. People shouted and pushed toward the back of the theatre.

Sabrina sneered at me and cackled. "Very well, my little bitch. If I can't harm your friend, then I'll kill your lover instead!" With a gleeful screech, she thrust out her arm and pointed the golden dragon head at Kaine.

A blazing ball of fire shot out from the golden dragon's mouth, spitting sparks outward like a meteor hurtling through the earth's atmosphere.

"Watch out, Kaine!" But I hadn't gotten the words out of my mouth soon enough.

Kaine threw his body sideways. Even as fast as he was, he couldn't dodge the orb of flame completely. The ball missed his chest (and his heart!) and struck him in the leg. The fireball disintegrated, leaving a large gaping hole. Kaine fell to the floor. He clutched at his wound, ready to stem the flow of blood, but no blood came forth. Instead, a cloud of black smoke billowed out of the wound.

What few audience members were still running from the theatre ran faster. Thad and the other actors kept to the floor, terror making similar masks of their faces. At last, Jenn and Tuo began to move.

"You bitch!" I darted around the end of the orchestra pit

and dashed up the steps. Kaine tried to struggle to his feet, but fell down, yowling in pain. Jenn rushed to my husband's side, catching him before he hit the floor. Sabrina, laughing, whirled on Tuo, knocked him off his feet and scurried past him. Taking only seconds to recover, he rushed after her.

"Kaine, Kaine." I slid next him like a baseball player sliding into second base. "Kaine." Somehow, I couldn't get any other word out of my mouth. The rest of them were trapped behind the boulder of fear stuck in my throat.

Remarkably, he raised his hand from his wound and pressed his palm to my cheek to comfort me. Smoke trailed out of the wound again and I had to fight the urge to upchuck. "I'm okay, Chrissy-doll." He grimaced against the pain. "Or at least I will be." Waving his hand at her, he beseeched Jenn, "Go. Get Sabrina. Don't let her get away with the scepter."

Jenn shook her head. "Sorry. I stick with my friends and take care of them first. But don't worry. We'll find her."

He grumbled, displeased at her for not following orders. "Are you women always this stubborn?"

Thad, having herded the other actors off the stage, knelt beside us. "What the hell was that thing? I had no idea when I—" His eyes grew round as his mouth grew smaller and closed up shop.

Jenn and I exchanged a look. A blind man could see that Thad was holding something back. But Kaine was the priority right now. "Come on, C, let's get your man to a dressing room and sort out this wound."

Together, Jenn and I wrapped his arms around our shoulders, putting him between us. Although it was slow going—partly because my hubby complained about not needing help—we finally made it to Thad's tiny dressing room, a converted storage room. Gently, we lowered the glowering Kaine onto the fuchsia chaise longue.

"You should have gone after her. Now that she has the scepter, she's not going to hang around. She'll hop on her ship and head for the next galaxy as soon as she can."

The next galaxy? As in *The Final Frontier*? I checked Jenn's face to see if she'd heard the same thing, but she didn't seem fazed by his declaration. Funny thing, though, when I did the same with Thad, he had the same un-surprised face.

Since I was apparently the only one who'd heard Kaine's outlandish statement, I had to ask. "What are you rambling about? Did you hurt your head?" I reached up to part his hair and examine his head, but he slapped my hand away.

My hubby definitely wasn't the best patient. *Note to self: when Kaine gets hurt or sick, stay the hell out of his way. Or better yet, make Fitz the target of his grouchiness.*

"Chrissy..."

I frowned, unhappy at the sudden loss of the *doll* part of my name. "What?" Sure he was injured and all, but my tolerance for his attitude had run out about three minutes earlier. "So she really is an alien? Like from outer space-type alien?" I laughed. Yeah, you'd think by now that nothing could surprise me. After all, I'd gone from a solid skeptic of anything out of the normal to having encounters with strange beings, werewolves, mice-turned-humans, and best of all, running with dragons. What was a little alien compared to all that? Besides, I'd heard someone say she was an alien several times before this. Although, admittedly, I'd never really believed it until now.

"He's right, C. I wasn't sure at first, but I kinda thought she might be an Off-worlder."

Thad, still playing hide-and-seek with my glances, busied himself with cleaning Kaine's wound. Amazingly, the leg already looked better with the hole not as large as I remembered it. Was super-healing a dragon thing?

Kaine sighed and gave in to the situation. "Her Earth name is Sabrina Stellina because we don't have the physical capabilities to pronounce her real name, her Zeiwacian name. When she and I were together—" He paused to gauge my reaction, but I kept a straight face "—she was an intergalactic trader dealing with unusual artifacts from hundreds of planets. After we parted ways, I'd heard she'd gone rogue and teamed up with that traitor, Tuo, to steal the Scepter of Fire."

I sat next to him on the lounge, needing more than my own legs to support me. *A real alien. I met a real alien.* "But if you knew, why didn't you get it back from her sooner?"

"The theft happened while we were in Vegas." He suddenly appeared uncomfortable, but kept on. "Besides, the scepter was left in my care. I was ashamed that I'd allowed it to be stolen right out of my home. My former home. The one before the mansion. But I was too busy wooing you and let my guard down."

Wooing? I did love those old-fashioned phrases. I dismissed the wayward thought and refocused. I had to know if my suspicion was correct. "Did you buy the mansion as a present for me, for our new home? Or because you wanted a new place, a safer place once you recovered the scepter?"

At least he had the decency to look sheepish. "Both."

First my husband marries me to give him an heir without bothering to ask me if I want children. Then he buys a house because he wants a safer place for his possessions. I had to wonder if I was one of those possessions. I squashed the thought, reserving it for later. "But that still doesn't answer why you didn't track her down and get it back straight away."

"Like I told you before, Sabrina is a habitual liar. Of course she denied having taken the scepter. I stayed up late at night, away from our bed—" he shot me an apologetic smile, "—getting reports from my friends who had tried following her, but they lost sight of her every time. We were lucky when we caught up with her. Unfortunately, they never saw her with the scepter. Finally they did see her with Tuo. He's always wanted the scepter so he could rule all the dragons in the dynasty. It made sense that he was involved. I had no choice except to wait for them to show me where to find the scepter." He whipped out his hand and clutched Thad's collar. "I didn't know, however, that someone had taken the scepter from Sabrina."

Thad squeaked, reminding me of Missy. I hadn't seen my assistant since that embarrassing night Kaine and I had made love on top of my desk, in front of Pam. Since the two of them were so closely connected, I'd assumed Pam had told Missy about the revealing show. Frankly, I'd avoided her. But I'd have to make amends soon.

"How did you get the scepter, Thad?" I checked Kaine's leg and saw the wound looked even better. Breathing a sigh of relief, I motioned for him to turn my squirming friend loose. "Talk, Thad. Now."

"I didn't steal it," he protested and tried to scoot away from Kaine. Kaine, however, growled a warning for him to stay put. "I, uh, borrowed it from my neighbor's house."

"Borrowed it?" Jenn snorted and rolled her eyes. "Since when does a leprechaun borrow anything?"

"Are you kidding me? Is there anyone in my life who is actually who and what I think they are?" I examined Thad from top to bottom. "You're a leprechaun? A pot-of-gold-at-the-end-of-the-rainbow kind of leprechaun?" I knew my mouth was hanging open, but I couldn't get it to shut.

Thad's mischievous smile said it all. "Chrissy, where do you think I get my money? You can't seriously believe my plays pay for my lifestyle. Shoot, most of the time I have to dip into my own stash to pay the other actors." He shook himself as though the idea of paying others disgusted him. "Please don't tell any of my leprechaun friends I play Robin Hood to starving actors. If they find out, they'll disown me and take away my ability to find gold. Then I really will be a broke actor."

Jenn patted her buzzing hip pocket. "I wish I'd unplugged Partner from Mini-Pam and left them at your house." She waved away the irritation. "Never mind. We need to stay on topic here, people. I'll bet Sabrina's not sitting around chit-chatting."

"She's right." Kaine centered his frustration on Thad, making him squeal again. "You say you borrowed it from a neighbor. Do you know who the neighbor is?"

"No. I never saw them. I, uh, just opened the door with a little magical dust and let myself in. I found the scepter hidden behind a secret door and knew it was the perfect prop for my play." That mischievous smile returned. "Besides, who'd expect a leprechaun to pass up a golden staff?"

"Who indeed?" Kaine lurched off the lounge and hobbled toward the door, shrugging off my attempts to help him. "I'm almost entirely healed. If you must come with me, then leave me alone."

"Where are we going?" Jenn asked, staying in step with Kaine while Thad and I followed behind.

"Obviously, Sabrina is Thad's neighbor. And since she was staying by the lake, I have a good hunch where we can find her ship. And if we find her ship—"

"We find her and the scepter." I grinned at him, happy to see his movements growing easier. I wasn't so sure, however, that I wanted to find Sabrina. Especially not when she still had the Scepter of Fire to use as a weapon.

Does Anyone Speak Zeiwacian?

"There she is!" Thad shouted and swung his arm out, striking me across my neck.

Choke. "Damn it, Thad." Cough. "Watch it."

Kaine growled from the back seat next to Jenn.

"Sorry. I didn't mean to—" But Thad's apology got lost in the frantic scramble of everyone jumping out of the car almost before I'd managed to slam on the brake. Kaine moved with lightning speed with Jenn taking a close second. Thad and I brought up the rear, hurrying to catch up with them at the top of a small rise. I caught up with the two leaders and almost slammed into Kaine's back. However, he didn't appear to notice. Instead, he stared down at the scene below us.

"Tuo's with her." Kaine nodded his head at the two figures standing on the dock. "Be careful."

Tuo Chow had Sabrina cornered at the end of the dock, and from the way he was waving his arms about, I knew the argument had gotten heated. I could hear his words, but couldn't understand what he said. Sabrina, her face a mask of fury, shouted at him in a strange language. "Is she speaking alien?"

A small smile broke the concentration on Kaine's features. "Yes. Zeiwacian is one of over a few billion different alien dialects."

A few billion? Would I ever get used to this new parallel world and its strange inhabitants? "Wow."

Jenn bounced on her feet, raring to go after them. "Kaine, let's go. If we're lucky, they'll stay involved in their argument and won't notice us. Let's not lose the element of surprise."

"Agreed." I took a step forward, ready to charge into battle, but Kaine grabbed my arm and tugged me back. "No, Chrissy-doll, you and Thad should stay here."

"No problem."

I scowled at Thad, wanting to berate him for his cowardice. "If you hadn't *borrowed*—" I made quotes around the word, "—the scepter in the first place, Kaine's people could've found it before all this happened. You are not sitting this one out."

"Thad and you can help by staying out of the way." Kaine nodded at Jenn. "Leave this to the professionals."

"The professionals?" I spit out the word *professional* as though it gave me a bad taste. "I understand Jenn is a professional, but how the heck are you a professional?"

Gold filled Kaine's green eyes. "I've done this kind of thing before. I can handle myself."

"Yeah, well, I'm a professional, too, ya know. I've been dealing with unpredictable and dangerous situations for a long time now. Without any help."

"Chrissy-doll, I don't mean to offend you, but telling an old lady that the crumbs left on the kitchen counter were made by a rodent and not her dearly departed husband raiding the cookie jar doesn't make you ready to handle the likes of Sabrina and Tuo." His face softened. "Besides, if anything happened to you... Don't you know how much I love you?"

I had a tear in my eye and my heart grew full of happy emotion. I couldn't speak when a flash of light, blindingly intense, blared outward from the edge of the dock. Feeling like I should've ducked, I turned to see Tuo lying on his back. His body was covered in the same black smoke I'd seen coming from Kaine's leg. But the blast he'd taken must've had more power behind it because his body had been thrown backward, all the way to the edge of the lawn.

Kaine shook me, returning my attention to him. "Do you see now why you have to stay here?" He kissed me then, hard, driving the breath out of me. Too bad for him, however, that it couldn't drive away my stubbornness. Turning on his heel, he jerked his head toward where Sabrina stood staring at Tuo, telling Jenn to follow. The golden dragon on the end of the scepter glowed brightly.

Kaine was halfway down the hill before I took my first step, dragging Thad along with me. "Damn chauvinistic men. Especially chauvinistic dragon men."

The element of surprise we'd counted on didn't last long. Sabrina looked up, saw Kaine and said something that sounded like a mix of French and a garbage disposal grinding up bones. With an evil laugh, she pointed the Scepter of Fire at Kaine.

I screamed, not only as a warning, but in surprise at what Jenn did next. She threw herself sideways into the air, like a gymnast catapulting over the pummel horse, placing her body in front of Kaine. A ball of fire erupted from the staff and sped toward them, blazing like a sun ready to explode into a thousand smaller stars. Kaine tried to pull her out of harm's way, but wasn't fast enough. The fireball struck her shoulder, flipping her backward, spinning her over Kaine to land in a crumpled pile at my feet.

"Jenn!" I knelt next to her, saw the whiteness in her face, the dark smoke rising from her shoulder, and sent a prayer skyward. "Please, don't let her be dead. Please don't let her be dead." But Jenn wasn't the only one I had to worry about. Thinking I could do nothing more for my friend, I tore my gaze away from her to see Kaine changing, transforming as he ran toward Sabrina.

The thought of losing my husband sliced through me. "No!" I flew (okay, not literally, but you know what I mean) down the hill, my heart in my throat and a stitch in my side. "Kaine!"

Sabrina spun the scepter in her hand, reminding me of a gunslinger spinning his pistol in a show of ability. "The Scepter of Fire is mine. Mine to take and sell to the highest bidder." She glanced at the still-smoking body of Tuo. "Too bad for Tuo he didn't want to pay my price." She giggled, mean and nasty. "And yet, he ended up paying an even greater price and getting nothing."

Kaine roared his anger, his transformation nearly complete. His clothes tore away, exposing scales running the length of his body. His head, no longer recognizable as human, grew, stretching the bones and narrowing the eyes. Claws shook shoes off and curled, ready to take prey in their grip. His tongue lashed out, licking his lips in anticipation. A tail slashed the air. At last, with the metamorphosis almost complete, wings sprouted on his back. I kept running and watched my husband the dragon take flight.

No longer looking confident, Sabrina screeched a high-pitched piercing sound that echoed in the trees surrounding us. I stumbled and kept going, getting closer to Kaine, who now hovered in the air above her. She pointed the Scepter of Fire, striking Kaine in the chest.

He shrieked, his tongue whipping out. Fire burst from his mouth, spinning in a whirl of white-hot fury toward Sabrina. She thrust out the Scepter of Fire again, blocking the flame rushing her way and turning it back on Kaine. His own fire hit him in his left wing. With a snarl of pain and anger, he dipped to the side, furiously flapping the other wing, struggling to stay in the air.

"Leave him alone, you skank!" I didn't care if she used the scepter's power on me. Anything was better than seeing Kaine hurt.

But I was a mere pest, unworthy of her attention. With a twirl, Sabrina changed.

The beautiful redhead was gone. In her place stood an ugly creature with two heads. Bulging eyes covered each of those heads, all of them moving in different directions. Limb after limb burst from the black-green body, ripping her clothes to tatters to expose a black-red puss oozing from open gashes in her skin. Her legs disappeared, either under her body or gone for good. I couldn't tell which.

I skidded to a stop directly under Kaine and watched, horrified and too entranced to tear my gaze away from her. She doubled in size, stretching until she was as wide as she was tall. Three tongues wiggled from each of the lipless mouths and flicked spittle at me.

"Oh, gross!" I'd had babies spit up on me, dogs barf on my feet, and maggots fall on top of me. This black-red gook, however, was the worst. "Keep your phlegm in your own mouth, you bitch."

Kaine cheered me and I have to admit I was as surprised as he was at my bravado. I guess getting spit up on was the last straw for me.

Sabrina garbled what I assumed was her native language, but I understood the threat clearly enough to duck. A fireball zipped perilously close to my head. She screeched her displeasure at her miss, and with another even higher-pitched shriek, turned her massive body around to face the lake. Pulling a round device from somewhere on her body—and I so didn't want to know from where—she pointed it at the lake and pushed a blinking red button. The button's color slowly changed from red to green. Water in the middle of the lake boiled, making waves that rolled toward the shore.

What the hell? Is she summoning a lake monster? Does Lake Lanier have its very own Loch Ness Monster? I watched, too intrigued to do anything else.

Instead of a sea monster, a spaceship broke through the surface of the water. Sabrina pushed the remote device again and the ship wavered, turning what I assumed was the front toward her. A luminous glow extended from the ship and across the water, stopping when it struck the dock in front of her. With a gleeful cry, she stepped onto the light path and shuffled toward the ship.

"Chrrriisssy-daawlll."

I guess a tongue like Kaine's dragon tongue must wreak havoc on pronunciation. I swung away from Sabrina and found it hard to stand. Kaine had changed again, not in appearance this time, but in size. Like the dragons of ancient lore, he grew, enlarging his body once, then twice, then a third time. The enormous dragon flapped his wings, pushing great gusts of air at me. I staggered, trying to stay on my feet.

Jerking his head, he indicated his back. He lowered to the ground, not actually landing, but only inches from touching down. "Gwet ooonn."

Is he serious? He really expects me to ride on his back like one of those heroes in a fairy tale? I took a step closer and stopped. "I don't think I can. What if I fall off?"

"I'wll catchsh youw."

"Not exactly reassuring, ya know. How about 'Don't worry, Chrissy-doll, you can't fall off. I promise.'"

"Chrrrisssy-dddoll, dwon't worrsy. Youw cwan't falls offt. I pwromize."

I scoffed at him. "Too small, too late, dude."

"Thwat's not hwow vthe swaying gwoes."

I gaped at him. "Seriously? Are you seriously flapping your wings, not to mention your gums, and telling me I've got the expression wrong? Who the fwuck cares?" I'd purposely imitated his current speech impediment, needing some way to needle him.

Yet instead of throwing back a nifty retort, he simply glared at me, then pointed one claw at the escaping Sabrina. She was halfway to the ship, walking on the beam above the water. He shifted, lowering his injured wing for me to use as a ladder.

"Aw, hell." I called to Thad to take care of Jenn, gritted my teeth and ignored the warning bells clanging in my head. Trying to hurry while taking care, I climbed on top of my husband—and not on top in the good way either. "You'd better not let me fall off, you big lug."

"I wonwt."

"Argh!"

Kaine lifted in flight and I grabbed the small tuff of hair at the bottom of his neck. Pressing my legs against his body as I'd been taught to ride a horse bareback, I lay closely against him and prayed the air whipping by me wouldn't drag me off.

"Twry to grab the scepter."

Is it my imagination or is his speech getting better? Maybe it takes a little time to adjust to the tongue's new size. Wait a sec. What did he say? "Did you just tell me to try and grab the scepter?"

"Yes. Swabrina is cwoncentrating on walking the light pwath. This is our best chance to snatch wit away."

Pff. My best chance, if you could call it a best *anything.* Yet I knew he was right. We couldn't let her get to the ship with the scepter. "Okay, dive bomb her and I'll pretend I'm grabbing for the brass, er, gold ring."

He pointed his head down, flapped his wings with extra gusto and dived downward. I held on and swallowed back a yelp of fear.

"Chrissy-doll."

"Yeah?"

"You should open your eyes."

I hadn't realized that I'd closed them. "Uh, yeah. That would probably be wise. Oh shit!"

Suddenly Kaine stopped flapping his wings and curled them to his side. Dipping one side lower, he turned, speeding toward the shuffling Sabrina, who had her two heads looking toward the ship. I dug my nails into the rough scales on his neck and shifted my weight the other way.

Please don't let me fall off. Please don't let me fall off. Closer we flew, faster with the wind blowing my hair straight back from my head. I squinted against the wind battering my eyes and watched Sabrina's grotesque figure growing closer, bigger, until at last I reached out to grab the staff.

As though she'd waited for just the right moment, Sabrina whirled around and pointed the Scepter of Fire at us. A huge fireball burst from the golden dragon's mouth and spun our direction. Knowing I could do nothing to stop the fireball, I closed my eyes and waited for hot burning torture to envelope me.

Kaine's body rocked underneath me, loosening my grip and sending me sliding down his back toward his tail. I opened my eyes and screamed. Kaine, his head twisted around to see me, lifted his tail. My butt rammed against it, stopping my slide and my impending freefall off his back.

Black smoke filled my eyes. The fireball had missed me, but had struck home elsewhere. *Kaine!* Wiping my eyes and peering through the sooty fog, I gaped at the hole in his right wing. "Kaine. Both wings." As if he didn't already know.

He didn't answer. He couldn't. His eyes were closed and short pants of flame puffed from his mouth. With a growl that filled my heart with an overwhelming ache, he tucked his head, sending us into a downward spiral.

"Kaine! Please pull up. Kaine, can you hear me?"

We plummeted toward the lake. I fought the dizziness brought about from his spin and got ready for the impact, watching the water grow closer. I knew the end was near for one or both of us and I couldn't let that happen without saying what I had to say one last time. "Kaine, I love you."

At that moment, he lifted his head and I saw love even within the glowing gold. "I love you, too, Chrissy-doll." Seconds before hitting the water, he curled his body upward with a groan, slowing the descent until he abruptly stopped only a few feet above the water.

"Omigod, you saved us."

"Swim, Chrissy-doll, swim." With a great shake, he threw me off his back and into the water.

The shock of plunging into the water wasn't as great as the shock that Kaine had thrown me off. I sank several feet before finally getting my bearing and breast-stroking to the surface. "Why the hell did you do that, Kaine?"

He hovered above me, tilting his head toward the lake's edge where Thad had commandeered a small row boat and was pushing it into the water. "Thad will help you."

"But why did you drop me? We have to stop Sabrina." My

heart squeezed tightly in my chest. "Kaine, you're still smoking." Real fear, colder than I'd even known held me in its grip. I could barely whisper his name in question. "Kaine?"

He flapped his wings twice, putting himself several yards from me. Casting me a pain-filled look, he closed his eyes and fell into the water.

The waves from his impact carried me away from him. "Kaine! No!" I struck out, battling a second wave and swimming as hard as I could. I had to get to him. Sabrina's victorious laughter spurred me on, but my arms ached from my ride. I couldn't move forward.

Exhaustion overtook me, almost a relief against the heartache tearing my heart open. Tears streamed down my face and I gazed at the spot where he'd gone under. I stopped treading water and drifted under the waves, ready to join him in death.

I kept my eyes open under the water, hoping to get one last glimpse of the man, the dragon I loved, but the water was too murky. I cried out, losing air to give one last plea to bring him back to me. *How can I have finally found the man of my dreams only to lose him so soon?* A pain, greater than I'd ever experienced, sliced into me, cutting through me like a dagger to my soul. *Kaine, where are you? Please, don't leave me. Take me with you.* I sighed, releasing more of my air, and prepared to die. I closed my eyes, letting the emptiness enveloping me take over.

I wonder if dragons and humans end up in the same afterlife? I hope so. Kaine and I had so little time together. Our children will never have their chance to live. Goodbye, Kaine. Goodbye, my love.

Something grabbed my hair, yanking on me, and I yelled, making me expel the little air I had left in my body. I tried grabbing whatever was dragging me toward the surface, but I simply didn't have the energy to fight. Darkness closed in on me and I let it come.

A hand struck my cheek, jolting my eyes open. I jerked up, sputtering, coughing and spraying water everywhere. I blinked in the bright sunlight.

"Sheesh, Chrissy, don't get me all wet. I hate getting wet."

I gawked at Thad, then glanced around the rowboat. "Where's Kaine? Did you find him, too?"

"Well, he ain't in this dingy, sister." He noticed the anguish in my face and softened. "I'm sorry. I haven't seen him since he..." He tipped his head toward the place in the lake where Kaine had fallen.

"He's gone. Dead and gone." An evil cackle sickened me.

A terrified expression on Thad's face turned me in the direction of the voice, the witch of the lake, my husband's murderer, Sabrina. She'd made it to her ship and stood outside, holding the Scepter of Fire like a queen surveying her kingdom. "Only a strong person wielding the Scepter of Fire can kill a dragon, especially an enormously powerful dragon like Delcaluca." She lifted the scepter, then brought it down on the ramp of her ship with a *thud.* Thrusting out her chin, she shouted, "I, Sabrina Stellina, Zeiwacian citizen, killed the dragon, Kaine Delcaluca, leader of the Dragon Dynasty. Now I will control all the dragons of the universe."

Fury hotter than I'd ever felt broke free in me. I wanted nothing more than to take that alien bitch down. I stood up, balancing in the small boat and pointed at her. "I'm coming after you, you color-changing whore. No matter how far you go, no matter how long it takes, I will kill you."

(In retrospect, I had more guts than sense at the moment, but you can understand how I felt, right?)

Sabrina arched an eyebrow—or what I thought was an eyebrow—on one of her heads. "You? You're going to kill me? A poor pitiful Earthling? I don't think so." She took a step forward, coming off the ramp and back onto the light path. "As a kind ruler, I'll do you a favor and put you out of your misery."

Thad slapped a palm over my mouth, stifling my angry retort. He whispered in my ear, "Have you never heard the expression *live to fight another day*?"

"You'll thank me for letting you die before I send my army of dragons over your land, extinguishing all your pathetic lives." With a wicked grin on both her faces, she lifted the Scepter of Fire and pointed the golden dragon head at us.

Whip Lashed!

"Oh, shit! Row, Chrissy, row." Thad snatched up the oars and started rowing. I paused, unwilling, even in the face of certain death, to let her escape.

"Ow!"

Pain shot up my leg and I whirled on Thad. "What the hell?"

"I am not going to die in an ill-fated attempt to kill her." He jabbed his hand toward the other set of oars. "Now row!"

Grumbling, I plopped down and took the oars. "Someone has to take her down. Earth is doomed if we don't." I knew I sounded like a second-rate actress in a third-rate sci-fi flick, but the truth is the truth no matter how corny it sounds.

Thad opened his mouth to argue but ended up choking on the wall of water that washed over us. Once I'd gotten the hair out of my eyes, I swiveled around and saw the only thing that could ever have made me happy.

Kaine, glorious and golden, flew in circles around Sabrina, lashing out with his claws and flaming her with his personal blowtorch. The alien tried to dodge his blows, but couldn't. She was too awkward to keep up with the speeding dragon. But she wasn't one to stay cowed for long.

Letting his flames scorch her and his claws rake her,

Sabrina stood up and thrust out the Scepter of Fire. The base of the scepter flashed into flame, sending a golden-red streak up the staff toward the dragon's head. The streak hit the golden tip and a dazzling light zapped outward, illuminating the dimming light of the evening.

Kaine roared, leaned backward in almost a sitting position, and lashed out with his tail. A fireball blazed past him, narrowly missing his head. He struck back and pounded Sabrina, hitting first one head then the other. She screeched, flinging her arms outward and clutched her heads in her hands.

The Scepter of Fire spun away, racing across the water with the speed of a missile. Kaine didn't move, looking at Sabrina and then the scepter as though trying to decide what he should do. At last, he bellowed, flapped his wings in one powerful move and flew after the scepter. The scepter, however, splashed into the center of the lake before he could reach it. Kaine dove into the water after the scepter.

"Go, Kaine!" I jumped up in the boat, shouting with glee, nearly capsizing it before Thad wrestled me back to my seat.

"Are you trying to swamp us? We already took in enough water when Kaine came out of the lake."

I grinned at him. "I would think as an actor that you'd appreciate a grand entrance." Who could blame my happy hysterics? One minute I'd lost my love forever, and the next, he was kicking alien ass.

"I'd appreciate a grand exit more. Especially her grand exit."

I followed his gaze to see Sabrina, shuffling into her ship like a pig being prodded into a pen. "Shouldn't we try to stop her?"

"Like how? Hit her on the head with our oars? Think that'll

do it?"

Maybe if we each took a head? Yet I knew it was useless. Instead, I took heart in watching her ship soar into the air, growing smaller and smaller the farther she got away from us and our planet.

After a hurried trip back to the shore, Thad and I secured the boat and rushed over to Jenn. Conscious again, she sat up, rubbing her head and groaning. "Man, my shoulder and my head hurt like hell."

"I thought you were dead." I laughed, hugged her to me, then leaned away from her to study her arm. "Not that I'm not grateful, but how is it that your shoulder isn't like totally obliterated?"

Pushing the smoking shreds of her shirt away from her arm, she plucked a strange silvery material underneath. "Special Protector Body Armor. Never fight demons or aliens without it." She glanced around, noted the missing Sabrina, and struggled to her feet with both Thad and I arguing for her to take it easy. "What happened?"

Thad and I took turns giving her an abbreviated version of the events after she'd had her lights turned off.

"Are you serious? I missed all that?"

"Oh, right. Like you don't have enough excitement in your life. Seriously, Jenn, learn to let others have some of the fun."

"Naw. Protectors are selfish that way."

Kaine, empty-handed—*empty-clawed?*—landed next to me and shifted back to human form. I quickly handed him what remained of his slacks, which barely concealed his package. A little pride zipped through me. *Yep, that's my hunky-junky man.* I ran my hands over his body, checking the areas that I thought might match up with the wounds I'd seen on his dragon form. Only angry red welts remained. "You're okay? But how?" I touched one of the welts, making him wince.

"We dragons are an indomitable sort. Thankfully Sabrina didn't know how to use the scepter to its full potential. Otherwise, I've be dragon dust."

Dust? Like demon dust? I shook my head. "Do not mention dust to me ever again."

Kaine gave me a quizzical look but thought better than to question me. Instead, he pivoted back to the lake, a frown marring his handsome face. "I should keep searching."

"No luck, huh?" I knew I should've worried about such a powerful weapon resting at the bottom of the lake, but I was too happy. My friends and my hubby were all safe, and for the most part, sound. What more could a girl ask for? The last thing I wanted was for Kaine be out of my sight again.

"No, it's useless. I can't see anything at the bottom."

"You're tired. Can't you get another dragon to search? Haven't you done your share?" *And then some?*

He sighed, fatigue etched in the lines on his face. "I'll have one of the water dragons search for it. They're better under water and trustworthy. If they find it, they can form a guard to watch over it."

"But guard it for how long?" I couldn't help but wonder if the dragons should destroy the scepter, if possible, or let Jenn have it for the Society to protect. But I didn't want to voice my opinion. Yeah, I know. It was a first.

"For as long as the world needs us to. We can't let the Scepter of Fire fall into enemy hands again."

"Ain't that the truth."

"Which is why the scepter must be turned over to the Society."

Kaine growled at Jenn, who snarled in return.

Great. Thanksgivings were going to be problem with these two at the same table. But I figured that was a problem for later. Right now, I was too happy that those two were all right. I couldn't help it. I gave Kaine a big hug. "Let's go home, okay?"

He pulled me close and pressed his lips to my cheek. "Yes, let's."

Jenn dragged Thad along with her and headed toward the car. "While these two sit in the front seat, let's you and me talk. I need an informant among the leprechauns. Not to mention a loan. You know, from that pot of gold you have."

I laughed, hooked my arm in Kaine's and followed our friends back to our car.

"I still can't believe it."

"What?" I slipped into bed, grateful to have my husband safely home with me. Remembering the black smoke pouring from him sent a cold shiver along my spine.

"That Jenn offered us jobs as Protectors." He blew out a breath, answered the beeping of his cell phone and texted Fitz a response. *"Leave us alone or I'll let the mice feed on you for a change."*

I smothered a grin. He'd finally put Fitz in her place, making her understand that I was his wife and going to remain his wife, with or without a baby. Although it had been Kaine's idea to have her leave him to search for Sabrina, she'd shown a big dose of remorse for not adequately protecting him and had even started treating me with a little respect. "What's so unbelievable about our becoming Protectors? After all, I'm used to dealing with weird stuff. And you... Well, you're you. Now that I know these things—these beings—are real, I can help the Society sort the real from the fake." I lovingly touched the tattoo on his neck. "And you can help bridge the gap of misunderstanding between humans and dragons."

"The gap of misunderstanding?" Kaine whipped out his tongue to lick the end of my nose. "You sound like you're making a speech."

"Don't be a smart ass." I snuggled against him again and took a sniff of his scent. No wonder he always had such a unique aroma. Eau de Dragon scent.

"So? What do you think about it? Want to protect the world from the bad guys like Jenn does?"

A few weeks ago I would've laughed at the question. Now, however, I got a thrill at the idea of learning to fight the villainous supernatural creeps of the world. I could even picture myself striking down a ghoul with a well-placed kick. "Ya know what? I think I would."

Kaine shifted so he could see my face. "Are you serious?"

I eyed him in return. "Are you?"

"I think I am."

"Me too." I pecked him on the cheek. "But I'd like to get something else done before we go to Protector School, or whatever they call it."

"Oh? And what would that be?"

I wrestled him on top of me, laughing at his surprised expression. "First, I'd like to get busy making an heir for my husband."

He inhaled and studied my face. In fact, he studied it so long, I started getting nervous. "Chrissy-doll, you know I love you, right?"

Relief flooded through me. "Sure I do. But I can't be responsible for the demise of your kind, so let's make a baby, you fiery stud. Besides, if having a dragon child keeps you alive and protects me from a terminal illness, then it's a win-won situation."

He kissed me then, sweet and soft, full of tenderness. "You mean win-win. But I need to know. Are you having my child only for the sake of the dragons? Or for my sake? Or perhaps even for yourself? Whatever the reason, I want you to know that having a child with you is second only to the pure delight I have when we make love."

"How about if I want a child for all the right reasons?" I searched his eyes, hoping to convince him of my desire to get pregnant.

"You should know something first."

Uh-oh. What now? And why is there always a catch? "Okay, tell me."

"When a human woman is impregnated with a dragon's child, she changes."

I frowned at him, wanting him to get on with the full explanation. "You mean besides the immunity against disease? But I thought you said the birth would be a human birth. So wouldn't that mean the woman would still be human?"

"Yes, both mother and child are human at the child's birth."

"Then how does she change?"

"She changes inwardly, not outwardly. She becomes dragon. As the child grows and becomes dragon, so will the mother. Chrissy-doll, *you* will become dragon."

I gasped, then immediately regretted it. I could see from his expression that he'd misunderstood my reaction. "No, no, Kaine. You've got it wrong. I like the idea."

"You do?"

"Sure. Because if I have your child, I'll be able to live a long time like you, and breathe fire and fly, right?"

"Well, dragons do more than those things, but yes, you would."

I nipped at his chin. "Ooh, sounds like a plan to me. Ya better get busy, dude, and knock me up. I've got a yen to soar among the clouds and not as a passenger."

Kaine laughed, his eyes morphing from gorgeous green to sparkling gold. "With pleasure." He slid his hands to cup my bare breasts and, placing his head between them, lustfully growled against me. I felt the wetness between my legs, and wondered not for the first time how the simple act of his touch and breath against my skin could thrill me so much. Slipping to my side, he ran his fingers through my hair and skimmed his other hand past the patch of hair to finger his way into my folds.

"Chrissy-doll."

The way he said my name sent delighted tremors through me. Of course those tremors were nothing compared to the ones he created by rubbing his index finger over my clit. I ached for the need of him, not only between my legs, but in my heart. I pulled him closer, crushing my mouth to his.

How I loved his mouth on me. I loved the way he managed to play with one part of my body while giving full attention to another part. The man could definitely multitask.

Soon, however, he broke away from the kiss, nearly wrenching my soul out along with it. He redeemed himself, however, by dropping down to kiss me again. This time in a hotter, wetter part of me. I gasped and gripped his hair, determined to keep him in place for a while. Sucking and licking me, he blew a breath against my throbbing nub, sending me over the edge into my first, and definitely not my last, orgasm.

"Oh, yes! Keep it up, Kaine. Oh, man, I love what you do with your tongue." Every man should have the tongue of a dragon so every woman could experience this ecstasy. Screw the old saying "my castle for a horse". I'd trade my castle for a dragon, this dragon, any day. I bit my lip to keep from giggling at the thought. "Kaine, make me come again."

Obeying my wish, he stood up and plunged into me, pleasing me in the power behind the thrust. Taking my face in his hands, he feathered sweet kisses over my cheeks, my eyelids, my lips. "Chrissy-doll, look at me."

I obeyed and found him staring at me, an urgency in his eyes. He called to me, asking me with his burning gaze to match his rhythm and equal his passion. I entwined my legs around him, moving with him, giving him everything I had. Squeezing, I clinched the muscles of my cave around his shaft, wanting everything I could get from him. Sweet sweat ran down his chest, and I couldn't help but lick one of the rivulets running down his toned abs.

"Kaine, we're doing it."

He laughed and kept pounding me, driving me inch by inch closer to the headboard. "I know. Hopefully you didn't just now notice, which, by the way, would be a major blow to my ego."

I tweaked his nipple and my big strong dragon yelped. "I'm not talking about having sex."

"Good. Because I'd much rather be having sex than talking about it."

I tried to tweak his nipple again, but he clamped a hand over it. "I'm trying to say something very serious. But if you don't want to hear it, then I'll just hush up and screw your brains out."

"Oh, ho. I'm not going to fall into that trap. If I say just hush up and screw me, then I'll get blasted for my insensitivity." Panting with his effort, Kaine sent me an exasperated look. "Still, okay, I'll bite." He arched an eyebrow. "And I really will bite if you want me to. What are you talking about?"

I grabbed his forearms and tugged his face closer to mine. "We're making a baby."

He froze in mid-motion to gape at me. "Uh, yes. You didn't realize that when we started?"

When he still hadn't resumed his motions, I wiggled my hips, getting him back into drive. "No, you don't understand."

"This wouldn't be the first time." He dropped onto his elbows, his hard thrusts gone, replaced by a slower, more loving moves. He kissed the rounded corner of my shoulder.

I captured his face in my hands and kissed him, pouring all my feelings into that one sweet kiss. "Don't you get it? I can feel it happening. We're making our baby *right now.*"

"But how can you know that? Are you sure?"

Is that a tear I see in his eye? I swallowed, his emotion overwhelming my own. "Trust me. I don't know how I know, but I do."

"Then we'll always remember this night as the night our son—"

"Or our daughter." I grinned at his surprised expression.

"—or our daughter came into being." He kissed me tenderly on the cheek. "I love you, Chrissy-doll." Kaine tensed, closed his eyes and cried out, heralding the climax sweeping over him. I arched against him, tugging him closer, wanting us to stay like this forever. My own release echoed his.

After the shudders were over, we lay unmoving for several minutes, both savoring this incredible moment in our lives.

"Kaine?"

"Yes, my love?"

Blissfully happy, I snuggled into his arms. "Let's have lots of kids."

"Seriously? Are you sure?"

For a moment, the old fear threatened to squash my new dream. Then I looked into his eyes and found the strength, the trust to push it away once and for all. "Absolutely."

He chuckled, held me to him. I smiled, and although I now knew that the things that go bump in the night actually were real, I felt completely safe wrapped in my dragon's arms.

Banged Anyone With Fangs Lately?

"Are we ready? This is the first time I've tried a conference call via my computer." I studied the monitor and waited for the picture in the upper-left corner to grow clearer. "Jenn? Skye? Can you hear me?"

Jenn waved from the upper-right-hand corner of the screen. "We're good to go, C. I've got you and Skye on my screen."

My childhood friend Skye Redding wiggled her fingers at her. "Me too. It's nice to meet you, Jenn, even if it is remotely."

"You, too, Skye." Jenn beamed from hundreds of miles away in Tulsa, Oklahoma. "C, you look great. Better than usual even."

I tried to keep a grin from my face and failed. "Thanks. I've got some news and thought I'd let you both in on it at the same time."

Both Jenn and Skye smiled in return and I knew my friends had come up with the same conclusion. Still, they waited for me to make the official announcement. "Girlfriends, I'm pregnant."

Jenn and Skye squealed in delight. Skye, effervescent as always, hopped up and down in her seat, excitement virtually radiating through the computer all the way from her home in Pismo, California. "Oh, Chrissy, I'm so happy for you."

"I bet Kaine's on Cloud Nine. Literally." Jenn's eyes grew large at her near-miss. "Uh, I mean... Oh, hell, you know what I mean."

Yeah, I know what you mean. Like a dragon who can actually fly and sit on a cloud. I shook my head at Jenn's *oh-crap* shrug and rolled my eyes. "Trust me. He is. Of course, this means I'll have to put off taking that job offer of yours, Jenn. Kaine says he'll wait and start when I do."

"What job is that, Chrissy?"

"Oh, uh, Kaine and I were thinking of becoming real estate agents." I inwardly winced and hoped Skye would accept my lame answer. Fortunately, Skye didn't question me further and Jenn pantomimed wiping her head in relief.

"No problem. I understand." Although never demonstrative in her affections, Jenn reached out and touched the monitor as though she were trying to touch me. "That's great news, C. Just great. I wish I was there to give you a hug."

Tears welled up in my eyes before I knew it. Probably just hormones. Yeah, hormones and the happiness of a friend's good wishes. "I wish you could too. Both of you." We sat for a moment, gazing at each other through the thousands of pixels connecting us.

"Well, since we're sharing good news, I've got a little bit of my own to spread around." Skye's dark eyes sparkled in her oval face, making her even more beautiful than she already was. At five feet five, she was a slim dark-haired beauty, with a perfect body to match. But it was her inner glow, her genuine willingness to believe the best in others that made her a special person. I'd known her since third grade, and even though we hadn't lived close to each other for several years, we'd never lost touch.

"Really? That's terrific, Skye." I leaned forward, ready to

take part in her happiness.

"I'm married!" Skye squealed and spun around in her chair. "Can you believe it? I. Am. Married!"

I shrieked, too, partly because I knew she expected me to. Jenn clapped her hands and grinned which was the most I would've expected from her. After all, she didn't know Skye from the cat in the moon.

"Tell us about him. Where'd you meet? How long have you known him? And why the hell haven't you mentioned him before now? Details, girl, details." I spoke to Skye at least once a month and felt a stab of alarm in the fact that she hadn't said one word about this new man in her life.

"I know, I know. I should have, but I only met him a few days ago."

My alarm spiked higher and I could see by Jenn's frown that she thought it was strange as well. "Wow. A few days? Um, I don't want to rain on your procession—"

"Parade."

"Whatever, Jenn." I scowled at her and switched back to Skye. "But aren't you moving a little fast?" Not that I was one to talk.

The brightness in Skye's smile dimmed. "I know how it looks and you're right." She leaned back in her chair and sighed. "But I couldn't help it. Dmitri's everything I've ever wanted in a man. He's strong, handsome, sensitive, virile, daring, funny, protective—"

"Okay, okay, we get it." I laughed. Let's face it, her enthusiasm for her man was contagious. "He's perfect. So where's this Mr. Perfect from?" No one was actually from California much less the small coastal town of Pismo.

"Well, you wouldn't know it by looking at him—" Skye held

up a photo of her and a very handsome blonde surfer-dude sitting on the beach under the moonlight, "—but he's from some place in Eastern Europe. My psychic said he has a deep red aura which means he's very grounded and strong-willed." Her light laughter echoed through the speakers sitting on my desk. "You know. The opposite of me."

Jenn snorted. "And he's a surfing kahuna from Eastern Europe, huh? Not likely."

I arched an eyebrow at my skeptical friend, warning her to behave. "Judging by his tan, he obviously moved to California to catch the rays."

"You'd think so, wouldn't you? But he gets his tan sprayed on. You know, for health reasons. Besides, he works from sunup to sundown. We rarely get together during the day, and when we do, we're always indoors. But I don't mind as long as we're together."

A tickle of anxiety nudged its way into my thoughts, but I firmly pushed it away. I was determined to enjoy my friend's happiness. "So can you remember the name of this country?" Not that I'd know it since I'm geographically-challenged.

"Um, let me think. Oh, yeah. He's from a place called Banat. It's part of one of those countries used in the movies a lot." Her face scrunched together as she tried to remember, then suddenly brightened. "Oh, yeah, how could I forget?" She continued, sounding like she was reading from a textbook. "Banat, located within Transylvania, is a region steeped in Romanian history and known for the beauty of its Carpathian landscape."

I saw the color drain from Jenn's face at the same time I felt it flood from mine. "Transylvania?" Transylvania as in Dracula's Transylvania?

"C." The warning in Jenn's tone was unmistakable.

"No, you silly. I told you. He's from Banat, not *that* place. Besides, all the Dracula stuff is pure nonsense." Skye's smile faded a little.

I shook my head and watched Jenn hurriedly scribble on a slip of paper. She slapped the note against her screen for me to read.

It doesn't mean he's what you're thinking he is. Do not say anything to her. Yet.

"Chrissy?"

Skye's worried look had me stumbling for words. "Uh, it's nothing, Skye. Just a little morning sickness."

"Oh, you poor thing." Skye rattled on about friends' cures for morning sickness and I plastered on a fake smile. Jenn and I exchanged a few more looks, but she remained silent. I sat quietly, nodding at the appropriate times, numb and not hearing anything else Skye said. One thought kept repeating in my mind.

Did my friend marry a vampire?

About the Author

Beverly Rae's witty, sexy, action-packed romances leave readers experiencing a wide range of emotions. As a multi-published author, Beverly is always working on her next book, taking the "usual" and twisting it into the unusual.

To learn more about Beverly, please visit www.beverlyrae.com. Send her an email at mailto:info@beverlyrae.com or join her Yahoo! Group to join in the fun with other readers as well as Beverly: http://groups.yahoo.com/group/Beverly_Rae_Fantasies.